THE SERENITY COMPOUND

By Kris Noel

Martin Sisters Publishing

Published by

Martin Sisters Publishing, LLC

www. martinsisterspublishing. com

Martin Sisters Publishing, LLC, Kentucky.
ISBN: 978-1-62553-006-6
Young Adult/Science Fiction/Fantasy
Printed in the United States of America
Martin Sisters Publishing, LLC

~ for Danny

ACKNOWLEDGEMENTS

Above all, I want to thank my family— my mom, my dad, and my sister, Shannon. I'll always be grateful for your support and what you've all done for me. Thanks for not telling me I'm crazy for wanting to be a writer (even though I might be). I also want to thank my extended family for their interest in my writing. I appreciate all of you and I'll always be grateful for your support and enthusiasm.

I want to thank the friends who have always been there for me no matter what. True friends are hard to find and I appreciate those who continue to stick by me. I want nothing but good things for all of you and I hope you all know I will always be there for you.

There's one person who hasn't been in my life for very long, but I'd like to thank you for everything you've done to support me. You've changed my life and given me the courage to put myself out there. I just want you to know how incredible I think you are and how grateful I am that everything turned out the way it did. I wouldn't change any of it for the world.

Finally, I'd like to thank Martin Sisters Publishing. It's been a pleasure working with you and I'm so happy you decided to take a chance on my novel. Thanks to Kathy Papajohn for carefully editing my novel and helping me improve my writing. I really appreciate everything you all have done for me.

Chapter One

Verus

No matter how long I've lived in Verus, the glowing fluorescent lights still mesmerize me every time I head into the main hub of the city. Today, I do my best to not let them distract me as I hurry to meet my friends at the local diner. A cool rain has begun to fall and after I lapse into a quick jog, I'm there in no time.

My sore muscles make it difficult to pull the door open, but I manage it. Once I'm inside the diner, the boisterous music immediately fills my ears. My friends find this particular type of music irritating, but I've always liked it. I wish I was talented enough to learn how to play something myself.

"Over here, Alva," a familiar voice calls. I turn to see Tessa waving at me from her spot in the small booth. Enzo sits across from her, grinning. I always love seeing him smile because his teeth are so straight and perfect. "What took you so long?"

I drop down into the booth next to Enzo and sigh involuntarily. Both of them watch me tie up my hair and remove my jacket.

I have known them both my entire life. Tessa is half Chinese and half Irish, giving her one of the most beautiful faces I've ever seen. I often find myself marveling at her breathtaking appearance, but I guess I don't mind mine either. I've learned over the years that no one cares about how you look in Verus.

"I was practicing," I reply, with a smile. I stretch out my arms and today my pale skin is covered in dark bruises. They vary in color between yellow, black, blue and pink, but I'm proud of them. They mean I'm getting stronger. "Can't you tell?"

I'm sure they've already noticed because a black eye I've been sporting since a few days ago is still present on my face. It's fading fast, but they know how I got it. I've been fighting.

Enzo stretches one arm above his head, giving me a mock cheer. Because he's wearing a tank top, I'm able to admire the tattoos all over his dark arms. His thick rimmed glasses rest over his hazel eyes and a skateboard is at his feet, which he is pushing back and forth. He flashes his dazzling white teeth again and rests his hand on my shoulder.

"Don't waste your time," Enzo says. "Last time I checked, you're already the best."

I peer around the room for a while before anyone says anything else. Some waitresses are busy at other tables, but it isn't too crowded for a Thursday night. Mostly all the kids who normally hang out here have school tomorrow. Enzo, Tessa, and I also have class, but we're only staying for a bit. I always like to meet up with them after school.

"Do you want anything?" Tessa asks.

I wave a hand dismissively before bringing my full attention back to them.

"I'm having dinner with my parents."

She shrugs and playfully kicks Enzo's leg under the table before pressing her hand down on the chrome table. She is so short her legs barely reach him.

I'm a bit taller than her, but nothing special. I think I have an average height and build.

Once Tessa lifts her hand, an interactive menu comes to life on the table's surface. She flicks through the electronic pages until she comes across the milkshakes. She selects a chocolate one and then swipes the menu away. The table returns to normal. It only takes another few moments before the waitress arrives with her treat.

"Some color does you good, Al," Enzo teases, pointing at my bruises.

Only after our presentations today, I learned that Enzo is part Egyptian and part Portuguese. I have some Portuguese in me too, but it barely shows. It's also a big deal at school to discuss and celebrate our differences. It has been so long since any of that mattered, but our teachers believe it's important to remember but never go back to such destructive thought.

"Don't call me Al," I hiss, raising my fist threateningly.

Enzo feigns fear, but he knows I would never hurt him outside of a fight.

"You know I'm stronger than you," I tell him.

"I know," Enzo replies without a hint of jealousy.

From my observations, I believe no one is ever truly jealous of anyone. I know that might sound strange to say to outsiders, but we have agreed that most of us are proud of each other. I remember the first time I felt jealousy, I learned quickly it wouldn't get me anywhere. If I want something, I have to work hard for it. I have to work harder than anyone else. It's my job to prove myself.

Tessa sucks up the rest of her milkshake and pushes away the empty glass. It's gathered up shortly by the waitress.

A moment later, Tessa leans forward, smiling, and asks, "Can we talk about our trip in a couple days?"

She brushes back her shoulder length black hair and stares at me, obviously looking for my approval.

"Yes," I say, with a laugh. "What about it?"

"We've never been outside Verus. Aren't you nervous?"

I've never thought about it like that. Sure, I'm nervous to see somewhere new, but if we're serious about joining the army, it's the right move. It'll prepare us for our potentially long careers.

"My dad went when he was my age," I continue, shrugging. "It's not like we'll see anything besides the training camp."

"I guess," Tessa replies.

Tessa and I watch Enzo lift himself from the booth and climb over the side. He pulls out his skateboard with his shoe and kicks it up into his hands.

"Better get home," Enzo says, peering toward the door.

The rain has died down a bit, so I know I should be heading back too. I don't want to get stuck in it again.

Tessa joins us on the walk back toward the Verus village. All the houses were built in the same area, so everyone is always near each other. Mine is the biggest, however, because my dad is an important citizen in the city. He is the commander of the Verus Army. There are constantly people in and out, staying over on a nightly basis. There are many parts of my home I can't even use.

I understand that no one assumes my dad's position gives me an unfair advantage at getting into the army, because it doesn't. I know my father has no influence in picking the new recruits. From my earliest memory, everything has always been done fairly in Verus and I don't think anyone worries that my dad's position affords me any special privileges.

Enzo and Tessa separate, heading toward their own houses, while I shuffle up to the gates leading into mine. After scanning in with the palm of my hand, the gates open and then shut automatically after I am inside. The front doors are opened for me by one of the housekeepers when I approach.

"Good evening, Alva," says a jovial voice. Our housekeeper, Joseph, smiles warmly at me as I step onto the plush carpet. "I was heading up to start dinner with Avery."

My twelve year old brother, Avery, is an excellent cook. He often spends evenings creating new dishes with Joseph. Sometimes I stop by to help, but I like to spend that time working on some of the broken down computers. It'll only be a matter of time before I can get them working again.

The long hallway leads to an even longer staircase that brings me to the second floor. Joseph follows behind me as I trudge up slowly. My body is sore and it begs me to rest after dinner. I know I can't - and I won't.

Avery greets me when I enter the kitchen. He hugs my leg so tightly it nearly goes numb. I have to pry him off before I can move toward the stove, where the strong smell of onions and peppers fill my nose.

"Sausage sandwiches," Avery explains while Joseph stirs something in the frying pan.

Avery has the same shocking blonde hair as my mother and I. He has a few freckles on his nose, which I occasionally catch him rubbing at in the mirror. I often have to explain to him that they won't go away and sometimes he cries about that.

Avery tells me, "Mom and Dad are setting the table in the dining room."

"Are we having guests?" I ask.

"No," Avery says. "Only us tonight."

I'm happy about that. We rarely all get to eat together without some sort of guest joining us.

We all head into the dining room to begin dinner. I see my mother and father are already sitting down. Joseph is bringing in the platters of food and taking his seat at the table. My father eyes me as I take my own seat.

"You've been practicing today, Alva," he says, beaming proudly. He elbows my mother who is still in her work clothes.

My mother is an electrician, so she is wearing a pair of dirty jeans and a blue collared shirt with her name on it. Her name is Ramsey.

"Looks like you're on the right track," my father remarks.

It's hard to explain why fighting is such a big deal in Verus. My education consists of simulations that represent real war scenarios where I, and others like me, might have to use hand to hand combat. Like my fellow students, I'll know how to use a variety of weapons by the time we turn eighteen.

Fist fighting is stressed. I've learned it'll keep us stronger than our enemy because we won't have to depend on weapons. We won't have to depend on anything but ourselves.

We haven't had a war in a long time, but our city continues to prepare. We have always been known for our army and it's prestigious to be a part of it. That's my only wish for when I turn eighteen. I hope the same for Enzo and Tessa because I'm not sure how I would get on without them. They are about as good as I am, anyway.

I rub my tender knuckles after my dad passes me a roll. He is the only one in my family with dark hair and dark eyes. Even his skin has a slight tan to it. My brother and I get all of our paleness from our mother. Tonight her identical hair is tied up in a tight bun and streaked with dirt.

My father peers at me. His commander uniform is pressed and clean, smelling of laundry detergent. He is always clean and tidy, unlike my mother. He holds such a high position of power, he has to remain organized.

"Are you going to pack tonight?" My mother asks, raising an eyebrow. "I want to make sure you have everything you need."

I open my mouth to speak, but my brother interrupts. He is often too excited and a bit selfish. He has trouble letting the conversation drift away from him. Typical twelve year old, I suppose.

"Diana is coming over to play," Avery spits out.

He picks up his napkin to wipe food from the corner of his mouth. He is neat and tidy, exactly like our father. I never picked up those same traits.

Diana is Tessa's younger sister and she's the same age as Avery. They are best friends and hang out almost every night. Sometimes Tessa comes, but I doubt she will tonight. I just saw her earlier and she told me that she has school work to do before our trip.

We'll be gone for a week total.

"What else is new?" I ask, leaning over to give his shoulder a slight shove.

He frowns and rubs where I touched him.

"You're rough, you know that?"

I smile and continue to eat my dinner. Most of my friends are rough, but that's nothing to be ashamed of. I know that Avery doesn't like it, but that's the way he is. He has always been gentle.

After eating, Avery helps Joseph clean off the table.

I resign myself to my room because helping with the chores are no longer my job. It was when I was younger, but Avery quickly took over when he was old enough.

As I leave, I hear my father say one of his favorite lines, "All little boys and girls should help with the chores."

I walk down the long hallway and push open the door to my bedroom. My floor is covered in clothes and there are computer parts all over my desk. I've recently been working on building a computer from scratch, so that's all I do with my nights. I find it incredibly relaxing and it's my way to unwind. My parents give me that time alone to get my thoughts together. They're not strict besides urging me to do school work on time. I know that they want to see me do well.

I enter into the bathroom connected to my room and wash the dried blood and dirt off my hands. I scrub at my face until it's nearly red. I smile at myself in the mirror. My teeth are nearly perfectly straight because I knocked a few of them out when I was a kid. They had to fit me with veneers and they've been straight ever since.

Part of me doesn't want my black eye to completely disappear because I like the colors on my face. I touch it tenderly, but it doesn't hurt much. Only a small stab of pain remains.

My hair is long and so blonde, it's nearly white, except for the small streak of blue that I've dyed myself. In the mirror, I'm also able to see how pale I am. Despite all my combined ethnicities, my Swedish ancestry seems to take precedence. I also realize how much I look like my mother.

I sit back down at my desk and run my fingers over the project I've been working on for the past few days. It's a little bit bigger than the size of my hands, but it's old technology. I wanted to work on something old so that no one would have anything else like it. My thumb finds the indent on the back and a red light scans over my skin.

"Alva Martin," an electronic voice calls. It sounds garbled and strange, so that's something I'll have to work on. "Welcome."

I wipe my forehead with a bandana that's sticking out of one of my desk drawers. Using some small tools, I'm able to unscrew the back of the computer and figure out some of the wiring. After cutting a red one, I use my small pen welder to attach it to another wire. When the voice calls my name again, it sounds much better. I grin, proud of myself.

Slipping on the back cover again, I place the computer on my desk. I spend some time packing up clothes for my trip and include the computer and some of my tools. Maybe I'll have some free time to work on it while I'm away, but that's unlikely. I'll be working a lot during the upcoming days.

My father comes to check on me a few moments later, but I basically have everything I need. I'm a light packer and whatever I don't have will be provided for me at the training camp. We're not supposed to pack much anyway.

I watch him move toward my open window and peer out at the garden. The flowers are blooming beautifully, but he seems worried about something. I can't place what it is, so I ask.

"I have a strange feeling," he says, without turning to me.

I want to roll my eyes, but I don't. Avery worries like he does, most of the time for no reason. I don't like being fussed over and I don't want him to make a big deal. I'll be back in no time. What I'm truly worried about is when I turn eighteen and I'll have to leave them for a longer than four days. Sure, I'll be able to see my father, but I won't be able to talk him like I can now. There will be a separation between us because he will be my commander, not my parent. I don't want to talk about my feelings with him yet.

There's no separation between men and woman in the army or in Verus in general. I've read about separation like that and to be in honest, it made me sick to my stomach. I know there was once a time when women were treated like inferiors and it seems so ridiculous to me. Personal space between genders isn't even something that is common. We're all comfortable and secure with being around each other. We even share the same changing room in gym.

We have never been made to feel shameful about our bodies, which never made any sense to me to begin with.

"Dad, I'll be okay," I reply, distracted. I accidentally burn my fingers with the welder and stick them in my mouth. As I get up, my dad extends his arms and drags me into a hug. I smell the fresh laundry scent on his clothes and breathe in deeply. No one else I know smells like that and it strictly reminds me of him. "Let me finish my homework."

I pull away and my dad nods after I plop down on my bed. His gaze lingers on me before he heads to the door.

"I'm very proud of you, Alva," he says.

I hide my smile when he finally leaves me alone. He tells me that often and says the same to Avery. Tonight, it feels more real. It feels like it's meant only for me. I shake my head and start to concentrate on the homework I have to finish. I know I'll be up for a few more hours completing it.

As I peer out the window where my dad had been looking, I see the sky is dark again. The clouds look strange and ominous; they cover everything in their path. I have never seen clouds look like this, but it doesn't worry me. I know they will be gone by the morning.

Chapter Two

School

This morning the sun is shining, but a pit forms in my stomach. I feel strange for some reason, almost like my father's negative thoughts have transferred to me. I shove my books into my backpack and head to the bathroom to take a long shower.

It's easy to see the bruised blotches all over me, but they usually don't take long to heal. I run my fingers over a strange looking yellow one that's almost gone, which is from a fight with Enzo when he jammed his knee into my thigh.

I rinse the shampoo out of my hair and turn off the water. I dry myself off quickly, and shove on my clothes, which is a simple pair of jeans and a white tank top. Since I don't have time to dry my hair, I pull on my usual beanie.

Joseph has breakfast prepared for me in the kitchen. He places a plate of eggs and bacon on the counter along with a glass of cold milk. Breakfast usually makes my stomach turn, but he forces me to eat it anyway.

Avery shovels a forkful of food into his mouth and glances at me from his spot at the table.

"You look tired," Avery says.

I don't like mornings much. I'd rather stay up late at night and wake up later, but I know that isn't an option in my life. There will be much longer hours in the army and I'll have to deal with that.

"Thanks. I have to get going," I reply. I let my fork drop on my plate, even though I haven't finished. I know I should bulk up more because my frame is too slender, but there's no use. I'm still strong and I'm not getting any bigger. I have been trying for a long time.

Avery tells me to a have a good day as I slip my backpack over my shoulder.

I find my long board by the door and wait to use it until I'm outside the gate. It's a nice day for it and I haven't outgrown using it. The board helps me get to school quickly and I'm certain Enzo has his with him.

I arrive at my school and stare up at the massive building when I hop off my board. It's an old brick building with a welcoming feel to it. The classrooms inside are much more advanced and filled with computers I could tinker with. The thought excites me and gets me up in the morning.

Tessa and Enzo motion for me from the stoop in front of the school. Some of the teens on the front lawn wave at me, so I return the gesture quickly and brush past them.

I sit down next to Tessa and groan because of the soreness in my body that jolts through me. I think they probably feel the same way, considering we've all fought recently.

"Happy Friday," Enzo says.

Tomorrow morning we will be on our way to the training camp, so there won't be any time to rest. Still, I know it will be enjoyable.

"Just have to get through today," I reply.

I pull off my beanie and fluff out my hair. It's dry and falls pin straight over my shoulders.

Tessa steadies herself on my shoulder as light trickles of rain begin to fall. I notice that the weather has changed quickly. The thick clouds blocking the sun and a clap of thunder get my attention. We gather up our stuff and head inside.

I slump to my locker alone and quickly dial the combination. I slip the books I need into my backpack and shove the others one away. My board fits in nicely at the bottom before I slam the locker door shut.

When I turn around, I see that someone is waiting for me. It's a girl my own age, Neddie. She looms over me, but smiles when I bump into her.

"Alva," she says cheerfully. Neddie has broad shoulders and stands nearly a foot taller than me, so it would be impossible to get past her even if I wanted to.

I have no problems with Neddie. She just reminds me of things I'd like to forget.

"How'd you do on yesterday's test?" Neddie probes.

"Not so well," I reply.

This is what I mean. I'm not doing so well in math and I haven't told my parents yet. They'll be upset with me, but math has never been my strong suit. Still, they'll worry I'm not trying.

She walks next to me as we head to class. I know what she's going to ask me.

"If I help you in math, will you help me with fighting?" she asks.

I nod and bite my lip. I'm uncertain about working with Neddie because I know she could bash my face in if she's trained properly. I know I'm being selfish and that's not a reason to be unhelpful, so I agree. If I can't beat Neddie at her best, than I don't deserve to be part of the army. I know we all must be strong together for it to work and competitiveness must stay by the wayside.

Trying out for the army is the most competitive I will get in Verus. Technically, I'm not supposed to want something that badly, but I can't help myself. I have to admit, I would be upset if I didn't make it. I'm not sure if that makes me a bad person, because we are all supposed to work together.

When Neddie and I arrive in class, I find Enzo and Tessa near the middle. I have my class with them because we are split into the same group. I have all my classes with the same ten people, so I know them all pretty well.

I'm rarely ever happy in the morning because math is the first class of the day. When our teacher passes our tests back, I cringe. I know I have one of the lowest scores in the class.

Fortunately, the teachers try to play to our strengths. They know that we all excel at different things and we aren't made to feel bad about failure in one subject. They have to know that we're trying.

"Tessa Yeung," Miss O'Brien calls before handing her the test. She has a habit of saying our full names, even though we've had her since we were kids. She continues with Enzo at the next desk. "Enzo Okar."

I can see that Enzo has a good grade. He's decent at mostly every subject.

Miss O'Brien tells us to access our lessons from our tablets, which are slim computers built into the desk. Some of them are scratched and cracked, but most of them are replaced every year. There's constantly new technology coming in and I'm interested in it all because I like knowing how things work. I like seeing the patterns.

The teacher shows us a few new problems and I barely pay attention. My brain nearly shuts off before I'm brought back by the bell. I can't believe I somehow let an hour go by without learning anything. I need to work on that.

Our next class is human sexuality. I don't mind it and it's a welcome change from health, which I took during the first half of the school year. I learn a lot about how things used to be and I'm glad that Verus has changed. I'm glad that we are lucky enough to all be equal, the way it should be everywhere.

Mr. Anderson teaches this class and he greets us as we all take our seats. I already know today's lesson is about gender identity because the material is already opened on our desks. We've talked about this several times before, starting in elementary school. I think most of us are well versed in what it means and how to treat people respectfully, so it's not something any of us have to learn.

For most of the beginning of the class, Mr. Anderson talks about the difference between male and female. He leaves the question open, but most of us can't think of anything besides physiology, if that even counts.

Psychologically, I know we can rarely find any differences between our genders. Based on older and archaic definitions that have long since been changed, I would have been considered more masculine than feminine. Avery might have been considered more feminine, along with Enzo and some of the other boys in the class. I know that's stupid. I know that we're all capable of the same things and we are a combination of everything we want to be.

I like knowing I can be whatever I want. I'm glad it will never be any other way. I'm happy, that if I choose to have children, they will experience the same freedom I do.

Mr. Anderson goes on teaching another lesson, but it's hard to understand something I've never experienced. We talk a lot about sexuality, which we are taught to see as something natural. He explains to us that it hasn't always been like that. He explains that often times, girls were shamed for being sexually active and boys were praised for it.

"Sometimes I don't believe you," Tessa calls, grinning.

Mr. Anderson smiles back and shrugs.

"It's still like this in some places. We are a self-sufficient community, so there's not much we need from anyone else. We're lucky," Mr. Anderson explains.

We are dismissed by the bell, without being given any homework. It's nice that we won't have to work on anything else before training camp.

Finally, we have a break for lunch and then we go straight to physical education. We find our usual table in the cafeteria and two other students join us. Harmon is easy to spot with bright red, curly hair, but Lonnie disappears next to him. Lonnie is introverted and quiet, so I know he likes to keep to himself most of the time. No one forces anything out of him, but when he does talk it's usually something funny.

Lonnie sits down next to me. I know he's always had feelings for me because he only ever smiles at me. He told me once, but I let him know I didn't feel the same way about him. That's usually how we handle those things in Verus and I'm pretty sure no one takes it personally. Sometimes you just don't feel the same way about someone else.

On the other hand, I've never had any feelings about anyone else. I don't know what it's like to be in love, but I guess I've seen it between my mother and my father. I've seen it in other partners in Verus, but I don't know if it'll ever happen for me. If it does, I guess I'll be accepting of it, but until then I don't care.

Lonnie offers me half of his sandwich, which I accept. I'll share some of my chips with him, like we usually do. From what I've observed, he expects nothing more and nothing less. That's the nature of our relationship and I suppose we're both happy with it.

After lunch, we all head to P.E. together. I drop my things into my locker in the changing room and pull out my practice clothes. I change next to Tessa and Lonnie, sliding my shirt on over my skin.

Tessa turns to me while she's still busy dressing.

"What are you choosing today? I'm thinking boxing," she says.

Lonnie looks at me too as I slide on my shorts. I can see that he has a massive bruise on his chest close to his heart. It seems like he is also interested in what my P.E. activity will be today.

I know Tessa loves boxing, but I like fighting without the gloves because I don't feel like I'm depending on something I won't have in a *real* fight. There's a greater chance of getting hurt that way, but our teachers never let it go too far. No one will end up with anything more than bruises or a cut lip. It's nothing like the fighting that sometimes takes place after school, where there's no one there to end the round.

We head out onto the mats and Lonnie goes right for the weights. He's told me he doesn't plan on trying out for the army, so he really has no use for the training. Neddie, on the other hand, finds me right away.

I grab some white tape from the side table and begin to wrap my hands with it. Even though I don't like to use any equipment, I'm too sore to fight without it today.

As Enzo, Tessa, and another girl, Cara, head to the punching bags to warm up, the P.E. teacher, Mrs. Rolands, approaches me and places a hand on my shoulder. She has a whistle around her neck and her long hair is tied up in a ponytail. I like to let my hair flow freely when I fight because it normally doesn't get in the way.

"You don't give yourself a break, do you?" Mrs. Rolands asks.

I shake my head. My adrenaline is pumping and I normally get a bit nervous before a fight, especially if it's someone like Neddie. From what I imagine, she has an incredible reach and one punch could knock me out. I don't want to get too injured before I head to the training camp.

Our teacher blows her whistle, calling mostly everyone in the room to attention. She turns to Neddie and I.

We will fight first, before I get a chance to give her any pointers. I want to see what she's made of. I want to see if I can mold her into something better.

When we're on our own sides of the mat, I see that everyone has gathered around to watch us. Lonnie gives me a thumbs up from next to Mrs. Rolands. I give him a smile in return.

I do a quick jog in place to get my heartbeat up, but I don't need much warm-up. My eyes go to Neddie's bunched up fists and I feel the fear that usually precedes a fight, pulse through my body. I remind myself that fear is good, fear will keep me quick and it lets me know I'm alive. I remember that Verus taught me to be strong, but not to be fearless. I know that being fearless is the same as being reckless, and being reckless will not keep me alive in the army.

Neddie's face is set with determination when the whistle blows. She might be confident she can take me, but there's no way to be sure.

I bite my lip when she approaches the center of the mat immediately. I jog around the perimeter for a while before making any sort of offensive move. I need to figure out what she will do before I act.

Neddie steps forward once more. Her fist barrels toward my face, slow and uncoordinated. I duck and jab an elbow into her side, hard. Neddie doubles over in pain, but she recovers quickly. I'll have to do something more than that to win the match.

"Stay quick, Alva," Enzo calls.

He's said this to me many times, so I know he means that I should keep moving around and make myself less of a target. I'm already aware of this, but hearing him say it helps remind me.

I leap back when Neddie tries to punch me again. When she misses, I use my upper body strength to push her backwards. While she's unsteady, I give her a strong punch on the jaw. I see the light go from her eyes as she falls to her knees on the mat.

Her skin is red, but there is no blood.

I back up when Mrs. Rolands blows the whistle. She raises my arm in victory, but I know it wasn't much of a fight.

"Good job, Neddie," I say, approaching her.

I extend my hand and she shakes it roughly. I see a bit of embarrassment on her face, but it's unlikely that anyone will make fun of her. She's learning and I'll help her get better.

Next time we fight, I'm sure it'll last much longer.

"I don't know how you do it, Alva," Neddie comments.

"I'll show you," I say with a genuine smile.

I spend the rest of the period giving Neddie pointers and practicing with her at the punching bags. I tell her to be quicker on her feet and try to read what I will do before she acts. I'm confident those things will help and we can move onto something else when I get back from training camp.

After P.E., we're given a few minutes to rinse off in the showers. I'm the only one who needs it, so I find myself alone under the cool water. It's refreshing and I'm excited to head to our next class. It's electronics, my favorite period of the day.

During that time, I'm able to work on one of my projects. Since my computer project is packed up in my suitcase at home, I work on one of the robots I started with Tessa.

After using the remote to ram our robot into the wall, I go to pick it up and place it on our workbench, where Tessa eases herself up on one of the stools.

The shop is a big room with high ceilings and all the tools you could imagine. I know how to use most of them, but the other more dangerous ones have to be used with adult supervision. I usually avoid them until they're absolutely necessary, because I like doing things on my own.

I turn over our robot, which is the shape of a small black box, and do my best to readjust the wheels. It's basically done, but we'll have to perfect everything before it's graded. Everyone already assumes I will get the best grade and they ask me to help them with their own projects. Even our teacher, Mr. Rodriguez has me work on extra things around the classroom. He thinks I should ditch the army idea and get a good job placement in electronics, but that's not what I want.

Our last class of the day is art/creative writing combined. Enzo is the one who excels at both subjects and I know that he's proud of that. He pulls out one of his paintings from the closet and places it on one of the long tables. I help him organize the paints and brushes before he gets started. I'm always in awe of anything he creates because I don't have the same talents. Tessa and I spend a few moments staring at the beautiful watercolors he has blended together on a canvas. His artwork is all over the room.

The teacher makes us move to a separate table to work on our stories. Mine doesn't make much sense, but I enjoy listening to Tessa read hers out loud to the rest of the class. It's a relaxing way to end the day.

The bell dismisses us and I head right outside with my long board. We'll be leaving in the morning, so I want to make sure everything is in order and that I get to spend some time with my family. Tessa and Enzo head home too in order to finish packing. Enzo carries his finished painting under his arm as he separates from us.

Tessa stops by my house for a little while and we eat some cookies that Avery has baked earlier in the week. We dip them in milk while he watches us with a proud look on his face.

"They're good, right?" Avery asks, giving Tessa a nudge.

She nods, her mouth full.

"You want to bake? Diana told me that's what you've been doing in school," Tessa asks.

"I want to be a cook," Avery says confidently. "A chef."

It's funny how different Avery and I are from each other, but I also appreciate it. He has been given the freedom to choose what he wants to do and he will do it. I'm doing the same. Our parents don't mind what we do, as long as we are happy and making smart decisions.

I help Avery clean up after Tessa leaves. Our parents are working late today. I know my dad has to be at the academy and my mom will not be home for another hour. I head to my room for a while to clean it up and make sure I have everything.

When my mom gets home, she comes in and sits on the edge of my bed. She looks out the window like my father did the previous night.

"The weather has been strange lately," she comments. I see that she has changed from her work clothes and has showered. Her hair is still wet. "I hope it's safe for tomorrow."

I know why everyone is making such a big deal out of my trip. It's because I've never left Verus and I've never seen anywhere else. There's not much of a reason to leave our city and people rarely do it unless they're in the army. My father has only left a couple times and he always tells us he can't wait to return. I'm fairly positive that my parents are worried about me.

"I'm sure it'll be fine," I say.

When my mom's eyes meet mine, I realize again how identical we look. My mother is a beautiful woman, with wide hazel eyes and a lovely smile. She still has most of her real teeth, unlike me. She always tells me that's because I was a bit rougher as a child than she was. I still haven't outgrown that roughness, and I'm not sure I ever will.

"I can't wait for you to get back," she comments. "I want you and Avery here with us."

I laugh.

"I haven't even left yet."

I can see worry is still set on her face, like it was on my dad's. Why is everyone having such a bad feeling about this? Why am I, too? I know they're making me nervous and I wish they would stop.

I walk over to my mom and give her a kiss on her forehead. She runs her fingers through my hair and then rests them on my cheek.

27

I don't want her to say anything sentimental because she's not usually like that, but she does anyway.

"Don't ever change the way you are," she says.

I'm surprised by this. Why would I ever change? How would I become anyway? I always act like myself and I always have. Nothing in this world would make that any different.

I nod anyway and finish cleaning. She leaves me alone, closing the door gently behind me.

At night, I sleep horribly. In the morning, my mind is still filled with cobwebs of nightmares as I wash my face in the sink. I can barely remember any of them, but I want to feel normal again. I've never felt so uneasy.

Enzo and Tessa are ready and eating breakfast with my family when I slump downstairs. I place my luggage on the floor and join them. My stomach definitely can't handle food this morning, so I don't force it.

"About time," Enzo teases.

Everyone else laughs, but I groan slightly. My head is pounding and something still feels wrong.

When we're done, my parents lead us outside. We'll be taking one of the army's personal planes to head to the training camp. My father had it arranged weeks before and they are the only people who handle transferring civilians to the camp.

It's a short walk to the academy and the hanger, but I don't head inside the school where I wish to one day enter as a student. I've been in it many times since I was little and I know it inside and out.

A small plane waits for us. I know it fits about five people and it's just going to be the pilot and us. The ride will only take a few hours, but that's the longest I've ever been in any sort of moving device.

There are only transfer trucks in Verus, no cars. No one needs them because everything is so close.

Once our luggage is aboard, I hug my parents and Avery goodbye. Avery lingers for a little while before letting go. I can see tears in his eyes and I wipe them with the bottom of my shirt. He doesn't need to cry because I'll be back in a week.

We load onto the plane and I watch my family walk away through one of the windows. Tessa sits next to me and Enzo sits at the seat across from us. The pilot, a young man in his late twenties, greets us and heads to the cockpit. I hold my breath, waiting for us to take off. I don't know what to expect.

After a few scary moments, we are up in the air. I see Verus from the sky. It's a small city with a brick wall that is a barrier around it. I feel safe there. Up in the air, I feel uncertain. I feel like I've lost control.

I don't know what it is, but I know something will go wrong. I know that something will go wrong soon.

Chapter Three

The Crash

While we're in the air, I find time to relax. Enzo is asleep within the first hour, but I'm thinking about what it will be like at the training camp. For some reason, I can't picture it. I can't even begin to imagine what it will be like. I try to push away the fogginess clouding my thoughts, but everything stays fuzzy.

Tessa watches me curiously as I begin to bite my lip. She finally starts talking when my lip begins to bleed.

"What's wrong? You look nervous."

I force a smile and wipe the blood on the back of my hand. It tastes like metal.

"Nothing. Just our first time away from home. I think I want to be back already," I say.

Tessa nods in agreement.

"I don't think I like leaving," she responds.

"We could be afraid of what we might discover. Maybe it will be somewhere better than Verus," I say.

Tessa looks at me with an eyebrow raised. She believes me for a moment, but then we both start laughing. This rouses Enzo, but he doesn't open his eyes.

"Quiet down. It's nap time," Enzo complains.

He turns away from us and is back to sleep. Tessa rolls her eyes, turning back to me.

"I don't think we'll see anything anyway," Tessa replies.

That's true. I never expected to see anything, so why do I feel like I will? Why am I dreading something unspecific?

My stomach churns again. I'm sick from being on the plane.

I try to distract myself by working my hair up into a ponytail. It is soft and smells flowery because it was just washed.

I think of home briefly before closing my eyes. What is my mother doing? Where is my father? Does Avery have Diana over? For a moment, I'm jealous of them.

"Do you ever feel jealous?" I ask, suddenly.

"Yes," Tessa says, after a while. "I know I'm not supposed to, but sometimes I am. I think it's natural."

"I remember learning that it's normal sometimes, but not when you wish to harm people," I explain. "Not when it overwhelms you."

"Do you think there are people like that? People who want the worst for everyone but themselves."

"Maybe." I shrug. "I wouldn't want to live like that."

"Maybe it happens when you truly care about something. You know we were always taught that you should never want something too badly. Maybe we've never cared that much about anything," Tessa says.

I feel guilty. I don't think Tessa knows how badly I want to be in the army. I've told her it's what I want to do, but I don't think she knows how horrible I would feel if I didn't get it. I might get jealous. I might get angry. I might not wish the best for everyone else. Does that make me a bad person?

32

She looks away from me and I'm fairly certain she wasn't trying to get information out of me. I don't think she has any clue about how I honestly feel about the army tryouts. I think it's best that way.

A little while later, I see Tessa is asleep too. I peer out the window and see that the sky looks dark again. I can't see anything below because the clouds are blocking my view.

It's strange being up so high and I still feel uneasy about it.

I can't wrap my mind around airplanes, even though I have a technical mind. It doesn't make sense for something to be up in the air like this. I think about the physics of it as another hour passes by.

I'm thirsty, but I don't feel like getting up for water. Tessa and Enzo are still asleep, so I contemplate waking them up. I decide against it because they both look so peaceful.

I notice that the clouds are not clearing up at all. I'm not sure if it's normal to fly in this weather since I know nothing about flying. A rumble of thunder somewhere far away concerns me. The plane remains steady however so I take a deep breath.

Enzo eventually stirs and nearly jumps awake. He looks at me with terror in his eyes and then calms down. I don't ask, but I think he was having a nightmare.

He stretches out and rubs at the top of his head. "How long was I asleep?"

"Around two hours. Three more to go," I say.

He looks distressed by this news. Flying is boring and there is nothing to do, so I think we all want the time to pass quickly.

"I can't take this," Enzo says, with a groan.

Enzo and I spend the next hour singing songs that we learned in Verus. A lot of them are silly, but I start laughing uncontrollably when Enzo recites all of them. He has a pleasant singing voice and I don't mind listening.

All the laughing jolts Tessa awake and she glares at us. She glances toward the window when we hear another loud thunderclap. It sounds closer this time, so I follow her gaze. The sky outside is darker than before and I know there's no way we can fly in this. I start to get out of my seat, but Tessa grabs my arm.

"I'm sure we'll land if there's a problem," Tessa says.

She doesn't sound confident.

"Can we fly in a storm?" I ask, right after another cluster of thunder. It crackles and I shudder violently. No one says anything, so I continue. "Is this normal?"

More silence.

I see a flash of lightning and then reach over to close the small beige blinds. I do not want to see the storm. I do not want to see where we are headed. Everything will be fine and we'll be at the training camp in a couple hours. Besides, the plane seems to be traveling perfectly well.

We end up distracting ourselves for another hour, but the storm doesn't die down. It keeps getting stronger. I can see my friends are not taking flying through the storm well. They both look frightened.

I think it's best for me to stay calm. One of us has to.

It is best to know fear than to be fearless. I remember this as I close my eyes. I am fearful, but I am alive. I'm smart enough to know fear.

The plane shakes violently—only for a moment. I refuse to look up at my friends.

My fingers dig into the arms of my seat, but I remove them to buckle myself in. I hear other buckles being snapped, so I know they must be following my lead.

"Why aren't we landing?" Enzo asks.

Of course, no one has an answer.

I hear strange noises coming from the cockpit, along with the sounds of the storm. Alarms are blaring, but still I keep my eyes shut. Another violent shake causes me to latch back onto the armrests, so my nails are tearing at the fabric.

I try to think of being in a fight where I have so much control over the situation, but it's just not the same. I'm helpless and I'm far away from home. My decision to remain calm is dissolving.

The plane starts to dive and I nearly black out. I can't look at anything. I can't see what's happening. It is hard to breath as the plane plummets, but there is nothing I can do. I knew nothing is going to be okay and I was right. I should have stayed home. I should have never gotten on this plane.

I hear screams, but they aren't mine. The noise in my ear is loud and the sound of air rushes past me. I think that part of the plane has been torn off or the alarms are blaring louder. I hear the pilot shouting something, but he is too far away to see what he is shouting about.

That's when I black out completely.

It's hard to breathe when I wake up. I feel pain all over, but at least I feel something. I don't remember much. I don't remember anything at all at first. I keep my eyes closed and outstretch my fingers. They are okay. I do the same with the rest of my body and everything seems fine. Still, there is a pain in my stomach unlike anything I've ever experienced.

When I open my eyes, I'm blinded by the sun. The storm is gone and I can't see anything. I think for a moment that I'm blind, but then why can I see bright lights?

Dust stirred up by the debris clouds my vision so I blink a few times trying to see better. I see parts of the plane strewn out everywhere and see that I'm lying far away from any of it. What is left of the plane itself is a crumpled heap in the middle of an apparent desert.

The thought of Enzo and Tessa startles me into action. We were in a plane crash and they might not be alive. None of us should be alive, but if I made it, perhaps they did too.

Before I can find them, I have to deal with my own physical condition. I pull myself painfully up off the dirt and look down. My white shirt is stained with dark red blood and a piece of scrap metal is sticking out of my side. I nearly cry out at the sight of it, but instead I grit my teeth.

I'm not sure if I should pull it out or not. I'm not sure if that will do more damage, but I can't move an inch with it in. My hands shake as I grasp onto it. I'm terrified and I want to cry, but I don't. I know that won't help me.

I yank the metal from my side and fall to the ground. I allow myself to let out a few sobs as I see the blood pool into the dirt. I need something to tie around the wound, so I push myself up and stumble toward the wreckage. I find a loose t-shirt flung from someone's luggage. After securing it tightly around my stomach the best I can, I begin to take in more of the situation.

I see someone's body lying under a seat and I run forward as quickly as my body will let me. Enzo's dark skin is instantly recognizable. I try not to panic. Amazingly, I find that his glasses are somehow intact when I roll him over onto his side. There is blood coming out of the side of his mouth.

"Enzo!" I cry. He doesn't move. I push the seat off him and try to analyze his condition. There is blood on his shoulder, but I don't see it anywhere else. I continue to shout at him. "Wake up!"

I begin to shake him violently. I know it's probably not a good idea, but I need to know he's alive. He can't be dead.

Enzo's eyes open suddenly and he struggles away from my grip. I try to calm him, but he pulls away from me and stands up. He is weak on his feet and his hand goes to his shoulder. After a moment of looking around, he sits back down on the dirt, so once I discern that Enzo will survive, I begin to look for Tessa.

She is much harder to find. Her body is deep within the wreckage and she is still strapped into her seat. I fumble with the buckles and ignore my own pain. Enzo comes to help me and he carries Tessa away from the wreckage. Once he places her down, I look for any major damage.

Tessa is covered in cuts that are bleeding slightly, but nothing serious from what I can tell. I push her hair from her face and see that a large welt has formed on her forehead. Her eyes flutter open uncertainly at the touch of my fingers grazing her injury. I understand that it is the pain that forced her awake, but I am glad she is alive.

The pilot, I think. If the three of us are alive, he must be alive too. I search the area around the plane, but I don't see him anywhere. Finally, my eyes spot some feet from underneath hat used to be the fuselage. When Enzo helps me pull the metal away, we see the shocked look on the pilot's face. His eyes are wide open and his mouth is gaped in a surprised expression. I have to look away from the death I see in his eyes.

I bury my face into Enzo's shoulder, but I don't cry. I'm happy to be alive, but being one of the few survivors also makes me feel guilty. I didn't even know the pilot's name.

Something else confuses me when we all gather back together in the hot sun. How did the three of us survive with only a few minor injuries? My side throbs painfully and Enzo's shoulder is bleeding, but nothing serious at all. It's a miracle we aren't dead. How is it possible?

I peer around and see something in the distance, but I can't make out what it is. It might be a town. There might be people around, I think hopefully.

Enzo and Tessa are watching me from where they are sitting on the ground. I have my hands on my hips, but I reach up to wipe the sweat off my forehead. It is mixed with blood.

I grab a piece of my hair and see it is even more shocking in the sunlight. Some of my white locks are stained red with blood and the blue streak looks nearly purple.

"I can't believe this. What are we going to do?" Enzo asks, echoing my concerns.

Tessa is strangely quiet as she looks at the ground.

"We need to get somewhere safe," I say more to myself than to my friends.

"We didn't die," Tessa says in a low voice.

We are all quiet for a little while longer. I'm not sure if I'm in shock because I'm shaking slightly and I can't stop. I try not to think about our precarious situation and move around to gather up some luggage.

Mine is somehow still intact, but I do my best to gather up the rest. I pull what's left of Enzo's clothing back into his backpack. I can't find Tessa's at all.

I sit down next to my friends and stare up at the sky. I'm still in disbelief about the crash, the sunny weather, everything.

I've never seen such barren land before and the sun blinds my eyes so I can't determine what the landscape consists of. Something is glinting on top of a cliff far ahead of us. It looms over us, so I realize that was what was blocking my view. I think there's a building up there. I think we can find people there.

I'm completely unsure of how to get up the cliff, but I see that it slopes to the right and there is a winding road up the side. It will take a while to walk and it's hot.

Although I had locked my fear away in order to help my friends, I start to become scared again. . I'm most terrified of the fact that I saw all this coming. I knew something horrible was going to happen. I had predicted it.

I don't tell my friends this. It wouldn't do any good, anyway.

I'm beginning to feel woozy but I start to see something in the distance. A few people are walking toward us. They are hard to see due to the blinding sunlight.

"Someone's coming," Tessa says, standing up. "Maybe they saw the crash."

As my vision finally begins to fade for real, I see her arms stretch to catch me. I've lost too much blood and I can feel it's wetness on my pale hands. But I must stay awake. I must find out who's coming. I can't die here, not when we're so close to being rescued.

I only last a few more seconds before my vision fades completely. I feel someone grab my arms to keep me up, but my brain is fuzzy.

The last thing I remember is warm hands on the side of my face and the sound of someone's muffled voice.

Chapter Four

Day One

My chest is tight, but I try to breathe deeply anyway. I can't seem to get enough oxygen because something is wrapped tightly around me, almost to the point of cutting off my circulation.

I know that my lips are parted because a low groan comes from my throat. As I try to turn, I feel someone's hand on my shoulder. It feels cold against my bare skin.

"Stay still." It's a man's rough, booming voice.

I continue to lie on my back but I force my eyes open. A man with skin paler than mine is staring down at me. The bright lights in the ceiling behind make him appear less than real.

"You are healing," he tells me, in a voice only slightly less rough than his order.

"I'm fine," I choke out.

I'm in pain, but it's nothing I can't handle. I peer down at myself and see that I'm wearing a strange hospital gown. I fumble to pull it off, but the man grabs my arm.

"Leave that on. The girls cleaned you up. They washed off the blood," he tells me.

This man's voice is not gentle or caring. I'm finally able to focus on him and the room. I see that Tessa is on a cot beside me, resting peacefully, and Enzo is asleep across the room.

It's a large room with one other empty cot. The floors are made of wood and windows expose the hallway outside. Through the windows, I see a boy walk by, but he does not peer inside. The smell of pine stings my nostrils.

The man looming before me is strong and a thick brown beard covers some of the pale skin on his face. His eyebrows are raised at me as he crosses his arms over his chest. He is wearing a thick flannel shirt buttoned up to the neck and his brown pants are pressed neatly. Part of him seems out of place, almost like he's from a different time. He frowns at me before sitting on the edge of the bed. He doesn't look at me and he puts his hands on his lap.

I have never met anyone like him. I know right away he is from somewhere very different than Verus.

"What is your name?" he asks.

I see him peer toward the door and he snaps his fingers together. A boy who was standing in the hallway shuts the door.

"Alva," I say. "Alva Martin."

I ease myself up carefully against my propped up pillow, but still he doesn't look at me. I feel strange, uncomfortable. I blame it on my injuries and the uncomfortable premonition that still hasn't gone away.

"I'm Alexander," he tells me. "And where are you from, Alva?"

"I'm from Verus," I say quickly. I feel like I'm being tested, but I don't know what for. I have never been questioned like this. "Do you know where that is?"

He shakes his head and then his eyes linger on the floor. He seems to be figuring something out.

42

"Your friends are from the same place?" Alexander asks.

"Yes."

He pauses for a moment before continuing.

I don't feel right asking my own questions because something feels off. Something tells me to be quiet.

"This is a no fly zone," Alexander explains. "I'm guessing your plane got caught in the storm and got off-course. Where were you headed?"

"To a training camp. I'm not sure where it was. We weren't told. I ... I never thought to ask."

He stands up but doesn't say anything else. When he heads for the door, someone opens it for him.

The pit in my stomach is becoming bigger. In fact, it's growing at a rapid pace. Why didn't he tell me what is going on? Why didn't he tell me where we are?

Now that he's gone, I'm free to pull off my gown and analyze the situation myself. I stand up and let the gown drop onto the cot. Thick white tape is wrapped completely around my chest, covering the fabric of my bra. My underwear is the only thing on the bottom half of my body. I wonder where my clothes are.

I turn to the hall window because I feel eyes on me. I see a boy staring back at me, his face bright red. He looks embarrassed and turns his eyes away immediately. I didn't even get a good look at him.

Why would he look so embarrassed? Why didn't he come inside to say hello?

Without putting my gown back on, I make my way toward the door. Luckily, it's unlocked and I'm able to slip into the hallway. I turn to the right, but see that it's a dead end. Left is my only option, toward the swinging door that leads somewhere bright. The number of lights in this building is unbearable.

When I slowly push through the swinging door, I see that I am standing in a kitchen. There is a large stove unlike anything I have ever seen. It's not electric like ours at home, it seems to be wood or coal burning. Everything looks strangely old fashioned.

The three boys sitting at a small table stop laughing and gaze at me with the same embarrassed expression the first boy had. They, too, look old fashioned. They are wearing long sleeved, blue collared shirts that are buttoned up to their necks, and the same brown pants that Alexander was wearing.

Clean. Pale. Vanilla.

They make *me* stand out from the crowd.

The boy with the darkest hair is staring at me, looking me up and down with a strange expression on his face. He's angry and I'm not sure why.

"What is wrong with you?" He shouts.

"Asher, calm down. She's probably still confused. She was just in a *plane crash*," the red haired boy says.

I see he is shorter and bulkier. I assume Asher is the angry looking one still staring at me.

"That doesn't give her the right to walk around like *that*," Asher shouts. "Look at her. Bruises all over!"

I'm not sure why he is raising his voice or what he's talking about, but I know I look startled. Their refusal to talk to me directly confuses and frustrates me, so I decide to speak up on my own.

"Where is this place?" I ask.

Asher laughs again, a cruel laugh. No one has ever laughed at me like that before and I'm not sure I like it. I feel my fists bunch up tightly.

"You're in Shiloh. I think you'll be here for a while," Asher says.

He stands up and approaches me, walking around me in a circle. I don't know what he's looking at. I can't figure out why he's doing this. I think for a moment he's challenging me to a fight and studying potential adversaries like I do sometimes.

44

I turn to him and he stops in place.

"Take me to Alexander," I demand. "Where did he go?"

He blinks and for the first time, I realize that he has a dangerous expression on his face.

His friends looked shocked by what I just asked.

My brain begins to hurt again. I can't handle this place. I can't figure it out.

"You don't ask to see Alexander. He asks to see you," Asher explains, his lips curling into a satisfied smile. "Don't make that request again."

"Take me to him," I demand, in spite of Asher's threatening words.

Why can't I see him? Isn't he supposed to be helping us? I don't care that this boy is trying to tell me what I can and cannot do.

Asher's hand flies out toward my face before I'm able to react. I'm not expecting it. His palm claps loudly against my face and I stumble back in shock. He slapped me. He started the fight.

He is laughing for only a moment before I clench my right fist and connect with his jaw. Asher falls to the ground and grabs at his face. I wonder why he would strike out at me in such a way, considering it barely hurt me at all. Why would he start a fight in the weakest way possible? And now, it's over. He can't lift himself up off the floor.

Hands restrain me before I can do anything else. The two remaining boys grab my arms and start to drag me back into the hallway.

"What are you doing? This isn't how a fight works," I say, pulling away.

We are back in the hallway and they are staring at me like I'm crazy. The two boys exchange glances. The red headed one points back to the room where my friends are.

"Go back to the hospital," he says, breathing heavily. "Stay there until Alexander comes back for you. I'd say get some rest."

I don't like how he's speaking to me, but I decide to head back to my friends. If they are awake, I want to talk to them. I want to see if they know something I don't.

When I make it back inside, I watch one of the boys through the window. He locks the door. I'm trapped and I'm not sure why. I watch him leave and see that my friends are still asleep.

There's nothing much I can do besides go back to sleep myself.

I wake up sometime later and immediately feel that my cheek is still stinging uncomfortably. I'm sure my skin is red where Asher struck me.

The light in the room is dim and I think it's nighttime. Since I slept all day, I don't wish to sleep any longer. I peer over at Enzo and see that he's staring back at me.

He's sitting up and his shoulder is wrapped in the same thick gauze as my chest.

"The door is locked," Enzo says in a hoarse voice. "I tried it, but it's locked."

"I know," I respond.

I run my fingers through my hair in an attempt to remove the knots. I see our bags in the corner of the room, our salvaged luggage. Enzo watches me as I go grab my own. I rummage through my suitcase and pull on a pair of jeans and a shirt to throw on over my bandages. I feel much warmer.

I smile when I see my computer is still intact. After shoving it back inside, I go to stand next to Enzo's cot.

"I think they drugged her. Maybe she was worse than us," Enzo says pointing at Tessa.

Deep scratches are still apparent on her face.

"What happened after I passed out?" I ask.

46

"That man…Alexander. He introduced himself and brought us here. We're in a small town called Shiloh. He said he'd explain when we were all awake."

"He didn't say anything else?"

Enzo shakes his head. I'm left feeling even more confused than before. He forces a smile and holds onto the side of my arm.

"We'll get home soon," Enzo says, trying to comfort me. "They need to send another plane and we'll be home again. I can't wait to be out of this nightmare."

We see Tessa stir and she peers over at us with groggy eyes. Other than looking tired, she appears to be okay.

I'm glad she is awake. I'm grateful we're all in this together.

"Alva," Tessa calls. She pushes back her blanket and then places a hand on her forehead. "You're okay."

I smile. Tessa's first concern is my safety. I wonder how scary it must have been to see me pass out like that. I wonder if they thought I was going to die.

"We're all okay," I remind her.

"This headache," she says, cringing.

I see that she has a glass of water half full on the side table next to her. My own throat burns for some, but I can wait. I won't ask for hers.

We all get dressed into our clothes from Verus. I let Tessa use mine, since obviously hers were lost somewhere in the plane's debris. I try not to think of the plane crash because I know it'll mess with my head. I have to focus on getting back home for now.

The three of us wait until Alexander returns, which doesn't take long once we are all coherent. I wonder if he has someone watching us and I'm not sure why that would be necessary. Maybe he's holding us as hostile enemies until he gets to know who we are.

Alexander motions for us to follow him into the hallway. We walk through the kitchen, but this time no one is there. I see a spot of blood on the wooden floor and I wonder if that is from Asher. I wonder how he is dealing with losing our fight.

From the kitchen, we make a sharp turn to the right through another door. It leads to a fairly big dining room where there is a long table surrounded by thick wooden chairs. A plain chandelier hangs from the ceiling. Three plates have been laid out for us, full of delicious smelling steaming food.

The three of us head for it immediately. Alexander takes his place at the head of the table. He watches us carefully as we start to eat.

I fork up some steamed carrots and mashed potatoes as Enzo cuts into the meat. My mouth waters. The food reminds me of home. It reminds me of my brother, Avery specifically.

Once we are finished, Alexander finally begins talking. It seems to me like he wants our full attention, so I give it to him. I would like to have some answers.

"I'd like to start off by talking to you, Alva," Alexander says, his eyes boring into mine.

"Yes?" I ask, in a small voice.

"No fighting here," he tells me. "You cannot fight with the boys here in the compound."

I don't understand. Asher hit me first and he started it. Maybe Alexander has already scolded Asher for his behavior, so I nod. Asher was the one out of line and he is being punished for it.

"Okay, I won't fight," I say.

"You'll figure out how things work here soon enough," Alexander says.

I don't understand that comment either.

"Won't we be leaving soon?" I ask.

Enzo places a tight hand on my leg under the table. There's a chance he senses something is off.

"I already told Alva this is a no fly zone. However, we will allow planes in to pick you up after two weeks. The landscape to

48

the left of Shiloh is a military testing zone where explosives are used. You weren't supposed to be flying over here to begin with, but I understand it's not your fault due to the storm."

I feel the knot in my chest loosen. For some reason, I assumed Alexander's news was going to be worse than that. I'm interested in learning about a new place, so I'm not too upset about staying in Shiloh for two weeks. It's only a week longer than I expected to be away.

Enzo's hand loosens from my leg and he smiles at me.

"We can stay here?" Tessa asks.

Alexander nods, but he does not smile.

I find it hard to imagine that he ever smiles. I try to judge his age and I guess late twenties, early thirties. It's hard to tell because of the beard.

"I figured we can learn from each other," Alexander says. "I'd like to know about Verus and I'm sure you'd like to know about our home. You can join the kids here in their classes, but you'll have to follow our rules while you're here. There's nowhere else to say in Shiloh, so I'm afraid to say you don't have much of a choice."

"And where are we?" I ask. If this place is part of Shiloh, why does he keep talking about it as if it's something separate? "Is this a school?"

"Sort of. I'm the leader here at The Serenity Compound. I raised all the kids here since they were little. Now, they're all between sixteen and seventeen. They were all orphans when they came here. I make sure they receive an education and are happy and healthy. They all arrived at the same time, so we're family. We all work together here."

"You want us to take classes?" Tessa asks.

"Yes. It's the only favor I ask in return for letting you stay here. You might find some of it useful," Alexander responds.

Tessa, Enzo, and I look at each other. I don't know what harm it would be to learn about these people. I could even tell people about it back at school in Verus. It could make up for the extra week that we will miss because of the crash.

"Anything else?" Enzo asks.

"I ask that you follow my instructions at all times. I want to make sure you stay safe during your time here at Shiloh. My word is final while you're here." He looks at each one of us in turn. "You must respect what I say and do while you're here."

"Fine," Enzo answers for us. "But what's the big deal?"

"We might do things a bit differently around here, but I need to make sure you'll respect our culture. You shouldn't judge us for what we believe in."

I'm not sure why he's saying this to us because we have been taught not to judge practically since birth. I've never been disrespectful to anyone. I've never teased anyone. I've never hated someone for being different. That's something Alexander needs to learn about us, too.

"Why would we judge?" Tessa asks.

Alexander shrugs and smiles for the first time. It seems like he's finished because he stands up. On our way out, he holds on tightly to my shoulder.

"I want you all to rest tonight. I also want you all to get used to the idea that in two weeks, you might not be going home. That's the first thing that we believe in here."

I let Alexander's words sit with me until we are back in the hospital room. I'm not quite sure what to believe because only moments before he told us that we'd be picked up in two weeks. Is he lying to us? Why would he do that? I notice my friends look as confused as I do by Alexander's words.

"We aren't going home?" I ask. I am quickly finding out I'm more talkative than my friends. I've never had to ask so many questions in Verus. "You said two weeks."

"You said you'd respect our beliefs, so here's the first one you'll have to try and grasp. Here, at The Serenity Compound, we believe that the world is going to end within two weeks. We call it, 'The Culling'."

"The Culling?" I ask, hesitantly.

"A sort of...moral cleansing," Alexander responds.

I try not to say anything. I try to be respectful like Alexander told us to be, but it's too *ridiculous.*

I don't want to any questions. I don't want him to think we can't handle being here. I know we are good people and we can blend in with the rest of them. I hope we can pretend to believe him for the next two weeks.

"What happens if it doesn't?" I ask, as Alexander turns to the door.

He turns back and gazes at me.

I can't place his look. I've never seen it before.

"It will," he replies. "It will happen, but if a plane comes in two weeks, then you can get on it. You'll be free to go, obviously."

After Alexander leaves us all alone, we just stare at each other in bewilderment.

I'm still not particularly frightened, but I have read about something like this. I think The Serenity Compound is a cult. It's possible a lot of its members are brainwashed, but I know they're harmless. The world will still be standing in two weeks and I'm certain of that.

I can't wait until the plane arrives and we can fly far away from Shiloh.

Chapter Five

Day Two

As expected, I have a hard time sleeping. I toss and turn and I'm pretty sure I hear voices in the hallway. Some of them sound distorted and strange, but I don't get up to investigate. I have to sleep. I have to heal and be well rested in the morning.

After a while, I slip off the t-shirt I'm sleeping in and toss it to the floor. The sheets feel smooth against my skin and I cool off enough to doze off. I'm in and out of sleep for the rest of the night.

Once morning hits, Alexander brings a few sets of clothing into the hospital bathroom right after waking us. He stops before leaving to say, "Be ready in an hour. We are always ready at dawn."

Enzo starts laughing when he looks over at me.

My eyes are puffy and I can't help but feel groggy. I have often discussed with them how much I hate the morning.

"You shower first," Tessa says to me. "You need to wake up."

I trudge to the bathroom in the corner of the room while pulling my luggage behind me. I don't know why I'm so upset about getting up early for two weeks because it would have happened during training camp, anyway. Still, I would have liked to get up early for camp. I would have looked forward to it.

When I enter the bathroom, I can see it's pretty big with plenty of space to walk around. I analyze the shower for a bit before stepping inside. I know that it's somehow run by solar power and I'm curious how it's set up. I can ask Alexander if that's something they will need help with.

I let the water run until it's hot and I strip my clothes off. I pull at my bandage. My wound hurts and is barely healed, but I'll have to change the bandage anyway. It's too thick and constricting for me to do anything.

Luckily, the bleeding has stopped, but obviously the wound is still tender. I'll have to be careful in the shower not to tear it open again.

I step inside and feel instant relief. I know for a few moments I can forget about everything that has happened. I can close my eyes and pretend that I'm at home. My mother is waiting for me downstairs. My father is about to check up on me before I head to school. Avery will hug my leg before I head out the door. I miss it all.

I feel silly immediately. My family will see me again and I know I have nothing to worry about. But I still worry. I still feel like something isn't right.

The mirror is still clear when I step out even though steam is rising to the ceiling.

There are some sort of special vents, like we have in Verus. They keep the glass from fogging.

As I peer at myself in the mirror, I'm happy to say I still recognize the person staring back at me. It's still me. I don't know why I was afraid I'd lose myself after the plane crash, but I'm still completely intact. I smile for a moment before I finish getting ready.

I use a hairdryer on my hair until it falls at my shoulders. When I peer over at the clothing left for us, I cringe. I hold up a blue dress my size that will fall beyond my knees and zipper up the back to my neck. Without thinking, I opt for my own clothes. I figure that Alexander only left those clothes because he thinks we don't have much with us.

Since it's getting hot out, I pull on some shorts and a blue tank top. I shove on my socks and boots before gathering up the rest of my stuff. Tessa steps into the bathroom as I'm about to step out.

"Didn't Alexander bring in something for us to wear?" Tessa asks. She picks up her dress and gives it the same look I did before turning back to me. "We'll be sweating in that."

"I don't think we have to wear the clothes he brought us. He didn't say anything," I reply.

Tessa shrugs and her eyes wander up to my hair. I know she loves braiding it, so I let her. She fixes it into a beautiful French braid, interweaving my blue streak into it. She smiles at me briefly before I leave her alone to shower.

Once Enzo and Tessa are ready, Alexander returns. His eyes fix on me first and he looks displeased.

I decide I don't like that look. I don't like when someone disapproves of me. It's something I rarely had to deal with in Verus.

"I left clothes for you in the bathroom. I didn't think I'd have to explain any further," Alexander says, with a bitter edge to his voice.

"We like our clothes," I explain.

Enzo nods. He is wearing what Alexander has left for him, but his sleeves are rolled up and the top buttons are undone. I don't think that's how Alexander meant the clothes to be worn.

Alexander looks annoyed.

"I thought you were all going to do what I asked. I'm afraid I can't let you stay here if you don't follow my instructions. This is *very* important to us. You're being disrespectful."

I gulp. Alexander is making me feel weird again.

"I didn't know…I didn't think I'd be able to work in the clothes you brought us," I reply.

"You don't even know what work you'll be doing yet," Alexander says.

"Do you really want me to change?" I ask. I don't know why I'd have to. I don't know why wearing his clothes is so important. "Can I just wear mine for now?"

Alexander stops talking about it, so I assume he agrees for now. I hope he doesn't bring it up again.

"I have breakfast ready for you three. The others will eat later. I don't want you to meet them all yet," he says.

After he leaves, I tell my friends I want to stay behind. I'm not hungry. In fact, I feel a bit nauseous. I know eating breakfast won't be good for my stomach.

Tessa and Enzo head out and I sit back down on my cot. I think about closing my eyes for a bit, but decide against it. For some reason, I don't want Alexander to think I can't handle it. I want to prove myself to him. I want to prove that I can blend in with his other students. How different could they be?

Besides believing that the world is ending in thirteen days from now. There's a chance Alexander was only kidding. I'm sure he wasn't, but still, it puts me at ease for a few moments.

As I'm shoving my luggage back into the corner, I feel someone in the room with me. He barely makes any noise, so I'm not sure how I realize he's there. I stand up quickly to face him.

There is a boy around my age. He is dressed like the rest, but with a darker blue shirt. His hair is combed out neatly, parted far to the left. It suits him and makes him much more handsome than Asher, the boy I punched out.

I watch as he looks at me and shoves his hands into his pockets. His eyes are the deepest blue I've ever seen. I don't know why, but for a long moment I stare back at him, unable to say anything.

"Alva?" He asks. "Or Tessa?"

"I'm Alva," I say quickly.

There is something calming to me about the boy. I think he must be around my age, but his clenched jaw makes him look older, around eighteen. He is strong and lean, making me believe he must have trained as a fighter. I see his hands look as though he has thrown a few punches. I want to ask him questions about it, but I don't.

"Barnabas," he says. He walks closer to me, but keeps a reasonable distance. He seems uneasy around me and his eyes trail up to my hair. "How old are you?"

I find myself wanting to know what he's thinking.

"Sixteen," I say. "And you?"

"Seventeen." He flashes a smile briefly, but then goes back to being reserved. His hands go back into his pockets and he leans on the heels of his black shoes. "I like the color of your hair. I've never seen anything like it."

The smile is back on his face as he continues to stare.

I see his mouth open, but he stops himself from saying anything else. I think he is struggling with something. Of course, I can't figure out what it is.

"I like it, too," I say, breaking the silence. "Why are you here?"

His expression turns serious again.

"I'm supposed to give the three of you a tour. Alexander sent me. He wants you to meet me first."

"Why?" I ask.

"I'm a leader here. Well…that's what I'm training for."

"So, are you a commander?"

That's the only thing I can compare it to. If the compound is like the army, Barnabas must be a commander. But then, what is

Alexander? What is his role? He must be something more important than a commander, something big.

"I don't know what that means," Barnabas replies honestly.

"You have nice eyes," I say, changing the subject.

I'm not lying. They are somewhat mesmerizing to me. Barnabas looks away and I think he might be uncomfortable. When he turns back, I see that his cheeks are light pink. I'm not sure why my comment embarrasses him.

"Oh," he replies quietly. "Thanks."

Yet another thing I don't understand. It doesn't make sense that complimenting his eye color would appear to cause him so much stress. Has no one ever said anything before? Am I offending him in some way?

I don't say anything else and I take another step closer. The separation between us is straining our conversation.

He watches me closely, following my every move. His eyes fall down to my boots and then back up to my hair.

"What are you looking at?" I ask, a bit angrily.

I'm not used to people watching me this way. He seems startled by my question and looks back down.

"I'm a little fascinated by you," Barnabas admits. "I mean...I've never seen anyone like you."

What?

I try to figure out how I'm acting differently than what he's used to, but I can't guess. What am I doing that's so fascinating to him? I have to admit that I'm a bit fascinated by him in return. He is different, but I don't know if I like it. I can't put my finger on it.

I hear someone clear their throat and my attention snaps to the door.

Alexander is glaring at Barnabas.

I open my mouth to say something, but Alexander motions him into the hallway. He closes the door, but it doesn't snap shut all the way.

I move as close to it as possible without them being able to see me through the window.

"Aren't you supposed to be the smartest one here?" Alexander hisses. "Your curiosity is alarming…there is nothing you can learn from these people. They can only learn from us."

"I want to know what it's like in Verus. I want to know why they act so strangely," comes the boy's voice.

"Remember what I told you," Alexander says. "It's our job to teach them the right way. I am being too forgiving already."

I don't hear any response from Barnabas, so I move back toward my cot. When Barnabas reenters the room, I see his face is set with determination. Luckily, Tessa and Enzo walk in behind him and I'm grateful for their presence. I don't want to say anything to offend Barnabas after he was scolded.

Barnabas's gaze darts between Tessa and Enzo, but he doesn't linger on them as long as he lingered on me. I don't know what that means. I don't know why he finds me more interesting than them, but I figure Alexander frightened him into showing little interest in anyone.

They greet each other and Barnabas starts the tour.

I enjoy hearing him talk. To me, he has a commanding voice, despite his shyness.

He takes us past the kitchen and into the main room. It is more like a living room, with a few comfortable looking couches and several rugs on the wooden floor. There are some instruments in the corner and Enzo smiles. He likes playing the piano and sometimes the guitar, which I know from our time together at home.

He pushes open the main doors and we step into the warm air onto a wraparound deck. I see it's high up and that we are on the top floor of the compound.

I peer off the side and see a green field down below. It's surrounded by a low fence that separates the field from a massive cliff. I recognize that cliff. My eyes go to the wreckage of our plane far, far down below. I feel numb for a moment.

Barnabas steps next to me and I can tell he's looking at me. He follows my gaze to the destroyed plane and lowers his eyes.

"That must have been terrible," he says. "I'm sorry about that."

"We're alive," I say briefly.

"That's a blessing," he replies. I want to ask him what blessing means, but I don't. I don't feel like talking at that moment. Eventually, Barnabas begins to speak to us again. "We're allowed time in the field for recreation after class. It's high up, so you'll have to be careful."

Tessa looks at me. She has the same tense look on her face as Enzo does.

My eyes go instead to the village to the left of us. I can barely see it from the angle we're at, but a cobblestone path winds up toward a cliff side town. It's one of the most interesting and terrifying things I've ever seen.

The houses are narrow, yet high, and they're all so close together. They are backed up all the way against the carved out side of the mountain and there is only a few feet of path separating the houses from the massive cliff. It winds all the way and seems to disappear into the mountain.

The last thing Barnabas shows us outside is the small chicken coup. There are only a few of them, but he explains that's where they get some of their eggs. He gives me a handful of seeds to feed one of them and I find myself smiling as they peck at my palm.

Barnabas leads us back inside. He heads down the stairs in the middle of the main room and we follow him. We enter into a long, dim hallway. As we walk, I can see into the open doors lining it.

The first room is a class full of girls. Someone is talking, but it sounds like an adult woman. They are being taught something.

Their eyes follow me as I pass by the door.

"What are they doing?" I ask, as we pass by another classroom full of boys.

I can't make out what they're talking about.

Barnabas turns to me before answering, his hands behind his back.

"Class. You'll be attending tomorrow," Barnabas says with a grin. He clears his throat before speaking again. I see that we are standing at another metal staircase that leads down into darkness. He sees me peering down and steps in front to block my view and then continues. "We only go down there to sleep. Nothing else. It's too dark to do anything else."

"Can't you put lights down there?" Enzo asks.

"No," Barnabas says quickly. "No lights, that's the rule. You'll have to get used to it."

"Okay," Enzo replies hesitantly.

He looks at me and raises an eyebrow. He wants me to ask more.

"Why does it need to be dark?" I ask. "I'm good with that sort of stuff. I could fix it."

"Our visions," Barnabas responds, cutting me off. "Our nightmares…well, I'm not supposed to call them nightmares. They're a gift. Alexander tells me mine are a gift."

I can see him struggling with something, but he doesn't say what it is. I don't ask because it seems personal.

His jaw is tense and his hands wring together uncomfortably.

"Visions? I've never had visions," I say.

"Alexander will make sure that you do," Barnabas says. "You will around me."

I don't like the way that sounds. How could Alexander force me to see something I've never seen before? And what are visions? What will I see while I'm at the compound? The thought frightens me, but I do my best to push it aside. I try to tell myself I'm overreacting.

Nothing that they do here at the compound can possibly affect me. It's *their* tradition. It's what they believe in, not what I believe in.

Barnabas brings us back to the first floor and he tells us to pack up our things. He brings us to the massive bathroom that we enter through the main room and I see that long lockers line the walls.

He opens three empty ones and steps aside.

"Girls come in at six a.m. and boys at seven a.m. Usually, we keep our daily outfits in there, but you all have much more stuff than us. Leave what you want to be cleaned in one of the hampers." He points to one of them along the wall. Only a few white towels have been thrown inside. There is a stack of them on a bench near the individual showers. I count four showers in total and three separate bathroom stalls. "Hopefully you'll wear our clothes soon. You'll have to get used to it."

I shake my head. I'm full of questions, but I can't formulate them. I see him staring back at me, his eyes searching me again.

"We'll be home before we'll have to do that," I say.

Barnabas frowns.

"It'll be easier when The Culling takes place if you start doing it now," Barnabas says.

Enzo clears his throat and looks down at the floor, away from us. Tessa gazes away, so I am the only one catching his glance.

"You really think that's going to happen?" I ask.

"I know it is," Barnabas says, wide-eyed. "We are trying to help you. Alexander thinks it will be difficult for all of you to assimilate, but I think you're reasonable people. This is what he's done to keep us safe."

"We don't need to assimilate," I say, angrier this time. "You can do whatever you want here, but we will only stay until we can go home. You can't make us do anything."

"No one is making you," Barnabas says softly.

He turns and we follow him out of the room. He waits for us to file out and then motions toward the couches.

"What do we do now?" Tessa asks.

"Enzo, come with me," he orders. "We're going to have a meeting with Alexander, you two will be told about your classes by Cassandra. She is Alexander's wife."

I'm surprised by this. For some reason, I never imagined Alexander to have a wife. I think he seems too hard and unforgiving. I don't know how I can already make this judgment, but I don't like him. I don't like when he's around. I don't like how he makes me feel.

I also don't like the separation that's being created between Tessa and I and Enzo. Why should he have a different teacher than us? It makes me feel helpless because I know I shouldn't argue anymore.

Once Enzo and Barnabas leave, we wait by ourselves. We wait for a good hour before Cassandra finally joins us.

She enters with a confident smile. Her dark hair is tied up in a bun, with one strand falling to the side of her face. She looks around twenty-something, which is clearly younger than Alexander. Her eyes focus on us and the smile quickly fades from her face. She gives us the same displeased look Alexander has been giving us.

Her long blue dress falls at her ankles where her black shoes peek out.

It's not a comfortable looking outfit and I stand by the decision I made to not wear it. I will never wear it, I decide. I will never wear that dress.

She clasps her hands together as she takes an unsure step closer to us.

"Stand up," she orders. I don't like the firmness in her voice. I obey, however, because for some reason I'm afraid not to. Her eyes analyze me first, but in a different way than Barnabas did. He seemed curious, but she looks at me in disgust.

Cassandra continues to instruct us by shouting, "Put your arms at your side."

I let my fingertips touch the sides of my bare legs and peer up at her strongly. I will not be intimated by this woman I don't even know. I feel like I should stand my ground. Against what? Why do I feel so strange?

"What's wrong?" I ask.

"Those are much too short. You'll need to wear something longer. At least something that covers your legs."

"They're shorts," I say in disbelief. "Why do my legs need to be covered?"

She looks surprised by my question and her lips set in a short line.

Tessa immediately gives me a hard look. She is scared or angry with me.

"Tomorrow you will wear jeans at least," Cassandra says. "Do you have a jacket?"

I think of my leather jacket in my locker. It is brown and comfortable and it reminds me of my mother. She gave it to me as a gift for my fifteenth birthday.

"Yes," I say.

"Wear it tomorrow. Cover up your arms." Her eyes go to my hair, which she doesn't seem to delight in it like Barnabas did. Again, she looks angry while asking, "What is that? Can it be rinsed out?"

"No. It's permanent dye," I respond, raising an eyebrow. "It will have to grow out."

"Can we cut it out?"

I know I look horrified. Cut out a huge chunk of my hair? But, why? I've always liked it and no one has ever been upset by it before. It's only hair. It's only a color. I'm still me with or without it.

"No!" I shout. I pull my arms away from my side and back up a bit. I don't like being so close to this woman. I wait until I'm calm before saying, "It stays. I will wear the jacket and my jeans, but this stays."

Cassandra gives me a dangerous look, but turns to Tessa.

I go numb as she begins to critique my friend. I can't hear the words she's saying because they're so jumbled and I think I must be blocking it out. A strange feeling overwhelms me and I want to run away. I'm scared because I have never felt like this. I don't even know how to categorize it.

The woman's voice gets louder and I snap back to attention.

"You will have to get used to being without Enzo. He will be separated for now, but you will see him during supper. You will be given jobs and start them tomorrow after your classes. Since you make three extra people, we will need your help." She pauses for a moment. "Do you have anything to say about that?"

I know the energy is drained from me, so I shake my head. Doing a job will help get rid of the uneasiness I feel. Working with my hands will clear my mind. They must need some help doing something useful and there are many things I'm good at.

"Can we choose?" Tessa asks.

"No. I have already chosen. Tessa, you will be on cleaning duty and Alva will be cooking duty."

My heart sinks.

I'm not a good cook and I never have been. Avery would be thrilled at a job like this, but it's not for me. Am I supposed to object once more? I can't help myself.

"What are the other jobs?" I ask.

"Three boys train to be leaders, two hunt, and three work as mechanics," Cassandra says.

"Mechanics!" I blurt out. "I want to work with the mechanics. Tessa would be better at hunting."

That's my specialty. That's what I'm good at.

Cassandra, however, looks horrified.

"That is out of the question. You can't work as a mechanic and Tessa cannot hunt," she replies. "You won't fit in there."

"Yes I will. I'm probably better than anyone you got. I don't know how to cook, I'll be useless there."

Cassandra looks thoughtful for a moment and then a sly grin comes across her face.

"You both can choose your own jobs. If you make it past the first day, you can stay. If not, you'll have to do what I say."

Both Tessa and I nod in agreement. Why wouldn't I be able to make it past the first day? I know I'm good and Tessa knows she can handle hunting. Still, I know there is more to it. I think Cassandra assumes something terrible will happen to us. I clench my fists and think, *I can take it.*

Cassandra spends a little bit more time lecturing us on being on time for class and not taking too long showering in the morning because there are a lot of girls. She tells us how everything here is a system and we can't mess with that system.

I want to laugh. During the past day, I have absolutely destroyed their system. I haven't done one thing they've wanted me to. I hope that doesn't change any time soon. I also don't know why I'm taking so much pleasure in defying them. I should be respectful, but I can't when I think what they're doing is wrong. I can't change myself to fit in. Isn't that what I've always been taught?

We're not given much to do that day and we still don't meet anyone else.

Cassandra comes in later to rewrap my wounds and put ointment on Tessa's cuts. We are given some antibiotics to fend off infection.

66

I feel like everything will truly start tomorrow. I will know what the compound is really like and if I can ever fit it. I'm not sure if I care. I remind myself that we will be out of here in no time and it won't matter.

Still, I want them to like me. I want them to learn from me. I want to learn from them. I hope they have something worth learning about.

After being told to lie down in the hospital for most of the day, I know that it's almost nighttime. Cassandra told us that the first night in the basement is the hardest. Apparently, it's difficult to get used to the darkness. Darkness doesn't scare me, however, and I feel like I can handle it.

It's not until we are on our way down when I start to panic. Cassandra looms behind us while Tessa and I stand in front of the staircase.

The hallway is pitch black beyond the third step.

I'm not sure how I will find my room or where I should go.

"Keep your right hand on the wall at all times and you'll never get lost," Cassandra tells me gently. "You go straight until the second door. Yours is one of the easiest to get to. There are bumps on the wall letting you know when you reach your door. All you have to do is feel two of them in your palm and you'll be at your room. Your bed will be the only thing in there."

She explains the same thing to Tessa, except Tessa is the third room.

"Who is in the first room?" I ask.

"Barnabas. He is our finest student," Cassandra says proudly.

I wonder why that is, but I don't ask. What does Barnabas do differently from the rest?

"Any other rules?" Tessa asks, a bit sarcastically.

Cassandra doesn't seem to notice Tessa's tone.

"No lights of any kind and no talking. These rooms are for sleeping and visions only. I doubt you'll be blessed and pure enough to have visions, though."

These words bite at me. I'm not sure why. I wouldn't want visions and I'm not sure they're real, anyway. What does she mean *pure*? I wonder what it means to be pure. I have no idea.

I watch as Tessa goes down first and disappears. I peer at Cassandra, but she doesn't say anything. She waits for me to go ahead. I step on the first rung, my boots loud against the metal. I pause for a moment and then continue forward.

Within a second, I am engulfed in darkness.

Chapter Six

Day Three

I run my hands along the wall and feel it's jaggedness under my fingers. I try to will my eyes to readjust, but the darkness never goes away. No matter how long I look, there's never a hint of light or anything but pitch blackness. I have never experienced anything like this.

I feel my hand run over the first bump and I'm grateful that I had my palm high enough to touch it. I think about whether Barnabas is sleeping in the first room. I wonder if he hears my boots against the ground as I walk by.

When I reach the second bump, I keep moving until I feel the cool wooden door under my skin. I find myself getting frustrated. I hate not being able to see. I hate that no matter how long I look, I'll never be able to see. I feel like I'll go crazy down here.

I eventually find the door frame to my room and stumble inside. My side hits something hard and the pain radiates up to my chest. I have to stop myself from groaning because I know it'll disturb anyone who's sleeping. With my hands, I'm able to feel the soft, plush bed before me. After sitting down on it, I feel that there is enough room to take off my clothes and shove them into the small space next to me.

I take a deep breath after I'm underneath my covers. It's warm and inviting, so I immediately close my eyes. It doesn't matter. The darkness inside my eyelids is the same as the darkness with them open. I feel the softness under my palms and relax.

That wasn't so bad. That wasn't scary.

It was inconvenient and I don't understand it. I think for a moment it's a way to stop us from talking and staying up late when we are supposed to be sleeping, but I don't get why they are so controlling.

I have to remind myself that maybe it isn't cruel to them. The kids seem used to it. Barnabas didn't seem particularly unhappy. I can't judge them for that. I try to think of the things they would find strange in Verus.

My clothes, for starters. Fighting Asher was another thing frowned upon. The blue streak in my hair is still another.

I never gave any of those things a second thought back at home. No one cared. If I had fought Asher to hurt him for my own benefit, that would be different, but he initiated the fight. I thought that's what he wanted.

I try to clear my mind and I begin to drift to sleep. I'll have to learn more in the morning. I nearly laugh thinking about what a funny story this will be back home. I wonder if Lonnie will want to listen to it, even though I know he will. In the darkness, I think of Lonnie. I picture him sitting next to Harmon, whose red hair was always so hard to miss. I decide that Lonnie is one of my schoolmates that I miss most.

Lonnie never scolded me for what I wear or how my hair was. I think he liked me for me.

I think I fall asleep for a little while before I start to hear it. There's a voice in the hallway, a low murmur I can't make out. It sounds so far away. As I sit up and strain my ears, I still can't make out any of the words. A cold chill runs through my body but I stay where I am. I realize I'm afraid to move.

The voice disappears almost as quickly as it came, but I am left feeling unsettled. I thought no one was allowed to talk. What would someone be talking about now anyway? My body finally relaxes and I lay back down.

Alva.

I'm rigid again when my I hear my own name. It is almost soft enough to be a whisper, but I'm sure I heard it. The darkness is making me go crazy. It's making me hear things that aren't real.

I hold back the urge to cry by shoving my head under my pillow. I do my best to block out anything I might hear from this point on. I won't hear it. I will ignore it.

The night goes by slowly and I'm pleased when a light buzzing goes off near me. I'm able to find it with my hands to turn it off. I quickly slip on my clothes as I hear people beginning to stir in the other rooms. I shove my feet into my boots and stumble out into the hallway.

Shoulders bump into me painfully as people push by me. I feel a hand on my arm, someone grabbing onto my skin. Somehow, I know it's Tessa. She is the only other person here who would need help.

We walk slowly forward together, Tessa with her hand on my shoulder and me with my hand on the wall. I'm relieved when we make it to the stairs and Tessa lets go of me. When I step into the light, I have to shield my eyes. The lights above us are bright and blinding. I see that all the other girls have already exited the hallway and I can hear their footsteps going upstairs.

Tessa turns to me.

"That was terrible," she says breathlessly. "Barely got any sleep."

"I know," I reply.

We hurry along to catch up with the other girls, but when we reach the bathroom the stalls are already full.

The room is filling up with steam, but the windows stay clear like in the other bathroom in the infirmary. Two girls are waiting patiently in their pajamas, sitting on a bench that runs along the wall adjacent to the showers. They look up at us as we walk closer.

One of them smiles slightly, but the other one remains silent and turns away. The one who continues to look at us has dark black curly hair and bright eyes. She looks young and innocent, but, from the look on her face, our presence confuses her. She seems unsure about how to act.

The other girl, who is tiny and has dirty blond hair, nudges her as if she is doing something wrong by looking at us, and they both look away. I exchange glances with Tessa and she frowns. No one seems to want to know us. No one has even introduced themselves.

Almost all of the showers turn off at once, so I start to undress, but the curly haired girl turns to me.

"What are you doing?" she says. "Wait until you get in there."

She points to the shower. The four girls exit their individual showers dressed in their knee length blue dresses. Their gazes linger on me as they head toward the station to dry their hair.

A tall girl, with long limbs and a slim figure stops right in front of me. I smile, but she does not return it. The dress hugs her curves and looks good on her, to the point where I think it might be a different dress than what everyone else is wearing. I wonder why that is. I wonder why she can wear something different from the rest.

When she doesn't say anything, Tessa and I inch past her. I grab my things out of my locker and step inside my individual shower. I see that there's a separate changing room before the actual shower, which is lined with wooden benches, which are still wet from the previous girls. At least there is a clean white towel. I place my things down, strip off my clothes, and move aside the curtain that blocks me from the water.

The water is cold when I turn it on. It seems that all the first girls used up all the warm water, so I stand there shivering. I decide not to wash my hair because I do not want to spend time drying it this morning. I want to be ready at the same time the other girls are.

I clean myself with some of the soap and rinse quickly. I'm done before the rest of them. After I change into my jeans and tank top, I remember to slip on my leather jacket. I hope Cassandra will be pleased that I remember, but then I'm not sure why I care. I don't.

Some of the other girls are lingering in front of the mirror once I step outside. They are fixing their hair and talking quietly to each other.

My jacket clings to my arms due to the moisture that remains on my body due to my haste, but still, I'm not too hot. Tessa is out soon after me, so she spends some time reworking the braid in my hair. It looks as good as it did yesterday.

I notice Tessa didn't wash her hair either. I see the girls watch us while we move to the side of the room. I don't like their eyes on me. I wish they would stop, but they don't.

The tall, slender girl comes closer. This time I think she wants to talk.

"I'm Ester," she says.

Her voice is polite, but I'm not sure it's genuine. There's a smirk on her face that tells me she doesn't mean to be nice. I reach out to shake her hand, but she doesn't accept it.

"Alva," I say, instead.

"Tessa," my friend says beside me.

"We've never had anyone new, so I'm sorry if everyone is staring at you," she says, looking at both Tessa and I.

I nod. That makes sense. That explains mostly everything. I guess I would stare at them if they ever came into Verus, but I'm not sure I would do it so cruelly. It doesn't look like they are not interested in me. They look at me like they hate me.

The last girl finishes pulling her curly hair up into a bun and fumbles over near Ester. No one looks happy.

"The boys are coming soon," Ester says to everyone. "We almost didn't make it out in time. You're going to have to be quicker, Eden."

She gives the last girl with the curly hair a glare.

Eden. I try my best to remember.

Ester leads us back out into the main room and we sit down on the couches around the room. I slump back, exhausted, but I see that all the other girls have their knees pressed to together and their hands in their laps. I think Ester seems to be the best at doing this.

She gives me a hard look, but I don't move.

I do sit up, however, when the boys start piling in. They walk past us without saying a word. Enzo remains as silent as the rest of the boys. He does give us his biggest grin though.

I see Barnabas look at me briefly, but his eyes don't linger long. I see the slightest hint of a smile on his face. I think I must be imagining it. Ester is glaring at me with a look that I interpret as disapproval.

Asher stares back at me. His face is rigid and I can see the bruise on his cheek. Even his eye is slightly swollen. I shrug and he looks away, flushing red. I feel like I've already made an enemy. I've never had someone hate me so much right away. I've never had someone hate me so much, period.

But why is Ester looking at me like that? Why does she seem so fixated on what I'm doing? I also wonder why we're waiting. My stomach is empty and I desperately want breakfast. I start to get up, but Ester calls out.

"Where do you think you're going?" she hisses.

74

I stand there, unsure.

"Breakfast."

Some of the other girls giggle. I'm not sure why.

"We eat with the boys, so we wait until they're done."

"Really?" I ask.

"Sit down," Ester says. "We wait for them."

I sit down and Tessa puts a hand on my shoulder. She seems to have mastered the ability to do the right thing, unlike me. I'm not sure why everything I do is wrong, but it only makes me want to prove myself more. I hate failing, even if I don't understand the reason behind my failing. I hate being the worst at anything

About a half hour goes by and Ester, Eden, and a third girl get up. They disappear back toward the kitchen.

My blood boils because I don't understand why they are allowed to leave. I decide to speak up now that Ester is gone.

"Where are they going?" I ask the girl next to Tessa.

She doesn't say anything. No one says anything. They don't even look at me.

I start to smell food and I understand on my own. Their job is cooking and they are the ones that make the food in the morning. That is the job that Tessa gave up. I am grateful that she doesn't have to be with them because that would leave me alone with the mute girls.

Another half hour passes and the boys finally file out. Their line breaks apart and they start talking jovially to each other. Enzo finds us and I see that he is dressed like them.

I frown at him disapprovingly, like Alexander probably would at me.

He laughs and peers down at himself.

"It's not so bad," he says. "But I guess it's easier to wear this than the dresses they picked out for the girls."

"Where have you been?" Tessa asks, giving him a quick hug.

Some of the other boys watch us. The rest of the girls are gone.

"Just with the boys," Enzo tells her. "I don't like it. I want to be with you and Alva, but they said I couldn't. They said I'd have to get used to it for a while."

"I don't get why they separate us. In Verus ..." I start.

"We don't have to worry about it at home," Enzo says, cringing. "I know. That's why I hate it. I don't understand it."

"Did you get a job?" Tessa asks.

Enzo nods.

"I didn't want to hunt, so they said I could take care of the chickens. The cleaning girls used to do it," he explains.

Someone grabs Enzo's arm and pulls him away from us. It's Asher. He steps in front of Enzo and gets close to me. I can feel his hot breath on my cheek. His dark hair flops over his forehead.

"Don't ever touch me again or I'll make your life miserable here. Got that?" Asher says, with a cruel smile.

"What are you doing?" Enzo asks, his face flushed with anger. "Why are you talking to her like that?"

I've rarely ever seen Enzo angry like that back in Verus.

"Because soon enough the three of you will realize I can do whatever I want. You're the ones who have to learn your place," Asher hisses.

I feel my face get hot. I want to do something, but I'm not sure what. All of my frustration comes from the fact that I don't know what he's talking about. I don't understand why he is talking to me like this or what I've done so wrong.

"What's our place?" I ask.

Another boy comes up behind him, the short boy who was there when I punched Asher.

"Well, with the other girls," the boy says. "If that's not clear enough, I don't know what is."

"Shut up," Asher says, with a laugh. "The little girl doesn't know what we mean. They must be from somewhere screwed up."

Over Asher's shoulder, I see Barnabas watching me carefully. He turns away when I notice and starts toward the kitchen with two other boys. His hands are shoved into his pockets.

I hold onto Enzo and Tessa and we brush past the two boys. I don't want to talk to them anymore. I want to eat.

When we head inside the dining room, a bunch of people are already seated. Alexander is at the head of the table with Barnabas to the right of him.

One of the other boys who Barnabas was with takes the seat to the left of Alexander. He has a dark unreadable look on his face. He is a bit bigger than Barnabas with fiercer features. He does not have the lean build of a fighter, but the tall stature of someone who has done hard labor. I know the difference.

They are all dressed the same except for Barnabas and the two other boys. Their shirts are a bit darker, but that is all.

The girls crowd down at the opposite side of the table, around Cassandra. We are separated, but I chose a seat next to Enzo. The division between male and female starts with us.

I count everyone at the table. Nineteen total, including my friends and I. I'm guessing nineteen people make up the population of the compound, unless there are some more people hiding somewhere. I doubt it.

Alexander stares at us until everyone is completely silent. They all press their hands together like they are about to pray, so I hesitantly do the same.

"I'd like to thank you for keeping us safe and preparing us for the upcoming weeks. I thank you for the opportunity to rebuild this world in a pure way and making us worthy of living for you. We will try to help these three new souls and I hope you will help us in that journey. I know it will be difficult for all of us."

I see Alexander's eyes on me. I look away and watch Barnabas. His eyes are closed and he's biting his lip. I think he looks stressed.

"Any news for us Barnabas?" Alexander asks, keeping his eyes trained on me.

Barnabas opens his light eyes and leans over to whisper in Alexander's ear. Alexander smiles and looks around at everyone. Everyone stares back at him, waiting.

"Things are going forward as planned. The new souls will be accepted, but there is one who wishes to bring us down. There is one who can destroy everything."

I hold my breath as everyone looks at me. Why would Barnabas play such a cruel joke on me? Why would they all even assume that whoever it is, Alexander is talking about me? What plan? Who is Alexander referring to anyway?

"What?" I ask.

I hear Asher snort.

"It means nothing," Barnabas says unexpectedly.

Alexander gives Barnabas a hard look and surprises me by smiling. He is smiling at me.

"Alva, you will get along well here. We are not trying to harm you. We are not trying to make you feel uncomfortable. We welcome you all with open arms. In twelve days, you may leave and forget about Shiloh all together, if you wish. You'll be back home in Verus."

"Okay," I say. I don't know what else to say, so I focus back on the food laid out on the table. Eggs, bacon, pancakes, waffles. I'm hungry, so I add, "Let's eat then."

Some of them laugh and Barnabas cracks a small smile. It erases from his face when Alexander nudges him. They begin to pass the food around and everyone starts talking again. They're not as bad as they seem.

I should not have been intimidated by first impressions.

In order to lighten my own mood, I turn to Enzo and Tessa. They are already digging into breakfast and seem to be happy. Everyone else seems jovial and engaged in conversation, so we talk about a few things at home. None of the girls stare at me anymore. One of the girls even gives me a brief smile.

I notice that Barnabas is the first one to leave. He stands up abruptly and grabs on to his plate. I watch him disappear as he heads back into the kitchen. I don't know what he could be doing, but I don't ask. It seems out of place to ask.

I also think about why he whispered into Alexander's ear before. Why couldn't he speak to us directly about whatever was going on? I suppose it's another tradition, something I won't understand. I wonder who they are praying to because I don't think it is any god I have ever heard of. Some people in Verus are religious, but they've never done anything like this. This all seems unnatural to me.

Three girls never talk. I think they all look similar, small and meek, with pale skin and dark hair. I notice they barely ever look up from their food and they begin to gather up the dirty plates as people start to file out.

"They clean," Enzo says, probably noticing my gaze. "Cleaning duty."

"That's what I was going to be," I whisper back.

I see that we are close to being left alone with Alexander, so I decide to get up. Enzo and Tessa follow me out of the room and back into the main room. I'm unsure of what we should do next. There are only a few other boys sitting around, but I feel better when Barnabas and the two boys he's always with come in and approach us.

"They want to meet you," Barnabas says, motioning toward the two boys next to him. Enzo waves hello. He already knows them. The tall one with dark features that had been sitting across from Barnabas at the table eyes me. I can't read his expression. Barnabas motions to him and steps aside. "This is Demetri."

He has an uncertain glance and now I realize his eyes look sinister. I don't think he means well, but I'm not sure how I know that.

"Alva and Tessa. Nice to meet you," I say, answering for my friend.

It doesn't seem like Tessa's going to speak anyway. She's staring up at Demetri like he's a monster, so I elbow her to make her stop.

"I guess you can say that," he responds in a booming voice.

"And this is Asa," Barnabas adds, pointing to the boy to his left.

Asa is much shorter than Barnabas and his grin feels pleasant. He has a kinder look and seems eager to welcome us. He clasps his hand around mine.

"I'm sorry about your crash. I can't help but feel it was deliberate," Asa responds.

We all sit on the couches to talk. I'm glad we finally have some time to learn about them, but they all seem interested in us. That is, they all seem interested except Demetri. His face is rigid and I do not like the way he is looking at me. I know I couldn't beat him in a fight. He would crush me.

"Deliberate?" Enzo asks, sounding curious. "What do you mean?"

"Like it was done on purpose," Asa says. He does nothing but explain the definition to us, which I already know and I'm sure Enzo does too. He continues after Enzo stares at him, "It was part of the gods' plan. Do you know anything about them? Alexander seems to think you're godless."

"Some people who practice religion in Verus believe in gods. Some, only one God. Christians," Enzo explains.

Asa laughs.

"Our religion isn't mandated or created by man. It only started about twelve years ago. That was when all the visions about The Culling started."

"What visions?" I ask.

"Most of us have them because Barnabas is around," Asa replies, looking at me. "It is a gift."

That's the second time I've heard that. I peer at Barnabas, but he is looking at the floor. I want to talk to him because I am convinced that he doesn't agree. Whatever it is, he seems stressed out by it. I see his hands clench into loose fists.

When he peers up at me, he looks hopeful. His locks eyes with mine.

"No one has visions where you're from?" Barnabas asks.

"No...no, of course not," I respond.

I want to ask him more about it, but the boys are summoned by Alexander. Even Enzo leaves, so Tessa and I find the girls.

They are in the kitchen. The three mute girls finish up wiping down the dishes and place them in their rightful cabinets. None of them look up or acknowledge anything else going on around them.

I go to help them, but Ester grabs my arm.

"That's not *your* job. You gave it up," Ester comments.

She squeezes a bit too tightly, so I pull away. I don't mind. I just thought I'd extend a helping hand, but I guess I should listen to Ester.

A few moments later, we head down to the second floor. Ester leads us into the first classroom and all the girls take their seats. Tessa and I take the seats that are left in the back.

The classroom makes me feel claustrophobic. The lights are bright and overwhelming. The green chalkboard has an ugly brown tint to it. I have never been in a classroom like this and I don't like it. I feel trapped, unable to concentrate properly.

Tessa pinches my arm to get my attention.

"I can't wait to teach our class about this," she says, looking excited. "I can't wait to get back."

Before I can say anything back, Cassandra enters and looks around the room. She smiles at Tessa and me.

"Good. You found your seats," she says.

There's something about her appearance that makes her seem more pleasant to me than she did yesterday. I think she approves of the way I'm dressed.

"Yup," I reply.

"The first class you'll be sitting in on is Sexuality and Birthing," Cassandra explains.

I furrow my brow and she notices. I have never heard of such a class.

"Birthing?" Tessa asks, reflecting my thoughts.

"You know about babies, right? That's what girls have," Cassandra says.

This gets all the girls to laugh and peer back at us. I feel alien and my cheeks flush red.

"Not all females have children," I respond.

She raises an eyebrow.

"I guess not. If there is something physically wrong with them or if they're unwanted," Cassandra says.

She takes a seat on the edge of her desk. The girls turn their attention back to her.

"What if a woman chooses not to have a child?" I ask.

I know plenty of women in Verus who haven't had children and some who never will. I think they are mostly happy and they don't see it as something they must do.

Cassandra laughs again.

"We don't have that luxury down here. Not with 'The Culling.' There will only be us left."

I decide not to say anything. I'm too interested in her lesson and I want to see where it's going. I somehow know I will disagree with all of it.

She first launches into a speech about how female bodies are made for certain things compared to male bodies. She claims that girls are not strong because they're not meant for labor like men are. Cassandra tells us we are made out of man, therefore we are meant to serve them. Our happiness in life comes from the happiness of our mate.

I frown.

This goes against everything I've ever known. Even talking about girls and boys separately, as if one can be inferior to the other, makes me cringe. How could anyone believe this? But it seems like they all do. This is another one of their traditions that I can't stomach.

Tessa looks like she's about to burst and I'm sure I look the same way. I think of Enzo. Does that mean Enzo is better than us and has always been? Have I also been meant to serve him? Is it my job to keep him happy? The ridiculousness of that statement makes me laugh out loud.

Cassandra's face turns red as she looks at me.

"Something funny?"

Again, all the attention is on me, but I don't speak. I hear Tessa's voice ring out.

"This is stupid!" Tessa says. "I'm sorry. I'm trying to be respectful, but *this* is disrespectful. What you're saying is disrespectful. I am just as important as any of the boys here. I matter just as much."

"Don't say those things in front of my students," Cassandra says. She looks flustered. "Don't poison their minds with your nonsense. This is how things will be when we're all alone. This is how the world will be rebuilt."

"You can't rebuild the world like this. Listen to what you're saying. You're a woman. You're giving all of us a disadvantage," I reply.

Tessa nods.

I see some of the girls watching me curiously. They seem to be thinking about what I'm saying and not rejecting it, but Cassandra quickly regains control of the class.

"You're leaving in two weeks so it won't matter, right?" she says firmly.

I guess that's true. What do I care? Her kind demeanor returns when I nod, so she continues by explaining, "I will be talking to these girls about what will be expected of them and their partner, if they are chosen by one of the boys."

"Chosen? What does that mean?" I ask.

"The young men will choose a wife when the time comes. We will need to repopulate. To be chosen by one of the leaders is the best thing that these girls can strive for."

"Barnabas," Ester says, with a giggle.

Eden leans over and hits Ester's shoulder playfully. The other girls laugh and even the mute ones smile.

My stomach churns uncomfortably and my heart beats faster. It is a joke I don't understand. I want to know why she's said his name, but I'm not sure where my curiosity comes from.

"I think it is clear that Ester will be paired up with Barnabas," Cassandra says with a smile. "It will only happen if you keep up the hard work though. Right now, you are my best student."

"He will choose me. I know it," Ester says.

"Don't desire something that's not yours yet," Cassandra says gently. "He will pick you - in time."

My cheeks flush red and I feel hot. If I lived in Verus, would I be forced to be with a boy only because he "picked" me? Would he make me do something I didn't want to do? Would I be forced to have a relationship with him? The thought sickens me, a boy choosing me and forcing me to obey. I thought these archaic beliefs were long gone. I thought we were done separating genders in this way. I try to wrap my brain around it.

I see Barnabas in a different light. Would he do this? Ester seems willing, but it's not really a *choice*. I think she would have to anyway, regardless of what she wanted.

The thought of them together burns at my chest. This is a feeling I can't place. This is something I've never felt before.

But Ester is so…mean.

I feel sick. I can't believe I'm having thoughts like this, shaming Ester in my mind, making myself believe she is a horrible person. I feel furious with myself and furious with everyone else. I know they're making me start to think like this.

I clench my fists and place them on the desk. I can't identify any of these new emotions or sort them out. I don't want to hate Ester simply because she longs for someone and I don't understand it.

Ester is not mean, I repeat to myself. I should stop having horrible thoughts about her.

Suddenly, my hate turns to Cassandra and Alexander. I instinctively know all of this is their fault. The girls are not bad. They just don't know anything else. They've been taught by Alexander for too long to know anything else. If only I can show them there's another way…

I fume all throughout class. It's long and I can't concentrate. When it's over, I'm told that my working group won't be on until tomorrow. I don't know who I'm working with yet, but I hope it's not Asher. He is the only one I cannot be around, besides Cassandra and Alexander.

Tessa doesn't start until tomorrow either.

We head outside for a while, but I don't even find peace there. Not with the remains of the plane crash right in front of us. I get flashes of it and I feel sick. I feel us going down again. I feel the impact this time.

During dinner, we finally see Enzo. He looks exhausted, but still cheerful. Alexander eyes us suspiciously the whole time, so we don't get to talk much.

I try not to look at anyone, not even Barnabas, especially not Barnabas. I feel ashamed by my thoughts about him and Ester during class. It's not fair to hate them.

When it's time for bed, I enter the basement a bit more confidently. I'm not afraid of what lingers in the dark, only because I've already gotten through it once before. I'm more afraid of the light and of all the eyes on me all the time.

Tomorrow, I have to show them that I will not change. If anything, they will change.

I will help them understand that things can be better than what Alexander and Cassandra have forced on them. I will help them fight for their own freedom. I know they are capable. Deep down, I know that's what they want.

Chapter Seven

Day Four

I wake up feeling somewhat well rested and a little bit better about things. I'm not sure why. I decide that I'll contact my father today. I have to make sure that he will be on his way for us as soon as possible. Of course, I won't be able to do this until our break after class.

My thoughts linger briefly on the voices that disrupted my sleep once against last night. They were easy to ignore, but I still wonder who could be talking late at night. I want to know who was bold enough to break Alexander's rules and what they were discussing.

I want to ask, but I'm not sure anyone will tell me.

My fingers graze the basement wall until my feet hit the metal steps that lead up into the light. I think I'm the first girl awake because I slept in my clothes. I hear people leaving their rooms behind me.

When I make it to the bathroom, I see that I'm the only one there. I quickly find a shower and undress myself, making sure that my clothes find a dry spot. Today I will have time to wash and dry my hair. After I turn on the water, I smile to myself because it's warm, unlike yesterday. In that moment, the compound doesn't seem so bad.

I'm done quickly, so I dress in the same clothes from yesterday and run my fingers through my wet hair. When I exit the small changing room, I see someone staring back at me.

Ester's expression is angry. Eden and the third girl, Ariel, are standing behind her watching me curiously. Ester's arms are crossed over her chest.

I can tell by the way she's standing that she doesn't intend to hit me…at least not yet.

"You took my shower," she says immediately.

I see Tessa step into the room and stop short. The smile fades from her face as she watches the three girls approach me.

"I didn't know it was your shower," I say.

I try to move past them, but Ester bumps me back with her shoulder. She is strong, but I know I'm stronger.

"You were here yesterday, weren't you? You saw how it works," Ester says.

"Let me through. I'm not afraid to fight you," I reply, through gritted teeth.

Ester doesn't scare me. The compound might scare me, but she doesn't.

"Don't do it again," Ester warns.

She bumps past me once more and I fall back. I feel my cheeks burn red as I sit on the floor. I don't understand why they are acting like this. I didn't know it was that important.

Tessa heads over and helps me up. I gladly accept her hand and head over to the sink with her. I try to busy myself with drying my hair so we don't have to talk about it. I don't like feeling embarrassed. I don't like how Ester has made me feel. It seems pointless to embarrass and intimidate someone in that way.

Part of me wants to fight back, but I know I can't. Even though I consider myself a fighter, I know it's not in that way. I will not push back out of anger. I have to remind myself that Ester is not the enemy. She is as caught up in this mess as everyone else.

When my hair is dry, I let it fall loosely over my shoulders. I know we're expected to wear it up, so I guess this is my way of rebelling against Alexander. I'm not sure this is right, but I have nothing else.

I wait for Tessa and then we join the other girls back in the main room, but it's another hour before the boys are showered and we can eat. I try to hold back my frustration during breakfast.

"Why do we have to wait for the boys?" I ask Alexander after he finishes his strange prayer.

Barnabas and Demetri look up at me. Barnabas looks frightened, but Demetri looks amused. Alexander's face is red and he remains silent as he watches me.

"Are you that selfish?" Demetri asks, with a half-smile. I'm not sure why he's smiling. "You think you're better than everyone else?"

"No, but you do," I respond. "It seems logical for the girls to eat once the food is ready instead of waiting a half hour."

Demetri and some of the other boys laugh, but Barnabas has an unreadable expression on his face.

"Why would girls get to eat before us?" Asher hisses.

He looks like he wants to punch me.

Do it, I urge him in my mind. *I'll drop you again.*

"What do you mean? Why does it matter?"

Enzo grabs my arm. He looks tense and gives me a warning glance. I'm not sure why he doesn't want answers, too.

Alexander stops eating and folds his hands in front of him. Everyone's attention is on him.

"Is there no separation where you come from? Does Verus believe in something different?"

"Why would there be separation? There is nothing different between Enzo and me."

"Besides everything!" Demetri interrupts me. His eyes are burning into mine with anger. "How can you say something so crazy?"

Alexander nudges Barnabas, smiling. Barnabas smiles back and begins eating his food again. In a few moments, he looks up at me and the smile is gone. I'm not sure what he is thinking, but I feel like he is mocking me. Alexander and Barnabas obviously share a joke I don't understand.

My chest burns again and I stop talking. I look to Enzo and Tessa, but they are busy eating. Why aren't they sticking up for Verus? What are they so afraid of and why are they avoiding my gaze? Something feels off.

I drop my fork. I'm no longer hungry.

I know something is wrong with my friends. Enzo's nudge before and the scared look on Tessa's face during my interaction with Ester earlier come to my mind. I want to talk to my father. I want to make sure that he knows we are in trouble.

After we eat, we are ushered to class almost immediately. I slump in line, feeling more defeated than usual, until I find myself in the same classroom as yesterday. Cassandra joins us a few moments later and writes something on the chalkboard in large letters.

Religion.

Great, I think. Now I can finally learn about what they believe in. Now I can begin to understand what's going on.

"What is religion in Verus, Alva?" Cassandra says, already directing the attention at me.

I take a deep breath.

"I think it's a belief in something higher than us," I say.

It's my best guess and I think I might be wrong, but Cassandra gives me a surprising smile. It seems pleasant and genuine.

"Good," she replies. "It's the same here. We believe in a group of gods higher than us, a vision given to one of us here. There is one here who started it all."

I see Eden and Ester exchange smiles.

"Who?" I ask.

They all turn to look at me, except for Tessa. She is staring at Cassandra like I am.

"Barnabas," Cassandra explains. "His visions are what created this compound. It's his genius that brought us all together."

My mind spins. I was thinking Barnabas is Alexander's pawn, but now I'm not sure. Barnabas might be the one controlling everyone and making them believe all these insane things.

It's possible I was unfairly blaming Cassandra and Alexander.

No. There must be something else to it. Barnabas does not look or feel like someone who knows what he's doing. Alexander does. Demetri does. Asher does. But not Barnabas. He looks frightened and unsure sometimes. That is not how someone acts who is manipulating everyone.

Then again, I'm not too knowledgeable about manipulation. Everyone is upfront and honest in Verus.

My heart pangs thinking about home and I stop. I feel like I'm about to cry and I don't want them to see me break down.

"How?" I continue. "How did he start this place? I thought he was young when it opened."

"He was," Cassandra says. She changes the subject. "The images we have of the gods we worship and try to appease are from Barnabas's mind. They have shown themselves to him and only him. Those of us lucky enough to have our own visions have seen amazing things. We know that 'The Culling' is coming and we only have ten days left. This is it. This is what we've been waiting for."

I bite my lip. Tessa looks mesmerized and she doesn't return my glance. I don't think she will ever speak out against them again and that scares me.

"We are at their mercy," Ester says seriously.

Everyone else says that same thing back, except for me and Tessa. Is that some sort of prayer?

I decide I will not say it. I will not say it even if they ask me to.

"Would anyone like to draw what the gods look like on the board? I would like Alva and Tessa to see."

Of course, Ester hurries up to the board and accepts a piece of white chalk. She draws for a few minutes, sweeping lines up and down the board, and then steps back with a huge smile on her face.

I see the drawings for the first time.

I stare at the huge human-like creatures with massive drawn in eyes and pointy fangs. The image terrifies me, but I can't look away.

Is that what Barnabas sees? Are these the beasts that haunt his visions?

I suddenly feel bad for him and I understand that fearful look in his eyes that I sometimes catch. How can someone live like that, constantly seeing such horrible creatures? Something is wrong with him and I know he needs help.

"How do you know what they want?" I ask. "How do you know this is how they want the world to be?"

"I know. Alexander knows," Cassandra replies.

It's not much of an answer. I'm not sure why everyone else accepts that as an explanation for the compound and its harsh rules.

Cassandra leaves the drawing up on the board for the rest of the class, so I know it's being burned into my memory. I don't think the horrible image will leave me and it'll make sleeping tonight difficult.

She remains vague about the history of the compound and how Barnabas could have possibly started it all, but I hope I will learn soon. I can even ask him directly. I'm not sure if he will answer all the questions I have and I'm not sure it's worth asking.

I halfheartedly listen to Cassandra go on about the decaying morality of society around them.

I feel like she is talking about me. I feel like she is trying to make me react. I'm not sure I can help myself.

"Even though we believe in these gods, the aliens that will end our earth, Alexander and I still know that it is important to keep our own morals intact. This is what you all have learned well. The world outside of us is decaying and most of them deserve to die. We cannot have a society where girls don't respect their bodies and themselves. Most of the women outside of this compound are too sexually promiscuous and have been ruining the sanctity of marriage. This disgusts me. This should disgust everyone. We must all remain pure until the time is upon us. This is the only way we will be accepted into the light."

This is the most confusing thing I have heard since arriving in Shiloh. I'm not sure what she means by girls not respecting themselves or being sexually promiscuous. I have never heard these terms before.

I decide it's not the time to ask questions because Cassandra is staring at me. I think she expects me to protest and she is trying to make me angry.

She continues on and on until we are finally given our break. Cassandra tells us that we only have an hour to relax before we go to our jobs. Her threat about lasting more than a day lingers in the back of my mind.

I hurry back upstairs into the main room where I grab Tessa's arm and we head outside. It's a bright, sunny day and I want some fresh air.

Tessa seems to regain a bit of herself in the grassy field, recognition returns to her eyes.

Ester, Eden, and Ariel also join us outside. They don't say anything, but stand near the fence looking out over the cliff.

I watch as Barnabas wanders near them, squinting toward the bright sun. I find it strange that he is the only boy, but comforting. I think he doesn't believe in the separation and he feels comfortable with everyone being together.

Barnabas avoids my glance and goes to stand next to Ester. She greets him enthusiastically and he returns her smile. His white teeth flash and I stare. Is he happy? Is it because of Ester?

I see his smile fade when he finally catches my gaze until Ester grabs his arm and they begin talking again. I can overhear them, even though I try not to.

"Hi, Barnabas," Ester says.

"Hi, Ester," he replies quickly, running a hand through his hair.

He looks uncomfortable, like he's been forced into something. His eyes dart up toward the compound and I see Alexander watching everyone. After a few moments, he heads back inside.

Ester and Barnabas talk for a while, but the stiffness of their conversation stresses me out. I can't imagine ever talking to anyone like that, so I try to tune it out. Back in Verus, I never talked to anyone else unless I had something to say. I would only ask questions in which I was interested to hear the answer.

I give my attention back to Tessa. She is picking grass out of the ground and flinging it over her shoulder. She looks bored and restless.

"Tessa," I say gently.

She looks up at me.

"I think we should fight," I say, with a smile.

Tessa returns my smile and stands up, wiping off her pants.

"We need to keep practicing for the army, right?" Tessa says with excitement. She starts toward the compound for a moment before turning back to me. "I need to grab something."

I sit alone while I wait for Tessa to return. It looks like Barnabas and Ester's conversation is over and they are both staring awkwardly past the cliff. I see that Barnabas's eyes are focused toward the crash and it looks like he is thinking deeply about something.

When Tessa runs back, I see she is holding medical tape. She tosses it to me and I quickly wrap my hands before handing it back to her. I wait while she does the same. I notice now that everyone else is watching us.

Barnabas has his back pressed against the fence and his arms folded across her chest. Ester looks annoyed.

Tessa and I stand up to face each other, keeping a distance of a few feet between us. We desperately need to relieve some stress and continue to keep up our skills.

I have fought Tessa many times, so I know her style. She is good and we have both learned from each other. I know she will not be like Neddie and she will wait for me to make the first move.

"Say go," I demand, looking directly at Barnabas.

He looks confused at first, but eventually steps forward. He keeps a safe distance from us.

"Go?" he says.

Tessa begins to jog around our invisible circle, keeping her eyes on me. I keep my fists up near my head as she lunges forward. I was wrong. She makes the first strike. She's a little bit too enthusiastic about fighting again.

I block her fist is blocked with my arm and I punch into her side. My arm throbs a bit, but she stumbles back.

The smile remains on her face as she starts back toward me.

One of the girls gasps, distracting me, and I feel Tessa's fist connect with my lip. I somehow know that it's been cut open and it burns painfully. I peer down and see the blood drip onto the grass.

By the time the fight is over, I see blood trickle down from Tessa's eyebrow and she is laughing. We both start laughing uncontrollably until Barnabas steps over and stands in front of us.

He is watching me, wide eyed.

"You're bleeding," he says.

He reaches out toward my face, but Ester grabs his arm back. She steps away from him immediately and looks down at the ground.

"Sorry for touching you, but…" Ester looks up at me and then back at Barnabas before continuing. "You shouldn't touch blood. It isn't clean."

Barnabas nods and then smiles.

"It's okay, Ester," he says in a calm voice. He motions toward Tessa and I. "I think we should head inside and get some bandages."

I agree and we follow him to the hospital room. I can feel my lip is swollen. I find some rubbing alcohol to put on it. Barnabas walks over with an icepack and hands it to me while Tessa is in the bathroom fixing up her eyebrow.

As I press the icepack against my lip, Barnabas continues to stand in front of me. He looks curious again, with one eyebrow raised.

"Why did you do that?" He asks.

"It relieves tension. We have to keep practicing, anyway. We are training," I say.

"Training for what?"

I think about how Alexander told him to stop asking us questions. He is doing it anyway. I start to think that Alexander doesn't have as much control over him as I thought.

It's possible he *is* the one doing the manipulation.

"The army."

"You're going to be in an army?" Barnabas asks, amazed. "They let you do that?"

"Yes," I respond, somewhat annoyed. "Everything is different outside of Shiloh. Nothing has to be like this."

"I think I have something to talk to you about…" Barnabas starts, uncertainly.

I wait for a moment, but my eyes lock behind him.

Alexander has entered the room and he is walking toward Barnabas. His hand clamps down on Barnabas's shoulder and he yanks him toward the door.

"What are you doing in here alone with them?" Alexander demands.

I see that Tessa has exited the bathroom and is frozen near the wall. I think she is afraid again, perhaps terrified of Alexander. I feel it, too.

"He was helping us. We were fighting," I say.

Alexander turns to me, his expression dangerous. He eyes my new wounds.

"You were *what*?" Alexander says. "Didn't I warn you not to do that?"

Barnabas is looking down at the ground now, avoiding eye contact. He steps aside and let's Alexander pass. Alexander looks at him briefly and Barnabas quickly exits the room.

We are left alone with Alexander.

He is close to my face and I lift my eyes to meet his. I want to show him he doesn't intimidate me like he does everyone else, even though he does. Still, I will not look away.

"Meet me down in the first class room in five minutes. Tessa, you too."

Tessa is shaking a bit as Alexander leaves.

We wait a few minutes before heading down the stairs, passing Ester, Eden, and Ariel as we go. Ester frowns at me, but doesn't say anything. For a moment, I think she might be afraid for me. I don't think she likes seeing people get in trouble.

I try to remind myself that I don't belong here, anyway. Getting in trouble doesn't matter because I will be leaving. I can't convince myself not to be afraid. I can't push away my bad feelings.

I grasp onto Tessa's hand as we find the first classroom where Alexander and Cassandra are waiting for us. They break up their own conversation and both glare at us. He motions for us to take two of the front desks. Tessa continues to grasp my fingers.

Alexander steps forward with Cassandra slightly behind him. She looks angry, but his expression remains calm. His calmness is more unsettling than Cassandra's anger.

"What did I say about fighting?" Alexander asks, looking mostly at me.

It seems like everyone blames me for everything here. I am getting used to it.

"You told us not to," I reply. "But it was only between me and Tessa. We know what we're doing, so I didn't think ..."

"It doesn't matter. I don't want you to give those girls any ideas," Cassandra spats. She slams a hand down on my desk. "I've spent years raising them to be ready for everything that's coming. If you want to stay here, you need to respect that!"

I sit back as Cassandra yells at me. I feel like even she is unsure of her words, but Alexander watches her closely.

"I think they can have ideas of their own, without me," I say sharply. "I don't think they need to be a certain way to be ready for your end of the world."

"It's 'The Culling,' Alva. Can you follow our instructions on this? These children are impressionable and sharing your ideals will not help them in the future," Alexander says. "Besides, it's not my end of the world. It's everyone's."

I frown. I don't want to argue about the end of the world, but I do want to talk about Barnabas. I take my chances.

"What's going on with Barnabas? Why do you all say that he started this place?" I ask.

Alexander pauses and steps closer to me. He stoops down so I can feel his cool breath.

I suppress a shudder.

"He was five years old when I met him. He needed a home and I gave all the orphans here a home. That's all you need to know," Alexander says slowly. "Try to keep yourselves under control while you're here. You can't be beating each other to death here."

I know he's overreacting, but I keep quiet. The way Alexander is watching me is making me nervous. He thinks I'm a bad influence. He thinks I'm the problem.

"I'll try," is all I say.

He smirks and steps away from me. They both watch us as we leave.

Tessa lets go of my hand and turns to me before we reach the stairs. Her face is filled with anger, unlike anything I've ever seen before.

"Why can't you just agree?" She asks. "It's not our job to change what they do here. We want to go home."

I am surprised by her reaction. It takes me a moment to say something back.

"What if you see something bad happening to people? Are you supposed to stop it?" I ask. I'm not sure. "What if these kids are in trouble?"

"They're older than us. They can fend for themselves. Nothing horrible is going on here and they like it this way. Who are we to say it's wrong?"

Tessa starts up the stairs, leaving me alone. I wait a minute before following after her. I try to let her words settle, but something still feels wrong. It's still my belief that Barnabas is not happy and he represents them all.

One of the boys, Rufus, finds me in the main room as I sit by myself. I only know his name because I heard Asher say it one time. He was with Asher when I punched him out. I think he was one of the boys that restrained me.

He doesn't say anything to me and hands me some clothes.

I unravel them and see it's a blue jump suit that's about two sizes too big, which makes me think they're trying to push me away from the job.

I change in the bathroom and find three boys waiting for me back in the main room. Asher's glare is unwavering as I start toward them.

"You sure you want to do this?" Asher asks.

"Why wouldn't I be sure?" I ask back.

Asher smirks and points to the two boys next to him.

"Rufus and James."

James is quiet and I've never heard him say much. Rufus gives me a blank look like he did before. I'm not sure if he has much of an opinion on the issue.

I follow them down to the second floor all the way to the last room where there's a small kitchen with chairs and a chalk board—another classroom.

Asher points to the stoves. They are more modern, unlike the old wood burning stove in the kitchen.

I know more about these.

"Do you know how to fix anything? Might be too primitive for you since you're always talking about how progressive Verus is," Asher says.

I don't like how he's talking to me and I feel like Cassandra put him up to it. I'm sure he already hated me before, but now he can't keep the hate out of anything he says.

"I know how to fix it," I shoot back.

"We're replacing parts on all of them, so you girls can use them tomorrow. We're almost done. All you have to do is not screw anything up."

I ignore him and get to work. My back hurts from hunching over the whole time and my fingers are in pain from grasping the tools.

After a while, Asher makes me do all the work while he watches. I don't like the sly grin on his face. I don't like how he keeps his eyes on me. The whole time Asher hassles me and none of the other boys say anything.

It makes me feel uncomfortable.

When we get our break for dinner, I find out that Asher made us all stay much longer than anyone else. In fact, we missed any food at all.

He grabs my arm as I head to the kitchen to look for something to fill my grumbling stomach.

"Dinner is over," he says sternly. "If you miss it, you can't eat. Alexander's rule."

I scowl at him. He's the reason we missed it and I know he knew it would happen. I push past him and back into the main room. I am filthy, but I will have to go to sleep feeling dirty and uncomfortable.

I slump down on the couch, alone. I'm not sure where everyone else is even though I hear voices outside. It's nearly dark out, so I have no idea what they're doing. I'm too annoyed to find out.

While I am alone, I head into the bathroom and find my small computer from home. I know it works and I know I'll be able to call my father. I sit on one of the benches and wait for it to make a connection to my home.

I see my father's face on the screen and I want to cry.

"Alva?" He asks, frantically. "Is that you? How'd you call here?"

I force a smile, trying not to look too relieved. I don't want him to worry.

"The computer I was working on. It survived the crash...just like me," I say. I don't mean to add the last part. It slips out, but I change the subject as best I can, "Was Alexander able to contact you?"

"He did. He said you were all fine," my father says, still smiling. "I'm so glad to see you. I didn't think I could contact you."

"You might not be able to after this. I don't think it'll have enough juice to make another call this far, unless I work on some power source." I pause. "What did he say to you?"

"He says we can be there the exact second they say we can come. Normally I'd ignore this order, but I can't get another plane until then. The army has strict rules about taking a plane for personal reasons, especially when they're running drills and we have so few. That crash cost us a lot of money," he says.

"I'm sorry," I reply. I'm not sure why I'm apologizing.

"Don't say you're sorry," my father says, with a furrowed brow. "Besides, if we went without their authorization it would be considered an act of war here. Army protocol. We don't know enough about them yet to invade. We can't put anyone else in danger since we still don't know why your plane was off course. Are you sure you're okay, Alva? They seem a bit...off."

"They are. They're fine, though," I say.

I stop myself from complaining any further. I don't want to worry him, even though that's the exact reason I called. I want him to come, but I can't tell my dad to invade just because I'm having some bad feelings. I can't tell him to call for war if there's nothing really wrong with me.

"If they've done anything..."

"I'm fine, Dad," I say again. "I just can't wait to get home."

"I know. Stay strong." He smiles sweetly. He's never had to comfort me like this before, so it's strange for both of us.

"Okay. I should go, Dad. I'm getting tired. Tell everyone I say hi," I say. "I'll try to call back soon."

"Okay," my dad replies. "I love you."

I cut him off before I can say it back. I don't want to start crying. I start to put my computer away, but I see someone watching me from the doorway.

My heart skips a beat.

It's Barnabas. He doesn't say anything.

"I'm sorry," I say quickly. "Are you going to tell on me?"

He shakes his head and approaches closer. He sits down next to me and eyes my computer.

I smile and put it on my lap so he can see it.

"What is that? It's so small," he comments.

I hand it over and his strong fingers clasp around it. The smile stays on his face as he manipulates the screen.

"It's my computer from home. I've been working on it for a while," I explain. "I'm guessing Alexander hasn't taught you about these."

"No," Barnabas says. His expression turns somewhat sad. He looks up at me, eyeing my cut lip, and then stares into my eyes before asking, "What's your home like?"

"It's nice," I grin. "I wish you could see it. I wish you could see how things could be. You could be different if you wanted to."

"It doesn't matter what I want," Barnabas says softly. He hands me back my computer, looking conflicted. "This is what I'm supposed to be doing. I'm supposed to be leading these people and I've failed if I can't. This has nothing to do with Alexander."

"This has everything to do with Alexander." I place a hand on Barnabas's hand. This is the first time I feel like he is hearing what I'm saying. I think he might understand. "Even if you think the world is ending, Alexander is shaping you all the way he wants.

He is taking control, not you. He is forcing the way he wants everything to be on you and making you believe it's supposed to be that way. Just answer one question for me."

"What?" Barnabas asks, staring down at our hands.

"If this world were to end…is this the way you'd want it to be afterward?"

He pulls his hand away and stares up at me. His face is set with determination and he begins to look angry.

I think I've lost him. I've said too much and insulted him.

"It's not up to me, he says. Don't try to confuse me. Remember, we are at their mercy."

Barnabas stands up and leaves me alone.

I try to figure out who he's actually talking about, but I immediately think of Alexander and Cassandra. We are at *their* mercy, not some imaginary force that Barnabas seems to be obsessed with.

I don't see him for the rest of the night.

That night when I sleep, I have a dream about Barnabas. He is standing alone in a field, but his sleeves are rolled up and his shirt is somewhat unbuttoned. He is smiling. The sky is clear behind him. He looks the best this way. He is content.

I'm not sure why he is so happy, but it feels good to see him this way. I can feel the stress is gone from him.

That is the last nice dream I have.

Chapter Eight

Day Five

I hear my own name early this morning. I'm not sure how I know it's morning, considering it's always pitch black inside my room, but I just know.

Alva.

It's a cold, emotionless voice that I have heard before. I'm not sure if I am experiencing déjà vu or if I know this person talking. Who would be calling my name this early in the morning, anyway?

I grab hold of the side of my bed and stumble forward. I still haven't gotten used to walking the darkness, so I stub my toe on the wall. It hurts, but I don't curse to myself like I normally would. Instead, I dress in my dirty work clothes from the previous day and work on my boots. I decide to head to the showers early to avoid any confrontation with Ester and the other girls. They can't complain if I use them long before anyone's even awake.

The upstairs is still dark when I find my way up to the first floor. I see out the windows that the sun is beginning to rise. The light is barely up over the mountains in the distance, so I have some time alone and that makes me happy.

I take a longer shower than usual and fix my hair. I find some clean clothes left in my locker, but most of my stuff seems to have gone missing.

I give myself a few moments to stare in the mirror. My lip is still busted, but it isn't swollen. I'm starting to look different somehow. I look exhausted and somewhat beaten down in a way I've never experienced. This place is making me feel low. It's making me feel lost.

I hate that.

After spending some time giving myself a mental pep talk, I feel a bit better. I only have to keep going for nine more days. I have to keep my friends going. If I can, I have to convince the others that this place needs to be changed. I can only imagine how beaten and broken they must feel, even if they are doing their best to hide it. Or they don't even know how terrible they have it.

Barnabas might be the worst at hiding it. I personally believe he is the most aware of the deception going on around him. If he feels it, then I know I'm right in thinking something's wrong. I hope some of them would even consider coming to Verus when my father arrives.

I have to wait for two hours before everyone is done showering.

Tessa sits next to me after she's done and begins talking to me normally, but she is wearing the dress that all the other girls have on, which makes me feel out of place.

"Why are you wearing that?" I ask Tessa.

She shrugs and forces a smile. I know it is forced, but I can't figure out what's so different about her. What's wrong with Tessa?

"It's not so bad," she says. "I'll only have to wear it for a little while."

I realize I am the only one not wearing the uniform now because Enzo has been wearing it properly for a few days now and Tessa has finally given in for some reason.

"But why?" I ask, more forcefully this time.

She gives me an annoyed look.

"I don't want to act out for the sake of acting out. They're letting us stay here and it makes them happy, so why not?"

"I'm not acting out for the sake of acting out. I just don't think it should be a rule," I respond.

"It's easier for them...having the uniforms. It makes laundry easier and it cuts down on time searching for something to wear and trying to be different."

"What?" I ask.

I cannot process her words. I haven't been wearing my own clothes in an attempt to be different. It's what I like. Since when is it wrong for me to wear what I like?

Some of her points make sense, but she doesn't sound like the Tessa I knew back in Verus.

The strange attitude of my friends continues at breakfast where Enzo still sits next to me while we begin to talk about upcoming class that day.

"It's mending and sewing today. Girls are supposed to be good at it," Ester explains, mostly to Tessa.

Everyone is much nicer to her now and I find myself a bit jealous. She hasn't done anything different except wear the uniform, but now she fits in. Why are they treating me like this?

"Enzo likes sewing. You're good at it. Tell them," I interrupt.

At home, he has a sewing machine and he was starting to teach me. He's pretty good at it, but some of the boys start laughing and Enzo looks away from me without answering.

My insistence makes Enzo angry with me and the boys' taunts grow louder. Enzo has never been angry with me like this, especially not over something so stupid. Not something that's the truth.

"Drop it, Alva," Enzo says softly.

My cheeks flush red.

Everyone is laughing, except for Barnabas. His face is set in a frown as he watches me. Alexander nudges him and whispers something in his ear. Barnabas looks away and begins eating again.

It seems like he's always getting in trouble for no reason.

I start to think about home. I try to think that everything will return to normal once we're back in Verus, but now I'm not sure. Will Enzo and Tessa treat me differently once we're back? Will they change forever? Will Enzo start to treat girls the horrible way they're treated here? What if everything begins to unravel at home too because of what we've seen here?

I think we should leave. I think staying here is a mistake. But will Alexander chase after us? Will my father know where to find us? Panic sets in and I feel trapped. I don't know what to do.

The plane crash wasn't the worst thing that could happen, stepping foot in Shiloh and being rescued by Alexander was. It even threatens to destroy what we have back home. I try to calm myself down. I try to tell myself I'm overreacting. I try to remind myself that they can't touch us back home and my friends will return to normal. I'm making too big of a deal out of this.

When we are finally in class, everything I attempt to do is abysmal. I am not meant to sew. My fingers don't work the way they're supposed to and I keep pricking myself. The third time I cry out in pain, Ester approaches me. She sits down next to me and helps me readjust my fabric.

"You'll have to be good at this, you know," Ester says calmly.

"I don't. I don't need to do this," I reply, biting my lip.

Ester glances at me and puts one of her hands on mine. I am surprised by this kind gesture. Even though I try not to hate Ester, I still do. I'm thinking irrationally.

"I know this is hard for you, but it'll get easier. I think you'd make a good addition to our compound," she says. "You have to learn your place."

I don't say anything because I assume she is trying to help. Maybe she is trying to take me under her wing, but I don't think she understands that I do not want to be part of Serenity and I never will. I'll never fit in. I'll never make myself fit in.

I don't want to learn my place.

"Isn't there anything else you want to do?" I ask Ester quietly. "Besides sewing and cleaning?"

I don't want to get her in trouble and Cassandra is only a few feet away, but it doesn't look like she is paying attention to us.

"I want to be a mother," she replies, with a slight smile.

I think about that a moment. There is nothing wrong with that, even if I don't want to myself. I don't have any motherly instincts and I don't think I ever will. It's not something I've ever wanted for myself.

"What's so great about that?" I ask. "I mean, why does that mean so much to you?"

She gives me a surprised look.

"That's our job. All of us will become mothers when the time comes. That is our duty in life and what we were made for. Don't you want that, too?"

"What about the girls who don't want that?"

"They don't exactly have a choice," Ester says, frowning.

Her response disturbs me.

If I was somehow made to stay in Serenity, would I have to get pregnant? How would they force me into it?

"What do you mean?" I ask.

Ester's voice becomes lower.

"The boys chose the girl they want to…well, you know. If any of the boys choose you, you have to follow their orders. It's our duty."

"That's rape," I say, almost too loudly.

"What?" Ester asks.

Cassandra turns, but she doesn't say anything.

Still, I assume her ears are strained in this direction. I lower my voice so I'm almost inaudible.

"Do you know what that means?"

Ester shakes her head.

My heart sinks thinking about how they all will be treated in the future. I'm realizing that it's possible Ester has no idea what sexual assault is or the rights she has over her own body.

"The boys shouldn't have control of your bodies. It's different in Verus," I say. I struggle to explain so that she'll understand, "If you don't want to sleep with a boy, you don't have to. It's your choice."

"That's okay because I want to have a child with Barnabas. I want him to pick me," she says, looking confused.

"That's not the point. Do you want to have a child with Barnabas only because they all tell you that's the most respectable thing you could do with your life? Is it because Barnabas will be a leader?" I pause. "Or is this a choice you came to all on your own? Do you really want to be with Barnabas?"

She stares at me.

"Why shouldn't I want Barnabas? He's the best boy here. He's the one we all look up to, besides Alexander. Who else could be better?"

I shake my head. I'm not sure what else to say because I don't think she understands. It's not the sleeping with Barnabas that makes my head spin—it's that it might not be Ester's choice. I'm scared that she doesn't realize she has choices, that there's more to her life than just this.

110

In Serenity, she doesn't have any choices.

"Don't do it because they tell you to. Don't let them make you feel ashamed."

Ester shrugs.

"I'd feel ashamed if I didn't."

I feel nauseous.

Cassandra is closer now and she watches as Ester teaches me how to sew a straight stitch. When it is my turn, I am much better.

"See," Cassandra says, with a light hand on my shoulder. "You're learning. You might make a good woman after all."

My chest burns as I look up at Cassandra. I do not return her smile. I hate what she's saying. I hate how she makes Ester believe her greatest achievement in life will be having a child with Barnabas. I hate how those are Ester's only options.

When class is over, I turn to Ester and wrap her in a tight hug. I don't want to let go because I think I could get through to her if I tried harder. I'm too exhausted. I can't do this on my own.

She is surprised at first, but hugs me back.

"Thank you for helping me," I say. "Hopefully I can help you in return."

Ester smiles at me before leaving. I don't think she knows what I'm talking about, but that's okay. I think she's starting to have doubts about the compound. I guess that's all I can do right now.

I'm the last one to leave the room. Tessa doesn't wait for me and Cassandra leaves right after Ester. I know she saw us hug. There's a chance she thinks everything is going to be okay with me now, but she is wrong.

I see Barnabas sitting down with his back pressed against the wall. He is clutching his hands and I can see blood pooling down on the tile floor. He gives me a terrified look as I approach and scrambles to get up.

"I thought everyone was gone," he says breathlessly. "You should go."

He backs away from me, but I take hold of his hands and cup them in mine. His blood gets all over me, but I don't care because something is obviously wrong.

I can feel his eyes on me as I analyze his strange wounds.

I see he has a puncture wound through each of his palms. His warm blood pools in my own hands as I clutch onto him. Has he harmed himself? Is this some form of punishment inflicted by Alexander?

"What is this?" I ask. "Did Alexander do this?"

"No," Barnabas says quietly. "It's the stigmata."

I take off my jacket and ease him back down onto the ground. I sit next to him and press the fabric against his wounds. Hopefully, I can get the bleeding to stop.

"The what?"

"Stigmata. That's what Alexander calls them. I get them every once and a while if I had strong visions the night before. I bleed a lot."

He's talking about it casually, like it's normal. My concerned expression makes him look away.

"Alexander said you wouldn't understand. He told me not to talk to you about it."

"You listen to everything he says?" I ask.

"I have to," Barnabas says firmly. "He's the reason I'm alive. He's the reason I'm..."

Barnabas trails off, looking distraught.

He doesn't seem to want to finish the conversation, so I sit patiently next to him with his hands in mine. They are warm, but I don't feel any blood anymore. His fingers grasp at my palms.

"You should get your hands looked at," I say. "I don't want you to bleed to death down here."

"Should be about done," he responds.

I raise an eyebrow.

"There were holes right through your palms. I don't think you'll be okay for a while."

Barnabas shrugs and pulls his hands out from under my now blood stained jacket. When he raises his palms, there is nothing. No scars, no blood, no holes. Everything is as it's supposed to be.

My mouth gapes open as Barnabas stares back at me. I grab at his hands again and run my fingers along his palms, which makes him shudder.

"How did you do that? Did you trick me? What is going on? "What's going on here, Barnabas?" I reply angrily.

I'm not sure how he could have tricked me because I saw it for myself, but I am still angry. I stand up and back away from him slightly. I know I won't run because I want to know. My curiosity overrides my fear for the time being.

"I am the chosen one," Barnabas says bitterly. "That's what Alexander tells me."

So, Barnabas *is* special. Either that or he's a good liar and manipulator. Both of them seem possible.

I feel confused and my head aches uncomfortably. I have never seen anything like this in my life and I don't know what's real.

"I'm sick of this place."

Those are the only words I can muster while Barnabas looks down at the ground and then back at his palms. For that moment, I know I can't be around him any longer.

I hurry upstairs and see that a bunch of people are in the main room—Tessa, Enzo, Asher, James, and Rufus. They eye the blood on my clothes, but don't say anything. I go to the window and press my head against the cool glass. I don't want to talk to anyone, anyway.

"You missed lunch," Tessa says. "What took you so long?"

"I got caught up doing something."

"Looks like she had her period," Asher replies, teasing me. "That could be why she's a little sluggish today."

It's a horrible joke and they wouldn't have made it if they knew where it came from. They shouldn't have made it anyway.

I look over at Tessa and she opens her mouth to say something, but no words come out. Enzo doesn't even look at me.

"Why would you say that?" I say, turning to Asher. "Does it make you feel good to say things like that?"

He puffs his chest out as I approach.

Asher smirks and his arms reach out to grab me. He shoves me against the wall, leaving me gasping for breath. His grasp is much stronger than I thought it would be.

This is the first time I am truly afraid of a boy. This is the first time I am unsure of what he might do to me. Asher is the first boy to ever make me feel uncomfortable and weaker because I am a girl. I begin to feel helpless and terrified as he presses his body against me.

"I can say whatever I want," Asher says. "There's nothing you can do about it. I'm stronger than you. I'm more important than you."

I squirm, but Asher only pushes back harder. I try to imagine Enzo or Lonnie from home doing this to me, but I know they would never. I begin to wonder if it's ever crossed their minds. With all my heart, I hope that Enzo won't bring this sort of behavior home with him.

I wonder if I will still be this afraid at home or if my situation with Asher with stay with me forever. \ I think that something inside me is breaking down and I hope it won't affect my life in Verus. I don't want Asher to ruin my trust in the boys I have been friends with my whole life.

"Let go of me," I say through gritted teeth.

"Only if you promise to behave."

I use all the strength I can muster and knee Asher hard in the chest. I fight out of anger, not because it's something I like to do. I let my rage out and my fist connects with his jaw. He fights back for a while, but I am a better fighter. When he is down on the ground, I continue to punch his side. I don't want him to get up.

When I realize I am covered in more blood that isn't my own, I take a deep breath.

Everyone is staring at me, including Enzo and Tessa. I look up at my old friends and I barely recognize them.

"What is wrong with you? You're my friends and you watched. You're supposed to stick up for me because we're *friends*," I hiss.

The whole room is spinning and I steady myself against a doorpost.

I see that Enzo and Tessa look ashamed, but that doesn't make me feel any better. I know I'm about to vomit unless I steady myself. I feel a hand on my arm and the world returns to normal.

Barnabas leans in to whisper in my ear. He says, "Follow me."

At first, I think he's leading me to Alexander to be punished, so I run outside. I see the trail that leads around the massive cliffs and I take it. I hear someone running behind me, but I don't stop.

I want to find some answers somewhere in the wreckage. If I need to, I can find somewhere to sleep there.

"Alva, wait!" Barnabas calls. "Please."

I slow down and rest my hands on my knees, breathing deeply. There is not enough oxygen. I'm going to suffocate.

I feel his hand on my back, moving up and down soothingly. When I finally catch my breath, I turn to him angrily.

"What do you want? I don't need you to touch me either," I shout.

"I'm sorry," Barnabas says, ringing his hands together. "I want to go where you're going. I only wanted to talk to you."

"Scold me, you mean," I argue.

His eyes tell me he isn't going to do that. He smiles curiously at me and motions for me to continue on, so we start walking slowly along the dry dirt. It's not as hot as it was the day we were rescued.

My head clears.

"You can trust me," he says.

"Why should I trust you? You believe in the same things Asher does."

"Sort of," Barnabas replies. "Sometimes I think you're wrong and sometimes I think I'm wrong. I'm not sure."

I look at Barnabas. I try to figure him out, but he doesn't make sense.

His hair is wind tousled, so he looks more natural. He looks more like a boy and less like someone being shaped into a man. He doesn't fit in with the rest, despite appearances.

We walk in silence for a while. I wonder when someone will come for us and I constantly check back to look, but no one is following.

"Won't Alexander be angry with you for disappearing?"

Barnabas shrugs.

"He's never angry for long because I think he needs me. I'll make up some excuse."

After a long time, the hill begins to level and I can see the wreckage about a mile out. I am covered in blood and dust, but I make no attempt to wipe it off. I don't care about it.

I feel my skin burn as we walk. I know the sun will take away some of my paleness, like it usually does in the summer.

We walk for a while, remaining silent.

The wreckage is only a few feet away, but I pause and sit down in the dirt. I want to explore inside to see if anything's been left behind, but I am also afraid of the pilot's body. I don't think anyone's moved it.

Barnabas sits down next to me and peers up at the bright sky. He blinks and then stares back down at the dirt, thinking about something.

"I have to talk to you, but I'm afraid we only have this time. I don't know if I'll be able to back at the compound."

I watch him curiously as he runs the dirt through his finger. He stops and locks eyes with me.

"What is it?" I ask.

I see him swallow and his face sets with determination. He looks scared and I think he is only a frightened boy trying to act strong. I understand what he's feeling.

For some reason I can't put him in the same category as the other boys in the compound. There is something dark about the way they act, but that is not the case with Barnabas—unless he is tricking me somehow.

"I recognized you the first day, but I wasn't sure from where. It wasn't until yesterday that I realized. I tried to talk to you about it, but Alexander came around."

"Realized what?"

"A few years ago I had a vision about you. I knew it wasn't anyone from the compound because your hair was the same. It was about the bright blonde girl with the blue streak."

His hand lingers near my hair and he runs a finger along where I know the streak is. He pulls away and folds his hands together, probably since I scolded him for touching me before.

"What does this all mean?"

Barnabas shrugs.

"I became so infatuated with you that Alexander made me block it out. I eventually did. I don't know what it all means and it's driving me crazy. I was obsessed with the thought of you." Barnabas pauses and takes a few breaths. "I haven't told Alexander. I don't know what he would do if he found out that the girl I was having visions about was real."

"What were the visions?"

"You changed everything," is all Barnabas says.

He looks hopeful again, but his expression turns dark when he looks past me back at the compound. I think the sight of it frightens him, but there's nowhere else to go.

"What do you know? What's going to happen to me, Barnabas?" I ask desperately.

I believe him. He might be the only one I believe.

"There's no fighting Alexander. This is his town. He owns it, so he makes all the rules."

"He owns Shiloh? I thought he only owned the compound."

"He controls everything that happens here, including the air space above it. His family has owned this town for decades. They're all dead now."

I shudder.

If Alexander controls the air space then he could allow planes in whenever he wants, so I wonder if he is keeping me here for his own purpose.

"Tell him to let us go, then," I urge.

Barnabas shakes his head.

"You don't *tell* Alexander to do anything. He thinks that if he can convert you and your friends, he'll prove something. He believes you were sent to him as a challenge."

"I won't change. He has to know I won't change," I say.

But will I? I feel like I already am. I am more afraid than I've ever been in my life. My trust in others is faltering. I am feeling weaker, less certain. Is this what Alexander wants?

"Will he let me go in nine days, like he said?"

"He might," Barnabas says. "But don't count on that. I'm telling you...the world is going to be destroyed then. Only those with me will remain. I've known this my whole life and I'd bet everything on it. I already have."

"Why are you telling me this?" I ask.

Barnabas pauses for a while, trying to formulate something in his mind.

"You're the first outsider I've ever met. You're the only one who might understand how I feel. My visions...you're the one that saves me in them," he replies.

"Why don't you stand up to Alexander? Everyone will follow you. Everyone respects you the most."

Barnabas shakes his head violently.

"He'll tell them I've lost my powers. He'll tell them I'm not the chosen one anymore. Even though he is afraid of losing me, he still has all the information he needs. He still has everyone backing him…a bunch of kids he can create into what he's always wanted. A perfect society, according to him. He's been pushing his beliefs on us forever. I never questioned them until I saw how things could be. He knew you'd be dangerous and a challenge."

"How did he get you in the first place?"

"Before my parents died, Alexander was starting out as a psychologist here. He was my psychologist when I turned five. My parents thought I needed help because of all my visions I was having. I knew the world was ending, but everyone thought I was crazy. Alexander did, too…at first," Barnabas explains. "My stories were so detailed and intense that Alexander started to believe me. He started having visions of his own because I made him see. Alexander started calling it 'The Culling' and that's what we know it as. He was the only person who believed me and I loved him for it. I finally started to feel free. After my parents died, he started this school for orphans and brought in other kids my age. He was like a father to me. He made me feel like my visions weren't so bad, like I was helping people by sharing them."

"When did he start to scare you?"

Barnabas is surprised by the question, but he smiles slightly.

"He started punishing us when we acted out. We were not allowed to act like children anymore. He and his wife became stricter and they started imposing their beliefs on us. They started telling us we had to train for 'The Culling,' so we can rebuild the world in the right way. He said it was God's will, but I know it has nothing to do with God. We are being destroyed by something else…by another intelligent species. They're using my brain

119

somehow and I can see their plans. Whatever they want me to see I see."

I can feel the horror building inside of me. I know I am shaking, but Barnabas doesn't say anything. I look over at Barnabas and I see a trickle of blood streaming from his nose.

Barnabas reaches up calmly and wipes it away. He stares at it on his finger and says, "Too many visions today."

I can see how the visions exhaust him. I'm grateful that I'm not him, that I haven't had any.

"What do you think this all has to do with me? How will I help?"

"I don't know, but you do help me. You do in my dreams. I can't stop thinking about it and I know you're as important as me. Alexander can't know." He peers back up at the compound and grabs my arm. "Let's go. I'll tell him you were upset and this was the only way to calm you down."

I nod and follow him back to the compound.

It takes a few hours to get back and Alexander is waiting for us at the door. Cassandra crosses her arm and blocks my path as I try to follow Barnabas. I watch helplessly as he is taken away by Alexander.

"Where have you been?" Cassandra hisses. She shakes her head and points to the showers. "Rinse off and get to bed. You missed your job and dinner. I thought we were getting through to you."

I feel like a child when she gives me a disappointed look. I decide to play her game. I approach her and hug her tightly, like I did with Ester. I meant it with Ester, though. Being this close to Cassandra nearly makes me gag.

"I'm sorry," I say, forcing a cry. I'm surprisingly good at this. "I was upset about the crash. I miss my family."

"You also beat Asher unconscious. You will be punished." Her voice becomes soft. "Rest first. Get a good night's sleep."

I nod and slump off to the bathroom. I am much more determined than ever to help these kids because of what Barnabas told me. I will help him. I somehow know he wants me to help, that's why he took that walk with me and confided in me. I am finally filled with a purpose.

It's obvious he has no one else to turn to.

I shower, dress, and head down to the second floor. Instead of going down to sleep, like Cassandra assumed I was, I sneak into the closest classroom. I have to wait for Barnabas or I won't be able to sleep.

I hear footsteps about a half hour later. I see him pass the door and hurry out. He is startled by me, but he faces me in the light of the bright lamps above us.

His right eye is swollen and bruising quickly. I see a cut along his left check and his nose is bleeding again. He places both hands on my shoulders to keep me from turning away, which makes me think he's not ashamed to let me see.

"Did Alexander do this?" I ask.

He nods. He raises his hand to my cheek, but then lets it drop.

"Listen for the voices, Alva," he says gently.

His voice is soothing, so I close my eyes for a couple seconds. He turns away from me and heads downstairs.

I wait a few moments before following after him.

Chapter Nine

Day Six

I pass his room and wonder if I should stop inside. I know that wouldn't be a good idea, so I keep going. I strain to listen if he is making any noise, but there is nothing. It feels nice when I collapse into my own bed.

I'm so exhausted from our walk today, but my mind is going a mile a minute. All I can think about is Alexander and Barnabas and the things I've learned about today, like how Alexander is a psychologist. This thought terrifies me the most and I immediately know why it's been nagging at me.

If he's a psychologist he could be a master of manipulation. He knows all about the human mind and how it works, so it's possible he can read people.

Maybe he can read me.

If he figures out what Barnabas is hiding, it will be unsafe for everyone. I assume Barnabas thinks that I can save him and in turn save everyone, but I have no idea what I'm doing. I can change things, but I don't think I'd ever be able to stop it for good.

It's obvious Alexander has too much power.

I press my eyes closed and try to get comfortable. Once my body is still and my thoughts are calm, I'm able to fall asleep.

I'm quickly plunged into a strange wonderful dream involving Barnabas. It feels real and I can see myself standing in bright green field. I smile as the sun warms my face. I bend down and run my fingers along the cool grass, leaning down I know it smells fresh.

As I peer into the distance, I see Barnabas facing me. His hair is tousled from the wind, like it was yesterday, and his crisp shirt is unbuttoned a bit. I can see his prominent collarbone poking out from beneath the soft fabric. He closes his eyes and lifts his arms toward the sun. I smile again because he is smiling a wide, brilliant smile.

My heart leaps with joy because in my dream I know he is free. I know Alexander is nowhere to be found.

I start to see the dark clouds in the distance, so I call out for Barnabas.

He snaps to attention and tries to run, but arms grab at him—strange alien arms, with thick scales and sharp claws. Barnabas shirt is torn down past his shoulder and he is bleeding.

He is beckoning for me desperately, but I can't help. I can see the alien eyes as they sneer at me. Beady, black eyes lock with mine. My legs are stuck in mud and I am knee deep in the ground.

I am sinking.

I see the sky behind him turn black and lightning begins to strike, which isn't far away. It's getting closer to Barnabas's bloody heap of a body in the distance. He is not moving.

Why are they making me watch his murder? Why aren't they letting me help? Isn't that what I'm supposed to do? Isn't that what they want me to do?

"Alva," comes a strange, strained voice.

The lightning comes close, tearing up the ground beneath it. The world is collapsing. My world is collapsing.

"What do you want from me?" I scream.

"Pull him from their grasp," the mysterious voice says, no louder than a whisper.

I shake my head and close my eyes. I want it to stop. I don't want to hear the voices because they chill me to the bone. They aren't…human.

I wake up screaming. I try to take deep breaths as I rip the covers from my bed. I can feel something wet on my face, so I reach up. Blood is coming from my nose and I think it might be coming from my ears, too. I have no idea if it has stopped because it's so dark. I'm sick of the darkness.

My throat is raspy from screaming, but no one comes to check on me. I feel positive that I've woken everyone up.

I feel my arms and run my fingers over the scratches. They feel like claw marks and I know my finger nails aren't that long. Did something scratch me? Did I hurt myself on something? I shake my head trying to clear my thoughts. I've never had a nightmare like that before. It seems foreign and unnatural.

Pull him from their grasp.

The strange voice echoes in my head as I shove my boots on. What do they want me to do? I can't help. I don't have any sort of power here. I'm out of my league. I ball my hands into fists and sigh. I can fight my way out, but everyone? I can't take on everyone.

I shudder when I think of Asher. I never want anyone to touch me like that ever again. I will kill him if he does it a second time. I know that for certain.

I struggle my way up the stairs and find I'm the first one awake again. I head to the bathroom and check my face in the mirror. Blood is streaked on my skin from my nose and I see it on the sides of my neck. I peer down at my arms and see the claw marks are gone. But how? I felt them in the dark.

I head to one of the stalls and vomit. I don't have much to throw up, but it all comes up. I feel sick and feeling in the pit in my stomach doesn't go away. I know it won't matter how much I puke because I'll still feel sick. I'll feel sick until I get out of this place.

After showering the blood and dirt off, I dress quickly and go into my locker before anyone else comes in.

Panic runs through me as I search through my bag. There is nothing inside of it, except for the blue dress I refuse to wear. I let out a frustrated groan and toss it to the ground. I'll walk around naked before I put that damn thing on. I'll run away. I'll...

I cut myself off.

Something is keeping me here. My friends. My father arriving in eight days. Barnabas.

I'm not sure why he concerns me so much. He is crying out for help and I know he's falling apart every day. My thoughts linger on the holes punctured through his hands and the blood streaming down his face. I think about the black eye and how he smiled in my nightmares...the real smile, a smile that I know he could one day have.

I search everywhere, in every locker, for my computer, but it's gone. I head into the main room as the girls file in. I don't want to talk to any of them. I only want to find what is mine. I don't find it in the main room either, so I head outside for some fresh air.

I frown as I see something smashed into the fence in the small grassy area. I know immediately it's my computer, but I still run to it. I hold the fractured pieces in my hand gently, almost as if it could be put back together. I know it is hopeless. I can no longer contact my family through it.

My fury rises as I peer back up toward the balcony that surrounds the first floor of the compound. I can see eyes in the window and I know it's Alexander. I let the pieces fall back down onto the ground and I head calmly inside.

Cassandra and Alexander both confront me when I return. They take me into the hospital room for a talk. Luckily, it's brief. I don't have the energy for much more.

"We've asked for respect from you several times and it was my idea to see you punished," Alexander explains as I sit down on the cot. "Cassandra convinced me to give you another chance. She had mercy on you, I guess."

I peer up at him, expressionless. I don't want him to read me because I now know that's what he's good at.

Cassandra smiles at me, but it doesn't warm the frigidness I feel on the inside. I know she is only pretending to be nice and she is only pretending to be my friend.

"How can you punish me if I'm not from here?" I ask. "I live by different rules than you do."

"Can you ever stop arguing for a minute? We're trying to help you," Alexander scolds.

"Why do you think I'm in such desperate need of help? Why do you keep saying that?" I ask, keeping my body steady.

They have to know I'm strong. I'm not a child.

"You are a daughter of God," Cassandra explains. "We all need help, some more than others. I know you can be a wonderful person if you submit to what we're trying to do here. You could be a beautiful young lady."

The word cult floats in my mind again. The opinion that's formed in my mind is that they are strange people trying to disguise themselves as religious. I know truly religious people, followers of a god, wouldn't act this way. They wouldn't beat kids. They wouldn't try to stifle their creativity and freedom. I know the difference. They worship something different. They worship themselves.

I have to remember it's not religious people I hate—it's Alexander and Cassandra. It's their self-righteous attitude. It's their belief or lie that they're helping Barnabas, when they're actually destroying him. I keep telling myself they are dangerous.

"I *am* a beautiful young lady," I sneer. I pause and look Alexander in the eyes. "But you're afraid of me. You're afraid of what I might do."

"You won't do anything," Alexander says. "Or I'll extend the time of the no fly zone. I can do that, you know."

"I know," I say.

We watch each other for a few moments and finally it seems like he gives up.

"Don't threaten me because I can do much worse. You haven't seen anything yet." Alexander laughs and his face brightens suddenly. He acts as though he hasn't threatened me seconds before. "I know there won't be a problem from here on and you'll be well on your way home in eight days. Stay safe, Alva."

Cassandra and Alexander follow after me as I leave the room. I can feel their hard footsteps through the tile floor and they radiate up into my racing heart.

I wait twenty minutes and head into the kitchen with the rest of the girls. I take my usual spot next to Tessa and Enzo as we wait for Alexander and Cassandra to join us.

Asher is staring daggers into the back of my head. He's bruised and beat up, so I avoid his glance.

I start a conversation with Tessa as she takes a sip of her water. It looks murky and strange, so I've never had any. I usually wait and get some from the tap in the bathroom.

"How's your job been?" I ask. "How's hunting?"

"I was with Titus and Jethro," Tessa replies.

I peer over at Titus. When standing, he looms a few feet over me. He watches me curiously as I stare at him, but doesn't say anything. In fact, I don't think I've ever heard his voice. He is big and bulky and looks as though he could crush me with the palm of his hand.

Jethro sits next to him and frowns at me. I'm getting used to people not liking me here.

"How are they?"

"I think something is wrong with Titus," Tessa says. "He might have a learning problem. I changed to cooking, anyway."

She doesn't elaborate and turns her attention to Ester who smiles at me from across the table. She feels like a much different person than she did when I first arrived. It feels like she truly wants to be my friend.

I look at Enzo, but he is talking more with the boys than with me. His actions have begun to mimic theirs and I wonder if he's treating me differently now.

I think of how Enzo was back home. I know he was my friend and he cared about me. He played music and skate boarded. He made me laugh and sometimes fought with me when he wanted to practice. He didn't treat me differently than any of his guy friends. Now it seems like he's one of them and he is disappearing forever. I want the old Enzo and Tessa back. I wonder why they've changed and I haven't.

What have we been doing differently?

Alexander and Cassandra enter and we start breakfast. I peer at the seat next to Alexander, but Barnabas is suspiciously absent. Alexander says his prayer and we begin eating anyway. What has happened to him?

I'm about to get up and search for him, but everyone's attention turns to the door. Barnabas steps through and he keeps his eyes on the ground. The room is silent, but the bruises and cuts on his face are obvious. The damage looks much worse in this light and he looks ashamed.

I look away because I don't think he wants anyone to stare.

The silence only stays for a few moments before everyone starts talking again and digging into their food.

As usual, I only eat a little bit. I'm so nervous and tense today, I don't think I could force anything else.

My eyes wander back to Barnabas and I keep my head low. He stares back at me and eventually his mouth bends into a small smile. We have a secret. I smile back momentarily. We have a secret and we can change things. I can get my friends back. It's a little bit exciting.

His smile fades when he peers somewhere past me. I turn to see what he's looking at and see Ester frowning at me. Her hands are shaking and she drops her fork. She doesn't eat for the rest of breakfast and keeps her gaze on me.

As we step out for our small break before class, Ester grabs my arm roughly. She holds me until everyone leaves the room, except for the three girls who clean.

I know they are Junia, Daphne, and Margaret, but they do not speak. I'm not sure if they are allowed to outside of class. I wonder what the purpose of that is.

Barnabas watches me briefly before rushing out. He can't help me or get involved. It would be too suspicious.

I turn to Ester, putting on a brave face. Her palm comes straight at my face and the slap radiates throughout my body. I watch her in shock, but this time I do not fight back. I stand with my arms rigid at my side.

"How dare you," Ester hisses dangerously.

"What did I do?" I question.

Her eyes bore into mine and I feel her anger. I feel it everywhere around me.

"You tricked me," Ester shouts. "I thought you were my friend, but you were trying to get something from me."

"What?"

"Barnabas. Don't play stupid. I know it's what you're good at. You were trying to confuse me about what I should do with Barnabas, but the truth is you want him for yourself. I've never seen him smile like that at anyone, especially not after he's received punishment. What did you do to him? Did you confuse him too? He hasn't acted out in years."

Her words sting, but I know she is most likely talking out of anger.

"I didn't do anything to him," I say, defending myself. "I'm not like that. I'm not trying to come between you and Barnabas."

I try to analyze my feelings. Getting in between Ester and Barnabas was not my intention. I don't even like Barnabas, not in that way. I want to help him. I'm not stealing anyone and I don't even think it's possible to "steal" someone. I'm not trying to make Ester upset.

I try to think about what my feelings for Barnabas are, but I come up short. I've never cared about someone romantically and I'm not trying to start now. I'm pretty sure it's something you can't control, but I will try to control it anyway. There's no room for that here. It would be silly anyway; it would be illogical. I don't even know him.

But I feel like I do. Barnabas knew me long before I ever met him, but still he feels familiar to me, too. He feels comforting to me, like a friend would, but more than a friend. I can't explain it.

He seems to be the only one who believes me and has my back. I find myself confident that he is the only one not trying to change me in some way.

"You try to act like you're so nice and caring, but you're not. I can see right through you," Ester threatens.

I grab her arm this time to prevent her from leaving and she turns back to me.

"Can you see right through me? Can you see through everyone else, too? What about Alexander and Cassandra? What about Asher? You follow them blindly, but you haven't thought about what you're doing. Do you want to live like that?"

131

"Don't push your beliefs on me," Ester says, angrily. "You think you're so much better than us. You think you've got it all figured out, like we don't want to be this way. We do. I do. I'm fine here and I have a nice life planned out. I won't let some stupid, insignificant *girl* like you ruin it for me."

"Why are you talking to me like that?" I ask. "That's something Alexander forced on you. You think that boys are better than girls. You think we're meant to serve them. I can be stupid and insignificant without my gender having to be involved."

Ester pauses, looking flustered.

"I…" she begins.

"You're just as important as everyone else. Don't let them make you think you're not," I say calmly. "Do you even realize what you're saying?"

"Shut up, Alva," Ester shouts, regaining her voice. Her face is angry and determined. "Stop confusing me all the time, like Alexander said you would. Stop talking and leave me alone. Don't ever talk to me again."

Ester seems almost unreachable. *Almost.* But she made a point. Am I acting like I'm better than them? Do I have a right to step in and speak for them? What if Ester *is* happy here? Am I making a huge mistake?

I want her to know she has other options. Still, my chest burns when I think of her trying to force Barnabas into it. What if she tries something? What if she convinces him he belongs here? I hope she doesn't do something drastic. She can't tell Alexander what I said.

I watch the silent girls clear the table and I see the distressed looks on their faces. For a moment, Junia looks up at me and I see desperation in her eyes. I realize she heard what I said. I step closer to her and let my fingers run along the wooden table.

"Am I wrong? Should I leave it alone?" I ask quietly.

Junia's eyes find mine again. She has beautiful green eyes, almost hidden under her dark hair.

She peers around at the others, but they don't look up. She gives me the slightest shake of her head and I am filled with purpose again. I know some of the girls want out, some of the boys too. Just because Ester denies it doesn't mean it's not true.

When I head to our cooking class, I feel like everyone has turned against me. The mute girls don't look at me again and Tessa is sitting near Ester, Ariel, and Eden. I sit far away from them, near the back.

Cassandra notices as she enters the classroom, which happens to be the small kitchen Asher and I had worked on. I feel nauseous thinking about whether or not I'll be working with him later.

She gives us a task to make a bunch of practice dishes and I burn the food during my first try. As I struggle during my second attempt, Tessa comes to stand next to me. I notice right away she seems different again, a lot like her old self.

"You're helping me now? Why?" I ask.

I try not to sound too ungrateful because I want to have her around. I need to know she's okay.

"You need help," she says, with a slight smile. "I've been feeling strange lately, a lot of headaches."

I try to figure out why she's actually normal again. I watch closely as she presses a hand against her temple as we try to salvage what I've done to the food.

Cassandra eyes us, but doesn't step closer. She doesn't like when Tessa and I talk, apparently.

"Have you been taking anything? Did Cassandra give you something?" I ask.

I feel like this is a rare opportunity I have with her and I need to find out all I can. I'm not sure if I'll have another chance.

"No, I don't think," Tessa says, with a furrowed brow. "I've been having a lot of nightmares, terrible ones. I want to go home."

I put a hand on her shoulder. She is still there and I know I can't lose her again. It only takes a few moments before my thoughts go to the murky water and something clicks. I'm the only one who hasn't been drinking it.

"Don't drink anything they give you. Pretend like you're following their orders and keep on doing what you're doing. They have to think whatever they're doing is working."

"I'm scared, Alva," Tessa whispers, her voice shaking. "We need to get Enzo back and we have to get out of here. I don't want to become different again."

"Listen to what I say," is my response. I don't want to say much more because Cassandra might overhear me. "Stay strong. Just over a week left."

Tessa looks at me, her eyes wide. I think it's something I said, but I can feel the blood running from my nose again.

Cassandra approaches and puts a hand on my back.

"Go to the bathroom," she says gently, handing me a couple of tissues from her pocket. "Wash it off."

I hurry out while stuffing the tissues under the stream of blood, but a conversation stops me as I approach the steps. I recognize Barnabas's voice from one of the classrooms. As I peek through the doorway, I see that Barnabas and Demetri are having a tense conversation. I move to the side, making sure they can't see me.

I press my back against the wall, keeping myself rigid up against it.

"You can't. You have to leave her alone," Barnabas hisses.

"Asher wants to teach her a lesson, Barnabas. She won't stop acting out until she's put into her place."

"Don't do anything to her. You can't..." Barnabas seems to struggle with his words. "Don't do it. Don't hurt her. Tell Asher to just leave it alone."

"What's wrong with you?" Demetri argues. "We're going to do it and if you stand in my way I'll tell Alexander you're straying from your path. He'll know you're having doubts. She's making a fool out of everyone."

"She's just different," Barnabas says. "What are you planning on doing?"

"Are you going to tell her? I don't trust you, Barnabas. Are you really choosing some girl over the well-being of this compound? She's been out of line and you know it," Demetri says.

I hear Barnabas mutter a few curses. I didn't think his mouth was capable of forming those words. I've always seen him as soft spoken.

"Stop it, Demetri," Barnabas finally says, in a firm voice.

"Alexander wants you to be a man, so why can't you just do it," Demetri argues. "It's not going to be a problem for any of the other boys here."

I hear Demetri's laughter and then a shuffle of feet. I feel like they are physically fighting, but I can't step in. They can't know I've been listening.

The shuffling stops and I hear Barnabas's heavy breathing.

"Leave her alone," he says one final time.

I hurry upstairs and try to think about what they were talking about. From that conversation, I can only assume Demetri is planning something horrible for me, but I have no idea what it could be. I want Barnabas to tell me, but I can't count on it. I'll have to keep my guard up.

The anger in me builds until I make it to the bathroom. I ball my fist up and plunge it into the mirror. I find out quickly that it's not glass, but a thick plastic of some sort. I hold onto my aching fist and stare at the dent in the fake glass.

The dent branches out in cracks and covers my face. I cannot see any of my features as I stare back at my distorted reflection. I feel different and strange, but I don't step away from the spot on the mirror.

At the moment, I don't want to see myself. I don't want to see what I'm becoming.

Chapter Ten

Day Seven

I make it through the rest of the day and despite a dream-filled night, wake up feeling a bit more hopeful. My hand throbs and my head feels fuzzy from my lingering nightmare.

Last night I dreamt that Barnabas was being dragged away again. I followed his blood trail until I found his mangled corpse. I had been crying in my sleep and when I woke up, I wiped the remaining tears from my cheek.

I'm not sure I will be able to save Barnabas. I'm not sure why I care so much.

I only have a week left, but what disheartens me is if I was at the training camp I'd be heading home today. Still, there's only one week left before my father will be arriving. I hold that hope close to my heart as I find my way upstairs.

It is much earlier than usual, but I'm used to being up before the rest. I decide to take a jog outside to clear my head. I will have enough time to get back before anyone notices I'm gone.

Once I'm outside, I decide to head toward the town instead of down toward the wreckage of our crash. I have never been into town and maybe I can learn something about the compound if I visit. The dirt path turns into cobblestone and it becomes harder to jog, so I slow down. Also, I'm afraid of slipping and plummeting off the cliff to my immediate death.

I see the tiny shops lining the sidewalks, but they are not yet open. It feels a lot like a ghost town because it's so early and the sun is just beginning to rise in the distance.

My eyes peer up toward the apartments above some of the shops. Most of the blinds are drawn, but in some I see a few people watching me through their windows. They appear to be confused by me and unwilling to talk. Some of them draw away when I catch their eyes.

An elderly man and woman are fixing up a fruit stand up ahead, so I quicken my pace to catch them. The woman turns to me, frightened, but the man gives me a slight smile.

He runs a hand through his peppered hair and raises an eyebrow.

I notice the woman is not dressed like the girls back in the compound. She is wearing a blue t-shirt and a pair of comfortable looking jeans, much more modern. They don't seem like those in the compound. My heart fills with hope.

"Are you from the compound?" He asks. "You look about that age."

"Do I look like I'm from the compound?" I ask.

I would assume my hair and clothes throw him off because I'm not wearing the compound's "uniform," but I did come from that direction.

He laughs and shakes his head.

"I heard about the plane crash. Alexander took you in. That's nice of him," the man replies. "My name is Edward and this is my wife Penelope."

The woman smiles at me curiously and brushes her long hair out of her face. Her face is lined with worry, which is also apparent in his pale blue eyes.

"Are you supposed to be here?" She asks. "Does Alexander know?"

"What would happen if he did know?" I ask back.

I wonder if they are as afraid of him as I am. If so, why aren't they dressed like the rest of his followers? I think I know why. I feel like Alexander doesn't think they're worth saving if the world ends. I believe that he thinks that only the children he raised from a young age are worthy of rebuilding the kind of society he's thinking of. I think he's only interested in the completely brainwashed people.

"I don't want to see anything happen to you. I would guess you've realized by now how…strange he is," Penelope says.

I don't understand.

"Why don't you all leave then and find somewhere else to live? Why would you want to live in a town run by a psycho?" I ask them.

Help those kids, I think. *Why aren't you doing anything about it?*

"Alexander controls all shipments of what we need to survive in and out of here. He controls everything. Even so, it's not so bad here. It's my home," the man says gently. "I never wanted to leave. It's not like we have the money to leave, anyway."

"He's just a bit crazy," Penelope adds. "The world isn't going to end. He's been preaching to all of us but eventually he gave up when he started that school. He's made all those kids are as crazy as he is. It's Alexander's world that will fall apart next week, when we are still here and the world doesn't end the way he's been predicting."

I shudder thinking about how it must feel to be trapped in a town with a psychopath controlling everything, but they seem used to it. Alexander might not be much of a threat to them or he leaves them alone. My own head is spinning. I'm not sure about anything.

"Those kids aren't crazy," I say. "They're trapped. You have to help us."

"You'll be fine," the woman says, placing a hand on my shoulder. "You'll be out of here in no time. I've heard that your plane will be here within a week."

"Is that why you came here?" asks her husband, Edward. "For help?"

I shrug. I'm not sure why I came. I didn't expect anyone to talk to me at all. I never imagined meeting such normal people. At least Penelope and Edward are normal when compared to Alexander and Cassandra.

"I'm not sure. I was looking for a way out. Can I stay here? Maybe I can bring my friends?"

Edward puts his hand up to stop me before I can say another word.

"Alexander will come here looking for you and we wouldn't be able to hide you. He won't hurt you. He's someone with some strong beliefs. He's nearly harmless," Edward says.

Nearly?

"No, no he's not," I argue. "He beats them. He makes them sleep in a dark basement and punishes them if they don't listen to him. It's horrible."

Penelope and Edward exchange glances.

"Has he ever hurt you?" Penelope asks.

"No, but..."

"Then why are you worrying about what his followers allow him to do to them? It isn't your problem. He'd never *really* hurt one of those kids, so that's just their way."

I feel helpless again. I stare back at them with my mouth open. Is everyone crazy here, deep down really mad? Do they not care about what Alexander does to those children? *Their way. Their way.* I'm sick of hearing it. I don't think it's right to stand by while innocent people are being tortured. I feel like that's how most horrible things continue to happen. It's because other people don't step in to stop it.

I need to start taking matters into my own hands.

"Thanks for your help," I murmur.

I don't look up at them again, but I turn back to the compound that looms in the distance. I don't like the way the sight of it makes me feel. I feel like I'm going back to prison.

Before I can walk away, Penelope calls my name and tosses me an apple. I catch it and hold it tightly in my hand. It is ugly and slightly brown, not the fresh red apples I'm used to.

"If Alexander stops the food shipments, we're all in big trouble and not matter what we do, those kids will never admit to being abused because they really do believe the world is ending. They don't want to be left out in the cold when it happens. They'll never cross Alexander because they believe that he is their only hope for survival."

I turn away again and think about what Penelope said as I walk away. I believe she's wrong because I believe that Barnabas is already willing to stand up to Alexander. I struggle to come up with anyone else, but I come up short. I'm not sure if anyone would risk their spot in the compound. I'm not sure how deep their belief in the upcoming apocalypse goes.

When I make it back to the compound, I realize that everyone is done showering and already in the dining room. I know I'm not extremely late, but I don't want Alexander to question where I've been. I don't want him to take it out on everyone else at Shiloh.

I walk in slowly and see my empty seat. Enzo and Tessa look at me curiously and then back at Alexander. He doesn't look at me until I sit down. When he does, he doesn't say anything. Barnabas doesn't look at me either, but I assume this is because he sees that Ester is watching me.

"Where have you been?" Tessa demands in a whisper.

"I'll tell you later," I say.

I see her reach for her murky water and I grab her arm gently, which I think prompts her to remember my warning, so she whispers something into Enzo's ear.

I have a feeling they've been getting drugged. I know they never would have acted the way they have been acting if they hadn't been drugged.

Seeing them put down the water without drinking it makes me feel better about my friends. I relax a bit. As long as they are okay, we'll be strong enough to leave when the time comes. I still feel conflicted, however. Can I leave everyone behind and pretend like all this didn't happen, like Shiloh doesn't exist? I could make my father come back with the army.

After I shovel down my food, I meet my friends out in the main room. I find out that we don't have class today and we're free to do whatever we want until it is time for us to do our jobs that afternoon. I cringe thinking about going to work later, but I know I can handle it.

Asher is also in the main room, but he doesn't intimidate me. I'm not afraid of him. He may make me uncomfortable, but I'm not afraid of him.

Enzo dusts off the piano that sits near the back of the room and sits down on an old wooden bench in front of it, so we gather around on the couches and listen to him play for a while. It soothes me and reminds me of home.

For a moment, I close my eyes until I hear others join us. I see that Barnabas and Titus have stepped into the room.

Barnabas sits next to me and Titus sits on the other side of him. He watches Enzo closely as his fingers slide back and forth on the white and black keys. As Enzo pauses to smile back at us, Barnabas motions for them to switch seats. Enzo nods and lets Barnabas take his turn on the piano.

The song that Barnabas plays is haunting, yet beautiful. I find myself entranced by it and my eyes are locked on his fingers. Suddenly, I wonder if this is why his hands look so strong. Obviously, I was wrong about him being a fighter.

I can't look away. I watch him steadily until the song is over and I'm sure he has been playing for about ten minutes straight.

"Where did you learn to play?" I ask.

He keeps his eyes down on the keys where his fingers are rested. He looks sad about something, but I'm not sure what it is.

"My father started teaching me before he died. I taught myself from there," Barnabas says.

"You're very good," adds Enzo.

I'm impressed that Barnabas was able to teach himself so much on his own. I find myself thinking about the sad life he must have had, but I'm dragged out of those thoughts by Titus tapping on my shoulder.

He smiles at me for a moment, but doesn't say anything.

"Titus likes it," Barnabas says, swinging around on the bench to face us. "He's told me before."

I turn to Titus, surprised by the information. "So, you can talk?" I ask him.

"Of course I can," Titus says, blushing briefly. "I don't like to though. Talking gets me in trouble."

"You should talk more," I insist, smiling at him. "Do you know how to play the piano, too?"

Titus shakes his head, exchanging glances with Barnabas.

"No. I can't read music," he says, appearing embarrassed.

"I can't either, but grab that book right there and we can figure it out. Let's look at the classics one," I say.

Titus turns to the three music books behind him and seems to hesitate. I see Barnabas reach out for the correct one and suddenly I understand.

Titus can't read at all.

I'm not sure what to say or do, but I'm overwhelmed with an urge to help him. As I lay the music book across my lap, I lean toward Titus to whisper in his ear. I ask, "Why didn't anyone teach you to read?"

"Alexander doesn't let me attend classes. He says I'm not worth it. I've never learned. I was slower than the others, so he gave up on me."

He's saying it loud enough so everyone can hear, so I guess he doesn't mind Enzo and Tessa knowing too.

I frown and then bite the inside of my cheek thoughtfully. I think it's obvious that Alexander doesn't care about any of the kids at all. Titus was a slower learner than the rest, so instead of giving him the extra attention that he needed, his education was completely ignored.

I turn back to Titus and take his hands in mine.

"I can teach you," I say. "We can have our first lesson today."

"I don't know...I don't think Alexander would like that," Titus replies.

He looks at Barnabas.

"He doesn't have to know how to read," Barnabas responds.

I smile at Barnabas and he smiles back.

We head down into one of the classrooms and I spend most of the afternoon teaching Titus the alphabet. Barnabas, Enzo, and Tessa hang out with us playing card games while I work with Titus.

Every once in a while, Barnabas leans back in his chair to help Titus. It's a relaxing afternoon and I find myself appreciating the break from all the madness. For the first time in a while, I feel like myself again.

After Titus announces he's tired, we all sit back and talk for a while. We push some of the desks together and I slump over the side to rest my head on Enzo's shoulder. He rests his own on mine in return.

I feel I haven't lost them. I believe that they're okay.

I notice Barnabas watching us. He crosses his arms over his chest. His eyes narrow at me.

"What's Verus like? I mean, why do you hate it here so much?" He asks.

I raise an eyebrow and lift my head up, clocking Enzo in the chin in my haste. I hear him laugh and he gives me a small shove, but I focus my attention on Barnabas.

"Don't you hate it?" I ask.

Titus nods, but Barnabas shrugs.

"I never knew there was anything else until my...until I met you all," Barnabas says.

I know he's lying because he has already told me about the dreams he's had about me.

"What do you mean?" I ask.

"I was okay with everything, even though I wasn't happy. I always knew there might be more somewhere but I knew there was no use thinking about it."

"Barnabas, you can change things, you know. They all look up to you," I say.

"How would I change things? What would I do? If 'The Culling' is happening, I want us all to be safe. We're safest here, with or without Alexander. Maybe he's who we need to stay alive."

I shake my head.

"The world isn't going to end," Tessa says, with a sigh. "You have to get over that. You can't let Alexander control you just because you're afraid of being on your own."

"My fear is much more than that," Barnabas says bitterly.

"You can come to Verus," I suggest.

Barnabas looks hopeful for a moment before looking away.

"I wouldn't fit in there. Besides, I know I'm right. I've been seeing this since I was five years old. There's no way around it."

None of us say anything, but after a while, Tessa looks frustrated and reaches over to grab my hand.

"I want to go outside," Tessa says. "You coming?"

I shake my head. For some reason, I like being inside today.

"I'll go. You want to come, Titus?" Enzo asks.

Titus nods and everyone except for Barnabas and I stands up.

I busy myself with gathering up the scrap paper I used to teach Titus. I don't want Alexander or Cassandra to find it.

"See you later, Alva," Tessa calls as they all head out into the hallway. "Stay safe."

She gives me a pointed look.

I hear their footsteps clank up the metal staircase. I turn my head to look at Barnabas, but he's peering down at his palms. At first, I'm afraid there are more stigmata, but his hands look fine.

It looks like he is remembering something. Whatever the memory is, it looks like it was terrible.

"Why didn't you go with them?" I ask.

Barnabas shrugs.

"Wanted to stay here."

I nod and begin to tear up the little pieces of paper. I don't know why it's so awkward between us. I see Barnabas tense up when I move my chair closer.

"I overheard you talking to Demetri," I say without any more hesitation. "What was that about? What is he going to do to me?"

Barnabas looks at me wide-eyed. He opens his mouth to say something, but at first, he doesn't say anything. It takes a few moments before he speaks.

"I don't know. That's why you have to be careful. I think they want to hurt you in some way. If I find out what it is, I promise I'll tell you. I didn't know…" Barnabas stutters, looking ashamed.

"It's okay. I'll figure it out," I say, cutting him off.

I lean back in my chair and he continues to stare at me. It's obvious to me he has something else on his mind.

"I have a problem." He pauses for a moment, keeping his eyes low before continuing. "When we turn eighteen, Alexander is making us pick a girl to…well, he wants us to become men. My eighteenth birthday is in three days."

"He forces you into having sex with someone?" I ask bluntly.

Barnabas looks frazzled.

"We always knew it was part of the plan and we accepted it. Ester expects me to pick her. He's going to make sure I do it. Ester will tell him if I don't pick her. I don't think I can do it…I don't understand how he can force this on me. He says it'll make me more confident. Stronger."

Barnabas grasps onto my arm tightly.

"Then lie. Ask Ester to lie," I say.

"She won't. She'll be humiliated if I don't pick her. What would you do? Would you do it if you had to?"

I hold onto his arm.

"No. I wouldn't unless I wanted to. You shouldn't unless you want to, Barnabas. It doesn't seem like you want to," I say.

Barnabas appears relieved for a moment.

"What should I do, then?"

I think for a moment, trying to figure out his problem. I want to kill Alexander. For the first time in my life, I want to see someone dead. His mind is sick and I know something is wrong with him and that I should take that into consideration, but I still want to kill him.

Why would a grown man force Barnabas and the other students into situations like this? Does he really believe that having sex will make Barnabas a man?

"Why don't you tell Alexander that you pick me instead of Ester? I'll lie for you," I say.

He gives me a curious half-smile.

"Really? You'd do that for me?" He asks.

147

"Why not? Ester might be angry with me, but who cares. Say it was your choice." I pause and give his tense shoulder a squeeze. "It'll be okay. When we're alone, we can...talk more about Verus."

Barnabas laughs and releases my arm.

I think he's grateful for my friendship at that moment and I am grateful for his. I think without it, I would have gone crazy by now. At least one person from the compound needs my help and I'm happy I'm able to solve one of his problems.

"Have you ever..." he pauses, unsure of how to say it.

I know what he wants to ask.

"Does it really matter?" I reply.

He shakes his head.

When he looks back at me, his eyes are distant again and he looks deep in thought. Sadness crossed over his face. Suddenly, he pulls his chair closer and buries his face into my shoulder. He is silent, but I feel him shaking slightly. He could be shivering, but somehow I know that's not the case.

Barnabas is crying.

I wrap my arms around him and hold him tightly to me. The last person to press himself against me was Asher, but this is completely different. Barnabas is not forcing me to endure his presence. He is not invading my personal space. I don't feel powerless in this situation. Still, it makes me a bit nervous because I'm not sure if I can really fully trust anyone here. I'm not sure if even Barnabas will eventually turn on me.

It takes him several long minutes to calm down, but I hold him in my arms the entire time. Eventually, he turns his face toward my neck so that he can gaze up at me.

"Don't tell anyone. Please," Barnabas says. "I haven't cried in years. I'm not allowed to. I'm supposed to be...strong."

"You think I would tell?"

He shakes his head and pulls away from me.

I see the wetness on his cheeks when he reaches up to wipe it away. Even after he was crying, he still looks older than me. He looks like an adult.

"We should go," Barnabas says. "I think I've embarrassed myself enough already. I'm sorry about that, Alva."

"Don't apologize."

Barnabas places a hand on my back as we head out of the classroom. As we exit the room, I collide into someone coming in our direction.

Asher stares back at me and he looks scandalized. He looks past me at Barnabas walking out of the room behind me.

"What do you want?" I snap at Asher.

Asher's face is still covered in light bruises, making him look more evil than usual. There seems to be something sinister in his expression.

I quickly see that he's no longer interested in me. He locks eyes with Barnabas and they both suddenly stop where they're standing.

"Don't take too long getting ready for work," Asher says without looking at me.

I decide to leave them alone. I think Asher has something private to talk to Barnabas about.

After fifteen minutes, I walk back downstairs to meet Asher, Rufus, and James for work. Asher informs me that we'll be fixing some lamps for the rest of the evening. It sounds boring, but I get to work. It turns out to be an easy job.

After about a half hour, Asher sits next to me watching me work. I glare at him and tighten my fist around the screwdriver I'm holding. I don't want to be anywhere near him.

"What were you doing with Barnabas?" Asher asks, baring his teeth at me. I recognize that he has some motive behind his question. He continues before I can answer. "He's not supposed to be alone with any of you."

"He wasn't. Tessa and Enzo were with us right before you came."

"He seemed a little stressed out. What did you talk about?"

"That's none of your business. Why do you care anyway?" I ask.

Asher shrugs and raises his hands defensively. He places a hand over his heart and does his best to look innocent.

"He's our leader and I love him. I would follow him to the ends of the earth," Asher says, sounding sarcastic.

"I bet," I reply.

"Just want to make sure he remains the good and loyal Barnabas before 'The Culling.' I want to make sure he's following all of Alexander's instructions."

"Oh, and I'm sure you have everyone's best interests in mind," I say sarcastically.

"I do. More than you know."

I finish the lamp I'm working on and start to get up. I wipe my hands on my jump suit and give Asher a fake smile.

"I'm done, so I'll see you tomorrow."

"Wait," Asher says, grabbing my arm. He peers over his shoulder at James and Rufus. "Alexander wants us to reset the circuits before we leave."

I'm not sure what he means, but I nod. I follow them to one of the closets and he pulls it open. It's dark inside. He places a hand on my back, but I twist away.

"What do you want me to do?"

"There's a lever in there I need you to pull. I'll go pull the other one in the next room," Asher says, with a smile on his face that makes my blood curdle.

I start to protest, realizing that he's messing with me, but he shoves me into the dark closet before I can do anything about it.

I'm sure this is what they've been planning and getting trapped in this closet is the situation I was supposed to be avoiding.

150

"Hey!" I call out, as the door slams behind me. I run my fingers along the wall looking for the light switch, but I find none. I try to push the door open, but someone is standing against it. "Let me out!"

"Shut up," Asher calls back, his voice muffled.

I can hear them laughing and my face burns with anger. I know there's nothing he can do to me out there, but I still feel panic rise in my chest. I want out.

I slam my fists against the wooden door and feel it splinter. I punch it until I can feel that my hands are raw and bloody, but it still doesn't budge. Their laughter dies down and I hear nothing but complete silence.

"Asher! I'm going to kill you! Let me out!" I scream.

I'm serious. At that moment, I want to kill Asher.

It begins to feel like the darkness is swallowing me up. I sit down and wrap my arms around my knees. My chest feels heavy. I have trouble breathing. I have never felt this way before. It is overwhelming.

Suddenly, the visions begin. In the darkness, I feel hands on me. I jump up from where I'm sitting. Something with claws is grabbing at me from all directions. I feel it tearing through my clothes. I scream.

The claws continue to rip through my clothes. I feel them rake at my skin. Searing pain is coming from my arms and legs. I feel wetness that I instinctively know is blood. I am being torn apart and I can't stop it. I try to scream out again, but I can't find my voice. Sudden, the lights flash on. I see Alexander. The sight of him fills me with a sense of pure evil.

Then he is gone.

My body hits the floor hard.

After what like feels forever, but in reality is only a half hour, the door opens and Asher is standing over me. He has a sly grin on his face. I find that I can't speak. . My body is shaking uncontrollably.

Asher motions for Rufus to come help him and they grab me. Together, they carry me to the basement.

I'm going back down into the darkness, but there's nothing I can do about it. I still can't move. I still can't talk.

They bring me to my room, knocking my right arm painfully into the hard wall as we pass. Once I'm placed in bed, Asher lingers over me and laughs. His laugh is cruel and I want to strangle him. I want to do something…anything, but I feel helpless. I hear their footsteps disappear as they climb to the second floor.

It takes an hour for me to regain full use of my limbs, but I remain in bed. I'm too exhausted to get up and I don't want to show my face upstairs. I'm not sure what happened to me and I'm afraid it'll happen again.

For the first time since I arrived at Shiloh, I feel truly broken. I'm losing the fight I had in me. I want to give up and become one of them so the torture will stop.

Can I handle this for too long? How can I keep going when I feel helpless?

I close my eyes and feel myself drifting off. Before I can fall sleep, the image of Alexander flashes before me. The image makes my heart race and I rub my torn up and bloody fists in order to calm myself down.

I know I must destroy him. I know he is pure evil.

Chapter Eleven

Day Eight

When the irritating buzzing alarm goes off, I hurry up to the first floor. I head straight to the hospital room because of my throbbing hands and I can finally see them in the daylight. They are torn up and dried blood is caked over some of the scratches, making me wince when I wash them in the sink.

I dig into one of the medical drawers and find some ointment and bandages. I spend about ten minutes fixing myself up before I head to the main bathroom. My hands are nearly useless because they are bandaged so tightly, but the bandages are necessary because I don't want them to get infected.

When I sit and wait for my shower, I suddenly remember my full experience in the closet yesterday. The memory comes back to me in waves and I feel nauseous. I look down at my arms, but there are no cuts. I know there was dried blood on my hands. I saw it in the sink when I washed it off. I clearly remember being torn apart. I remember claws and hands all over me. Now there is nothing.

I shudder when Tessa takes a seat next to me.

"What happened? Are you okay?" she asks, grabbing my hands gently.

I nod and try to forget about my pounding headache.

"Nothing," I respond. "Just some of...them attacked me."

Tessa is silent as I try to work out what happened. I feel like *I'm* being drugged because what I experienced was real. I can still feel every scratch. I can see Alexander clearly. I can still feel the menace in the way he looked at me.

I need to figure out if everyone is being drugged, but I can't figure out how. It might be the food. I eat what everyone else eats though and I don't act like them, but *I am* having strange, uncontrollable visions.

I have to find out how Alexander is creating these visions. I also have to find out what he's doing to Barnabas, what he's doing to me.

"Fight back," Tessa says in a low voice. "Why didn't you hurt them back?"

I wonder why Tessa is asking me that since I haven't noticed her fighting back either. I try my best to push those thoughts away and remind myself that she isn't herself.

She's being forced to bend to Alexander's will, like everyone else is. I can't tell if I'm being stupid by not trusting her.

"The boys weren't attacking me. Something else was," I try to explain, but I can't figure out what happened myself, so how can I ever explain it to Tessa.

Tessa raises an eyebrow.

"Please don't tell me you're going crazy. You're the one keeping me sane," Tessa says.

I stare straight ahead without saying anything and watch the first group of girls leave their showers, so now it's our turn. I see Ester watching me carefully when I enter the changing room, but I try not to look at her.

I can't figure out a way to help Ester. I want to, but I can't. I know she's too dangerous and she could give me up to Alexander in a second if she felt like it. I don't want to push it.

After I'm done showering, Tessa helps me with my wet hair so that the braid hangs to the side. I slump out into main room. My clothes are dirty. My others haven't been so I have nothing else to wear. I know Cassandra is getting rid of anything that goes in the laundry, but I will not ask her for my things. I'll keep wearing these clothes for as long as I can.

At breakfast, a few things change. When I enter, I see that Ester is seated next to Barnabas instead of one of the other boys who is training to be a leader. This makes me nervous because I assume Barnabas hasn't told Alexander about his intention to choose me instead of Ester. I know she will be furious with me, but I hope she won't do something drastic.

I give Barnabas a questioning look, but he stares back at me blankly.

I see that Asher, James, and Rufus are all smiling at me. Asher looks a little happier than the rest, but they all seem delighted by what they have done to me. So, I'm not going crazy after all. I didn't imagine that they put me in that closet!

I hide my fists under the table and vow to only eat when they are looking away.

"As we all know, in two days Barnabas turns eighteen. He will take a gigantic leap into manhood and pick a partner to help lead us all during the upcoming apocalypse. This pair will be as influential in your lives as Cassandra and I have been during your years here. I'm proud of him." Alexander places a hand on Barnabas's back before continuing. "We only have six more days until everything we have been working to prepare for comes to pass. I know most of you are ready. The rest, I hope can catch up."

I watch him as Barnabas forces a smile at all of us. Is it my imagination again or is he avoiding my glance?

Alexander looks at me with a sly smile and I feel the hate I have for him. I bite my lip to prevent myself from saying anything. My eyes wander over to Demetri, who is also smiling at me. I'm surrounded by a bunch of animals who want to tear me apart. I am incredibly uneasy.

When breakfast is over, I hurry to catch up with Ester. I want to talk some sense into her. I want to discuss how she has to lie for Barnabas.

I catch her arm and pull her back into the dining room once everyone else filters out.

Eden waits for her by the doorway, but then leaves us alone when she sees the urgent look on my face.

"What do you want, Alva?" Ester asks bitterly, pressing her hands against the sides of her dress to flatten it out. "I'd like to enjoy my free time."

"Ester..." I start. It takes me a moment to build up my courage. "You can't do this with Barnabas. You can't let Alexander and Cassandra force you into this. Please, trust me."

I'm not sure what to say without giving Barnabas away. I can't put him in danger.

"Why would I trust you? I already told you they're not forcing me into anything. I'm sick of you talking down to me, Alva. I can think for myself."

But you're not. I take a deep breath, trying to figure out how to explain it to her. Alexander has been controlling them for too long. It will be hard to convince her of anything.

"What if Barnabas doesn't want to?" I say.

Ester raises an eyebrow.

"How would you know what he wants? He's a boy, of course he wants this. Something is wrong with him if he doesn't."

"That's not true," I say, still holding onto Ester's arm. I desperately need her to understand, so I keep trying. "That's what

156

they're teaching you. Maybe he will…eventually, but not now. Not like this. Can't you see this is wrong?"

"This is my duty, Alva. This is what I have to do to help him. It's what Alexander knows will help him. You don't understand how things work here."

"I know how things work!" I shout. "This isn't your duty. It's not anyone's duty. Don't you see how twisted it all is? Don't you want anything to happen on your own terms, inside of having everything planned out for you?"

"Everyone's controlled somehow. I'm safe here. It doesn't matter how people do things anywhere else, because in a few days, this is all we'll have. You're the one that has to understand. Don't you ever consider that you might be the one who's got it all wrong?"

I don't want a life of oppression. I don't want a life of someone telling me what to do at all times. I don't want to even think about Alexander having control over everything if 'The Culling' that he is predicting actually happens. I will no longer be myself. I will only be whatever he molds me into.

Anger builds up inside me and I say much more than I should.

"You have to lie for him. You can't tell Alexander."

She's like talking to a brick wall.

I think deep down she understands, but she won't show it. It's hard to give up something you've believed for years. Admitting that Alexander might be wrong would unravel everything Ester's ever been told.

Barnabas was able to let go because I think he always had some doubts. He was never completely under Alexander's control.

"If Barnabas is acting against his will, I will tell on him. That's also my duty. I won't let this place fall apart. If you say one more thing to me, I'll tell on you too. I care too much about Shiloh. It's my home," Ester threatens.

I let go of her arm and watch her go. She doesn't turn back.

I can't find Barnabas anywhere, but I find Alexander instead. He is standing in the hallway outside of the hospital room and he spots me right away. He smiles and motions for me to join him.

"I have to go to class soon," I say, beginning to back up.

"You have some time," he says.

I take a few steps closer.

"What is it? I don't think I've done anything wrong today."

Alexander forces a harsh laugh, keeping his eyes on me. He runs a hand through his beard thoughtfully.

"I'm not punishing you today. I think you've already done that enough on your own," he replies. "I just want to see how you're doing. I want to know how you're fitting in."

"I think you already know the answer to that," I say.

"I need you to get along with the girls. They all have a strong bond and I know they'll accept you if you let them," Alexander says.

"I don't have to worry about that. My father will be coming in six days and I'll never have to see any of you again."

"One of the boys told me you've been spending some time with Barnabas. I told him it's best not to get too attached. He has other duties to attend to and he has no reason to be communicating with one of the girls. There's nothing he can learn from you. I told him if he does it again, he'll be punished. At least if it's unsupervised."

I glare at Alexander. I know he is threatening me, but that also means that he is threatened *by* me. In some ways, I'm sure I scare him, which makes me feel more powerful. Still, I don't want him to take it out on Barnabas. I know that's why he's threatening me this way. He knows I won't put anyone else in danger.

"You mean his duties with Ester? You think I'm influencing him somehow," I say.

Alexander's eyes narrow.

"Ester is right for him. She is pure."

"And what am I?"

158

"You're not on the right path at this moment. It could change in the future, but nothing seems to be sticking in that small brain of yours," Alexander shoots back.

"I'm a lot smarter than you and I'll prove it," I whisper. "Also, I don't want to be on a job with Asher anymore. I'd like to switch to hunting. I insist on switching to hunting."

"Oh, you insist?" Alexander asks, giving me a strange smile. "You don't call the shots here, Alva."

"I refuse to work with Asher and the other boys. They *attacked* me. Tessa switched to cooking, so what does it matter? I'll head out with the hunters later and they can teach me."

"You better be careful, Alva," Alexander warns.

"Why don't you punish me, then? Why don't you kick me out?"

Alexander watches me for a moment before answering. He makes me feel uneasy. He is considering it.

"Don't test me."

Suddenly, I begin to understand. I think I know why Alexander is afraid to do anything to me.

"You're afraid to punish me because then everyone would have to know why. They'd find out that Barnabas is having doubts. You're afraid that I could bring down this whole compound," I reply.

I walk away from Alexander before he can say anything else. From the way he was glaring at me, I can tell that I'm right and that's all I need to know.

I make my way downstairs and find the classroom where all the girls are. We have another sexuality and birthing class with Cassandra today, so I groan and rest my head on Tessa's arm.

She suppresses a laugh as the lesson begins.

Cassandra teaches the girls about when they'll all be pregnant, so most of the attention is on Ester during this lesson because they assume she'll be the first one to have a baby.

I feel nauseous thinking about Ester carrying Barnabas's baby, a baby that he obviously doesn't want and one that she might not want either. If that happens, he'll be trapped here. He'd never leave. He needs to give Barnabas a good enough reason to stay stuck here. Barnabas needs some incentive to behave.

Something else nags at me, however. It's not because I know that neither Ester nor Barnabas should be forced into this. It's because it bothers me to think about Ester and Barnabas together.

The image of Barnabas smiling and looking up toward the sky lingers in my mind. I want to see him this way. I want him to look at me the same way he did that day. I've never felt this way and I don't know how to explain it. I want him to come back to Verus with us and start over. I want him to be happy.

I also worry about if I will be able to talk to him. Obviously, people are getting back to Alexander about our conversations and that is something that must worry Barnabas. We can't be caught talking again or he'll be punished. I don't know if I can figure out a way to speak with him again without anyone finding out.

I need to find a way for Enzo to give Barnabas messages, but what would I even say? I don't even have a plan.

When class is finished, I don't have much of a break before Titus finds me. Apparently, Alexander agreed to let me join his hunting group. I'm excited to start because it means getting out of the compound.

I get changed and meet them outside, where it's only Titus, Jethro, and I. Jethro holds a shotgun over his shoulder as he eyes me suspiciously. Jethro is as big as Titus with a much wider-set jaw. He looks like a giant to me.

"Do you know what you're doing, little girl?" His voice booms.

"I'm a quick learner," I reply.

"I'm not sure about that," Jethro says with a laugh. "You haven't learned anything here yet."

I exchange glances with Titus and he smiles.

We head up toward the cliffs, away from the village. We will be high up.

"Don't I get a gun?" I ask.

"No," Titus says. "Alexander won't allow it, but you can help us with other things."

A weight lifts from my chest. There are weapons in the compound and I can find them. Having a weapon is a great way to defend myself against Alexander. I'll be able to get Barnabas out when the time comes if I have them. I need to find out more later.

"What do you hunt here?" I ask, as we climb. It's hot and tiring. I see that the path keeps going up and up. "It doesn't seem like there's much life around here."

"Mountain lion, some big birds." Jethro answers. He eyes me and then walks ahead with his gun ready. "We haven't seen much around in a while. The usual game has scattered. Maybe they can sense the end is coming."

"I'm sure that's it," I say, a little bit more sarcastically than I want to.

"You're lucky Alexander let you join us," Jethro replies, glaring at me.

We walk for over an hour when Jethro makes us kneel down and wait. He sees something in the distance, but I don't catch it. Titus is close to me for some reason. I can feel his breath on me. The silence is overwhelming.

Jethro leans forward holding his gun at eye level. He fires a shot, but I don't see anything drop to the ground. I'm sure he hasn't hit anything.

"Want to go check it out?" Jethro asks, turning to me. "That's the only useful thing you could do."

I start to get up, but Titus clasps onto my arm tightly. He gives me a terrified look before turning to Jethro.

"I'll go with her. Wouldn't want her to do anything stupid," he says.

Titus nearly lifts me up with one swoop and keeps his hands on my shoulders so I'm forced to walk in front of him. I try to wiggle away, but he hisses in my ear.

"Keep walking," he says.

He doesn't talk again until we are far away from Jethro, but he still keeps his body behind mine. He refuses to let me step beside him. He swings me around to face him.

"What?" I ask.

"Are you really that stupid?"

"What did I do wrong?" I ask, surprised.

"Why would Jethro ask you to go check it out if we both know he didn't hit anything?" Titus asks, raising an eyebrow.

Realization dawns on me and my mouth gapes open. Jethro was going to shoot me. That was why Alexander let me go hunting with them. He wants Jethro to shoot me and he'd blame it on my inexperience. They'd say it was an accident. That would be better than Alexander being forced to kill me himself and then having to explain what happened to the others.

I grab onto Titus's arms to steady myself.

"Thank you," I whisper breathlessly. "Thank you, Titus."

We wait a few more moments before heading back. This time, Titus makes me trail behind him, so his body blocks me from Jethro's view.

When we reach Jethro, I shrug and try to stop shaking.

"Nothing out there. Must've run away," I say.

"Yeah," Jethro mumbles.

Sorry that you're so disappointed you couldn't kill me.

I wonder if he'll try again, but I definitely won't give him the opportunity. I know Titus is looking out for me, too. Six days, that's all I have to survive. Six days feels like a lifetime.

Titus keeps a hand on my shoulder the entire time because I think he sees how rattled I am. I have no way to defend myself.

Jethro has a loaded gun and I have nowhere to go. I even jump slightly when I hear his gun go off again.

This time, he has shot something.

I've never seen a mountain lion before, especially not a dead one. We all approach it slowly as Jethro swings his gun over his shoulder and I feel safe for the time being. I kneel down in front of it and run my hands across its soft fur. It's big and I don't know how we'll move it.

In one swift motion, Titus grabs it by its arms and legs and gets it around his neck and over his shoulders. He struggles slightly under its weight and has to adjust it, but we start the walk back. He has no real problem carrying it for over an hour in the searing heat.

"Does it taste good?" I ask.

"Yes," Titus replies. "You'll have to help me cut it up."

I swallow hard. I look at the dead animal and think about cutting into it. I'm not sure I can because it's too beautiful. I still can't even reconcile myself to the fact that we killed it.

When we get back, Jethro returns his gun inside and helps Titus move an old wooden table to the middle of the fenced in grass. He slams down the lion on the table and we are handed long sharp knives by Jethro.

Suddenly, I feel more in control. I hold up one of the knives and stare at Jethro.

Titus gives me a hard look before I regain control. I lower the knife before Jethro notices and I watch as Titus begins cutting.

It is an awful job, but I quickly get the hang of it by watching him skin the animal. It takes a long time before it is all done and cut up because my hands are still so messed up. My clothing is covered in blood by the time it's over and Titus reaches over to remove a piece of the animal from my hair. I nearly gag and take a step back.

"You did well," Titus says, as Jethro heads inside.

I help pack the meat into a cooler and watch Titus carry it inside. He looks at me one last time before bringing the cooler into the kitchen. I remain in the main room and glance around.

Everyone is already at dinner.

I opt out of attending dinner because my stomach is churning uncomfortable. Also, I don't want to be around everyone. I change my clothes, finding one clean shirt leftover from a locker, and fix my hair in the bathroom. I do my best to get all the blood out of it.

After dinner, Barnabas walks right past me. He looks upset about something, but I don't know what's wrong.

I want to talk to my friends privately before we go to sleep, so we make sure everyone is out of the room before we discuss anything. Most of them head outside on the balcony, but I'm not sure where Barnabas is.

"How was dinner?" I ask.

"I think Barnabas and Alexander had an argument," Tessa says. "Barnabas spent the whole time looking down at the floor and didn't eat. Alexander told him to stop acting like a child."

"We have to get these kids out of here," Enzo says.

"Most of them won't come. I tried talking to Ester, but some of them like it here," I argue.

"Titus and Barnabas at least."

"What about the other girls?" Tessa asks.

"How will we even do this?" Enzo asks back, raising his eyebrows. "Alexander won't let them out when we go to leave."

"We need one of those guns," I reply. "They had them for hunting. There were also some knives."

"We need to think this through," Enzo says.

"We will," I reply.

Tessa looks nervous, so I think the thought of action is terrifying her. I hope we are all able to recover from this experience when we are back in Verus. I hope we can all be happy again.

We talk for a little while longer, trying to figure out what to do, but we come up short. I need to explore the compound more. I need a solid plan to make it out with everyone who wants to come.

Enzo plays the piano for us and it calms me down. Now that my friends are on board with coming up with a plan to help everyone, I can relax a bit. It's nice to have people on my side. It's nice to know I'm not going crazy.

I head down into the basement with everyone else that night. I see Barnabas, but he doesn't look at me.

What did Alexander threaten him with? Did he threaten to punish me? Did he convince Barnabas to continue along his path to choose Ester?

I worry about that for a few moments while I lie in bed.

I peel off my dirty clothes so that I am lying only in my underwear. I find it most comfortable to sleep that way and my clothes are becoming stretched out and uncomfortable.

I'm only asleep for a few hours before a nightmare wakens me. I know I must have been screaming because I'm breathing heavily. Everyone died in my nightmare. Everything was gone and it was all my fault. I didn't help them. The voices that I heard in my dream were urging me to do something, but I don't know what. It's all becoming so frustrating.

I hear quiet footsteps heading in my direction and I know someone is in my room. I tense, thinking that it must be Asher coming to finish me off...or even Jethro.

There is extra weight on my bed. Someone has sit down on it.

I can smell Barnabas as he eases himself under the covers. He smells like fresh laundry and something else sweet, which reminds me of home. How can he smell like my home? To my knowledge, he has never been there.

He doesn't say anything as he scoots in next to me. I turn to him and he leans in close without touching me. I can feel his breath on my face.

"What are you doing here?" I whisper.

I know how important it is that no one hears us. Visiting somewhere where they sleep is strictly forbidden and even I feel nervous about breaking this rule. Alexander has made the basement into sacred ground.

"I heard you screaming. I had to talk to you," he whispers. "Do you want me to leave?"

I know only I can hear him and I feel more comfortable. I'm desperate for some company in this dark place. Suddenly, it all feels more bearable.

"No. What happened to you today? What did Alexander say to you?"

"I'm not allowed to talk to you. I think he's catching on. He's going to make me choose Ester. It's already decided. I can't do it, Alva. I won't do it. I'll be punished."

"How will he punish you?" I ask.

Part of me doesn't want to know, but what could be so bad? He's already been beaten.

"If you're really bad, he forces you to stay down here for a day or two in complete silence. There's a special room he puts you in. The visions are terrible and they all feel real. There's no way out. He can keep you down there for as long as he wants and no one will help you."

"Have you ever been in there?"

"Once," Barnabas replies cryptically.

I don't ask about it because I don't think he wants to talk about it.

"Do you think we're being drugged? Maybe Alexander is the one making us have these visions. That could be the reason."

Somehow, in the dark, I know Barnabas is shaking his head. I feel the weight shift on the bed.

"No. I've been having visions since before I knew him. That part is real." Barnabas pauses. "You have them too…you never told me."

"I have nightmares," I say. "Mostly they're about you."

"That's because you're like me. If Alexander knew…"

"He won't find out," I say.

"He'll say you're the antichrist and he'll lock you away. I've heard him say that before. He said that's what the girl from my dreams is. You're someone to distract me … someone evil."

"I'm not."

"I know." He pauses. "Alva?"

His voice sounds weak.

"What is it?"

"Do you mind if I sleep here? Do you care if I…"

Barnabas doesn't finish his sentence and suddenly I feel like I'm going to cry. I have never met anyone so lonely. I have never met someone so grateful to be in my presence. I wipe my eyes and turn away from him. I grab his arms and wrap them around me. He pulls himself closer and I feel his body pressed against mine.

It's warm and comforting.

He digs his arm under my neck and reaches further to force the palm of my hand open. The bandages cover most of it, but he finds the lines in my palm and runs his finger along them. He holds his other hand against my hip.

"Do you want to know about my dream? The one before I met you?" Barnabas asks in my ear.

"Yes," I say.

He begins to talk to me soothingly about the first dream he ever had about me. He describes me standing in a field. I am smiling and looking up toward the sun and I begin to laugh. Barnabas talks about my light hair reflecting in the sun and how the image always made him happy.

That's how I know he's telling the truth. I have had the same dream about him and I know it's all real.

Barnabas's voice helps me drift off to sleep. I think briefly about how I've never felt this way about anyone else. I care about my family and friends, but this is a different feeling. This must be how my father feels about my mother. This must be what it feels like to be in love. Somehow, I'm certain.

I know I can't leave him here to rot. I can't leave him at all.

Chapter Twelve

Day Nine

When I wake up, I remember instantly that it's Barnabas's birthday tomorrow. I know he will be eighteen and by the terms of the compound, a man. I believe that right now he is still a kid, helpless. I can feel his fingers still resting on top of my outstretched palm.

I have only five more days to figure out what to do before I will be returning to Verus.

I carefully unravel myself from Barnabas's grasp, in an attempt not to wake him. I pull on my clothes and head back up to the light of the second floor. In the bathroom, I find a blue work jumpsuit that I can wear for today because I plan to wash my clothes in the sink.

After I shower and change, I take my wet clothes outside so they can dry in the sunlight. The dry morning heat tells me that they'll be ready in no time.

Tessa finds me sitting on one of the couches in the main room. She eyes my clothing and laughs. I see she has returned to wearing her own clothes, which I'm sure Alexander will blame me for.

He's supposed to think he's still successfully drugging her.

"Good morning," she says, sounding cheerful. "Ester's mad you used her hot water again."

I know that Tessa is in a better mood because we are formulating a plan. We are on our way to figuring something out. Everyone feels less useless than before.

"She'll get over it," I say.

Tessa smiles and sits next to me, where we watch the boys filter into the bathroom. I don't see Barnabas with them, so panic pulses through me.

It's possible Alexander found out about last night and is punishing Barnabas.

I wait anxiously for the boys to finish and we all head to breakfast. I'm getting sick of the same old breakfast and the look of it makes my stomach uneasy. I want to know where Barnabas is.

He walks in a few moments later looking unruly. His hair is messy and his sleeves are rolled up. The top three buttons of his shirt are undone and his smooth skin and collarbones are visible underneath, just like my dream.

Before Alexander looks at him, he sits down clumsily and smiles briefly at Tessa and me. His cheeks are full of color and his eyes are sparkling.

I like him this way. I think that it is his small way of rebelling.

Everyone watches him for a few moments before Demetri gives Alexander a nudge. Alexander turns to Barnabas and instantly looks displeased. Alexander whispers something to him.

Barnabas fumbles with his buttons and even as he glances down at himself, there is still a slight smile on his face. He leaves his sleeves pushed up to his elbows.

After breakfast is finished, I hurry to the hospital room to rewrap my hands. I feel someone behind me as I walk, but I don't care who it is.

Without turning around, I dig into the medical drawer and pull out the tape and ointment I'll need. I unravel my bandages and see that my wounds are looking slightly better. I squeeze on some more medicine and focus on the tape. I turn around to see Asher watching me.

He sits down on one of the cots, keeping his eyes on me.

My heart skips a beat.

"You've lasted a lot longer than I thought you would," Asher says. "You're not as weak as the other girls."

"The girls are stronger than you think," I say quietly. "Some are even stronger than you."

Asher eyes my hands and grins.

"I still hurt you."

"You didn't do this," I remind him, raising my bandaged hands. "Why don't you leave me alone?"

He eases himself off the cot and walks closer to me. When he speaks again, I can feel his breath on the back of my neck. Why does he insist on making me feel uncomfortable? Does it make him feel stronger?

I think he is still angry I embarrassed him, but I know he deserved it.

"We'll find another way to hurt you. I'm not done trying yet," Asher says.

"You should stop. It's not going to work, Asher."

"Next time it'll be worse," Asher says, with a laugh.

Unable to control myself, I swing around and grab Asher by his collar. It hurts my hands, but I pull him around and slam his back against the wall. He closes his eyes as I raise my fist to his face.

"What happened yesterday was a one-time thing. If you ever do that to me again, I will *kill* you. Do you understand that? I will kill you, Asher," I shout.

Asher looks dazed as I let go of him. He regains his composure quickly and tries to put on a brave face.

I feel like he will never stop antagonizing me, no matter how many times I threaten him back.

"You need to be afraid of me, Alva. You'll respect me soon enough. You'll respect Alexander, too. He'll make sure of it. You'll need us at the end of all this."

I ignore him and finish wrapping my hands. When I turn back, he's gone. I feel unsettled as I put the supplies away and head back out into the hallway. Despite Asher being weaker than me, I know strength isn't everything. I'll have to be careful.

A half hour later, I find myself in sewing class again. This time Tessa helps me and we finish something together, which is an oddly shaped and uncomfortable pillow.

Cassandra comes over to praise me and give me one of her fake smiles.

I know she is planning something for me. I know she and Alexander have spent time deciding how to deal with me. They don't know that I am doing the same regarding them.

When class is over, Tessa and I pretend to take a while putting our sewing equipment away and cleaning our station. Titus and Enzo join us after their class is out, so I'm guessing this is something they set up.

"Where's Barnabas?" I ask, as they sit at a few desks across from us.

"He's meeting with Alexander, planning something for his birthday tomorrow," Enzo says.

I think this is an attempt by Alexander to keep Barnabas away from us, but I also know his birthday will be a big deal. I try to stop thinking about it as we get down to business.

"Titus wants to come with us when we leave. Maybe we can get Barnabas out, too," Enzo whispers, leaning closer to us.

"We have to," I say defensively. "We need to get Barnabas out. That's part of the plan."

"He's almost always with Alexander. No one pays any attention to me, but attention is always on Barnabas," Titus replies.

"I don't care. He doesn't want to be here," I say.

"You have personal conversations with Barnabas?" Enzo asks with a raised eyebrow.

"He talks to you?" Titus asks. "I know he's unhappy, but I don't think he would ever leave."

"He will," I reassure them.

Enzo shrugs and we start talking about how we will get people out.

It turns out that Titus knows where the weapons are kept, and he has access to them. He can't take them, however, when Jethro is with him. He'll have to take them at night.

I know it'll be dangerous.

"What if 'The Culling' actually happens?" Titus inquires.

We all exchange glances. I never thought of that as a real possibility.

"Then we'll still need weapons," Enzo says. "We'll still need to get out of this place. Alexander would have more control over everyone than he ever has."

We'll still need weapons.

For a moment, my thoughts turn to home. I miss my room and my computers. I miss my father and my mother. I want to talk to Avery again and I want him to hug my leg like he usually does.

The world can't end because I have to see them all again. I can't be left in a world with Alexander and Cassandra and their strict, terrible rules.

I spend the rest of my break teaching Titus a few more lessons and collecting my clothes outside. Since I'm already in my work

173

jumpsuit, when Jethro collects us I'm ready. He still makes me nervous because I wonder if Alexander has instructed him to keep trying to hurt me.

We take the long walk up into the mountains again with Titus trailing me closely. His eyes are always on Jethro and his gun, so I feel safer. We wait as Jethro pauses, raises the shotgun toward something in the distance, and lowers it. He eyes the sky and then turns back to us.

"Bad weather is coming. We should head back before we get stuck in it."

I wait for Jethro to take the lead. We haven't been gone for long and I'm glad our hunting excursion won't be dragged out any further. I don't want to see him kill again today. I especially don't want to be Jethro's target.

When we make it back, I wander into the kitchen where Eden, Ariel, and Ester are preparing dinner. Tessa helps, but she mostly talks to me. I can see that this infuriates Ester and she is constantly shooting us nasty looks.

"What are you doing in here, Alva? This isn't your job," Ester says. It annoys me that she has a habit of saying my name after everything. "Go and wait for dinner, Alva. Get changed or do something useful, Alva."

"I've already done my job for today," I say. I twirl and watch her stare at my jumpsuit. "I'm thinking about wearing a jumpsuit every day since someone keeps misplacing my clothes. You wear what you want and I'll wear what I want. That sounds fair, right?"

"That's not how things work here, Alva," Ester hisses.

I dig my hands into the deep pockets and lean against the sink, blocking her way.

Eden and Ariel are watching me curiously.

"You should be a bit more open to change," I say.

"You're not taking this seriously. This isn't a joke. Alexander and Cassandra are keeping us safe. That's all I care about, Alva."

174

Ester grabs onto the boiling pot of water from the stove and starts toward the sink. The smell of smoke is all over everyone's clothing.

"I'm not joking either," I reply.

I head into the dining room before dinner is ready and I see the mute girls setting up. The one I know is named Junia looks up and me and blushes slightly. I seem to make her nervous, but I can guess why. She's afraid I'll get her in trouble.

As I sit down in my seat, I feel a soft hand on my arm. I watch Junia lean over and place an empty dish in front of me like she did at all the other spots. I feel like she is making a gesture of some sort, but I can't figure it out. Is she trying to tell me something?

When the others leave the room, Junia moves in close to me.

"Alexander is afraid of you," she whispers.

Before I can say anything to that, a few other kids file in. Luckily, Asher, Demetri, and James don't realize she's been speaking to me. I watch her take her seat far away from me.

"Someone's eager to eat," Asher teases.

Demetri steps next to me and reaches out to press his thumb against my cheek. I flinch, but he pulls away quickly. I see that there is some sort of black dirt streaked across his thumb.

"You're a little bit dirty. You're going to have to straighten yourself up a bit," Demetri says.

The others laugh.

I clutch onto the sides of my chair.

"And I guess you think that's your job to tell me that?" I ask.

Barnabas steps into the room and looks right at us. His appearance is back to normal and he's looking solemn. He freezes where his is.

"It will be my job. I think one day you'll make an acceptable wife," Demetri says.

"Not *your* wife, though."

"God, I hope not," Demetri laughs.

I grab onto his hand and position his blackened thumb back over my cheek. I rub the dirt he had removed back on my face and let go of him.

He takes a step back.

Barnabas comes back to life when Titus puts a hand on his shoulder. They both look at me briefly before taking their seats. Demetri moves away a moment later when Alexander and Cassandra join us.

Everyone is present.

Alexander clears his throat to get our attention. He says a quick prayer and then looks around at all of us.

I hate seeing Barnabas sitting by his side and looking so dejected. It looks like he is worried about something.

"There's a new rule that goes into effect tomorrow. There will be no more unsupervised fraternization between the boys and the girls. Outside of your jobs, you will stay in your own groups. It's unbecoming for a girl to be spending time with a boy alone, anyway."

For a second I wonder if Alexander knows about Barnabas visiting me at night, but I know that can't be it. There's no way he would know. He must be referring to us all hanging out in the classrooms after our lessons. He might have seen us there or heard about it.

Probably from Asher.

No one says anything, but Barnabas's eyes linger on me. He looks down almost immediately, but I know this is about us. I know Alexander does not want me influencing anyone. He doesn't want Barnabas to learn anything new from me because he doesn't want his best student's mind to be poisoned.

But I know he's too late because Barnabas was never a full supporter of what he's been doing here. Now he has the courage to fight back.

I also think about Enzo. Alexander is making it more difficult for us to plan something, but I guess I can talk to Titus during our job. If we become desperate enough, we can leave messages or meet after dark. We will have to be careful.

Suddenly, I realize how much trouble I'm in and it all hits me at once like a sledgehammer. A few days ago, I thought I was only a guest in this place, but now I'm a prisoner. There's nowhere to go, nowhere to hide, and nothing I can do about it because Alexander controls everything. I know I have to keep myself calm.

Before bed, I'm brought before Cassandra in one of the classrooms. I don't feel like talking to her, but she has requested to speak to me personally. I sigh to myself, thinking about how she made Ester fetch me rather than doing it herself.

"Hello, Alva. How have things been lately?" Cassandra asks sweetly.

She motions toward one of the desks.

I have no idea what she could want to talk about, but I obey. I will hear her out. I know she's not *really* worried about my well-being.

"Fine," I reply.

Cassandra waits for me to elaborate, but when I don't, she only smiles wider.

"Good, good. I am worried that you are not fitting in. Ester says you have been difficult and not willing to follow the rules. She believes you've been spending time with Barnabas and putting ideas in his head."

"Barnabas can think for himself - and so can Ester, I'm sure," I reply.

"You're pretty smart for a sixteen year old girl," Cassandra says.

"No need to add the girl part on the end."

Cassandra begins to frown, all of the fake happiness gone from her face.

I have to learn to keep calm until five days are up. Then I'll be safe. Then I can speak my mind again. I can't do it…another one of my flaws, I suppose. I'm learning a lot about myself lately.

"What have you been saying to Barnabas? He's been acting strangely. He's been talking back to Alexander more. You don't understand how important this all is. You can't be messing with his life."

"Oh, like you are? You've been messing with Barnabas since he was five years old, like you've been doing with everyone else. He deserves to see another point of view."

"Stop it, Alva!" Cassandra shouts at me, causing me to jump. She seems embarrassed by her sudden outburst and forces another big smile before continuing, "I rarely have to yell at any of these kids. I never have to raise my voice."

"I …" I start, but she cuts me off.

"I'm giving you some advice," she pauses. "Because when you're still here in five days and everything outside has gone, you'll need us. You'll need us more than you ever thought you would. We'll be all you have."

"I don't believe that, Cassandra," I say in a low voice.

We stare at each other for a few moments, but Cassandra is the first one to look away. I make her uncomfortable, like she makes me uncomfortable.

"You'll believe real soon. And during that time, I'd like to embrace you as I would my own daughter."

Cassandra walks away and I can hear her footsteps down the hall. I place my forehead on the cool desk and take a deep breath. I can't stand these people anymore. I don't like being constantly on edge, waiting for something horrible to happen.

I clamor down into the darkness of the basement and find my bed. Tonight it feels a bit empty without Barnabas. I want to talk to him, but I don't leave my own room to find him. I hope he is not worrying too much about tomorrow. I hope he has it all figured out.

When I finally fall asleep, I dream of home. For the longest time, I see myself eating dinner with my family. It feels so real, but I already know it's a dream. In my dream, I peer over and see Barnabas sitting with us and smiling.

He's wearing clothes that we wear, something he picked out himself. His fingers are dirty from helping me work on something and he is talking to Avery.

I think this might be something that could possibly happen. It could be part of my immediate future.

The dream is ripped apart when we all turn to see the storm outside. The earth is crumbling and a tornado is coming straight toward our house. Barnabas reaches out to me, but it's too late because the house is collapsing in on itself.

I wake up screaming again and cry into my pillow.

I lie on my back and try to push the nightmare from my head, but it sticks for a long time. I hate thinking about my family because that brings them into this place. I never want them to suffer like this. I never want them to experience anything like this. I wonder if Tessa and Enzo are thinking the same things.

The only thing that gives me hope is the knowledge that we're planning something. Titus is in on it and I know Barnabas will want to leave too. I think about talking to Junia about it because of how she interacted with me today, but I don't know if that's dangerous. She said Alexander was afraid of me.

Right now, I feel like he doesn't have to worry. I haven't done much and most of the other kids hate me. Ester has made sure of that and Asher has vowed that he will make my life miserable.

I allow myself to take some satisfaction in Alexander's fear. I like to think he's also up late at night worrying for hours. I like to think it's because of me.

At least we will come up with a plan, I remind myself. *At least I have something to hold onto.*

I'm not sure what Alexander will do besides dividing us and making sure we can't speak, but we can find ways around that easily. Unless he starts getting vicious, we don't have much to worry about. I wonder how long it will take before I evoke his full wrath. I wonder how he will take it out on me.

I'm afraid my father won't have his guard up or that Alexander will do something to harm him.

The thought causes a lump to form in my throat. I hate thinking about putting my friends and family in danger. I'll have to stay strong. I'll have to make sure everyone makes it out alive. Never have I ever feared for my life like this.

I hope soon Alexander will know what it's like to feel like this. I hope he will soon fear for his own life. That's what he deserves.

Chapter Thirteen

Day Ten

It's morning again and I immediately discover it will be an unusual day. When I go into my locker, I realize that there's a white dress hanging there for me. It is sleeveless with a lace collar and falls above the knee. I like it, but I'm still not sure I want to wear it. I don't know if wearing it would be playing into their game.

Tessa comes up behind me holding an identical dress. After Ester showers, she is also wearing it. Clearly, all the girls are expected to wear the white dresses. It might have something to do with purity.

"We're required to wear them," Ester says harshly. She is staring at me. Again, her dress is a bit different. She has sleeves and there is no lace collar. "Alexander won't have it any other way."

"For today," I say.

I agree only because it's Barnabas's birthday. I will try to blend in today. I won't make anything worse.

My heart begins to race once I'm alone in the shower. Panic ripples through me because I'm not sure what I will do. I want to pull Barnabas and the others away from this freak show. I want to end it all before it gets worse.

What if Barnabas doesn't comply? Will Ester tells on him? Will he be punished?

I hold back a sob when I think about it. I'm not afraid of what Barnabas might do, but how he might be punished for it. I'm afraid that no one has any choice.

And they don't.

I let the water run over me for longer than usual, thinking about what my parents told me when I was young. I never understood why they told me because I've never been afraid for myself like this before, but now I know it must have happened often…before everything got better, a time in the past when women were still unequal like they are in Shiloh.

My mother told me that I was the only person who has rights over my body. She told me that verbal harassment is not flattery. If something makes someone uncomfortable, they don't have to endure it. No one owes anything to anyone else.

These words mean much more to me now. For the first time ever, I feel ashamed of myself and I know that's because of these people here. I want them to know what I know. I want them to understand me, but I can't make them. I can't help them.

I can't stand to think that my mother was wrong or that Verus steered us all in the wrong direction. I have to hold onto something.

I shake the thoughts from my head and do my best to get control over myself. I dry myself and slip on the white dress. I like how it looks in the mirror and it fits perfectly.

After I finish blow-drying my hair, I ask Tessa to French braid it. For some reason, I want to look nice. I'm not sure why. I feel cold and stiff and distant. More than ever, I want to go home.

Eden comes over and puts some light make up on my face. My cheeks look a bit pink, but I still recognize myself. I'm not sure why all this is necessary.

Right after everyone is done getting ready, we eat breakfast with the other girls and Cassandra joins us and sits at the head of the table. I hear the boys outside going to shower and dress.

"Today is a special day, as most of you know," Cassandra begins. "Barnabas is the first one turning eighteen. He will start on his journey to manhood and he has picked Ester to be his companion. They will be bonded for life and Ester will take care of his every need. She will serve him in every way necessary for him to become our future leader."

She smiles at me warmly, so I think she is pleased by my compliance.

Ester smiles proudly and some of the other girls congratulate her. I don't know why she's being celebrated. Her whole life has basically become servitude to someone else.

I don't want that. Even if I care about Barnabas, I would never be that for him. It's not possible.

"Thank you. I will try my best to be a good partner," Ester says, smiling gratefully back at us.

"That's all you can wish for," Cassandra responds, delighted.

Tessa and I exchange worried glances. The girls seemed to be so brainwashed, but I know not all of them agree. I think of the few words Junia and I have exchanged. I know she knows this whole thing is sick and she knows it shouldn't be like this. Junia and the other cleaning girls got the short end of the stick.

Ester seems to be benefiting from everything and has privilege here, while the others suffer. She won't realize how wrong it is until she suffers too.

"I would also like to thank Alva for respecting our special day. It's good to see her dressed nicely for once. I know this all must be strange for you," Ester says with a smile.

The sad part is I think that's Ester's best attempt at a compliment. I know it is a dig at me and perhaps she does know my feelings for Barnabas. I think she is being cruel.

"Is it strange? The way we celebrate manhood?" Cassandra asks.

"Yes," I say. "It doesn't seem to fit in with your morals."

I feel Tessa's hand on my leg.

"Why not?" Cassandra probes further.

I don't know why she is so curious, but she is. If she wants to know I will tell her what I think.

"I thought you wanted pure. I figured you'd be against something like this."

I don't agree with their definition, but I use her words

"Ester will be committed to Barnabas from here on. She will be pure in the eyes of God because she saved herself for him. I'm sure it's not like that in Verus and that's hard to understand."

Cassandra looks at us sympathetically.

I hate how she talks to me like I'm a child. I hate how it's obvious she already assumes everyone in Verus was horrible. I don't understand how virginity and morality are connected.

"I get it. I'll tell everyone about it when I get home."

I stare at Cassandra and she stares back at me. It feels like she's testing me. I want to know if they intend to let us leave, but she only smiles. I'm not sure if her smile is real.

We finish breakfast. I do my best to tune everyone out. I don't feel like listening to Cassandra anymore and I don't care what Ester has to say.

Tessa looks as low as I do. She barely eats anything.

I feel relief when we are all excused from class today to prepare for the events later on in the evening. I don't see Barnabas or any of the other boys all morning and I feel like this is somehow directly involved with me.

I'm certain Alexander doesn't want Barnabas to talk to me today. He is going to keep us separated until we leave. I'm not sure what he's planning.

I step outside with Tessa to get some fresh air and for us to be alone. We sit in some wooden chairs and peer out into the distance. It's sunny now, but I see clouds looming over the mountains.

"What do you think is going to happen tonight?" Tessa asks me.

I shrug.

"I'm expecting the worst."

"You think it's going to be that terrible?"

I narrow my eyes at her.

"If they're making such a big deal out of something, I'm sure we won't want to see it. I want to get out of here tonight," I say.

"Barnabas will be okay," Tessa replies.

Somehow, she knows I care about him. I nod and look away from her back at the clouds. It's starting to look like Alexander and Cassandra are right and the world will end tonight. Right now, I don't think that would be so bad.

When we head back inside, I see that the girls are moving all the wooden chairs into the main room. I spot some unlit candles are being placed around the floor and everything else is being moved out. The only thing left besides the chairs is the piano that Enzo and Barnabas played a few days ago. I run my fingers along the keys, wishing that it were a few days ago rather than today.

I notice that Ester isn't being made to do any work, but I don't complain because neither Tessa nor I are being asked to do anything either. I cringe as she walks around until she spots me and then does her best to smile sweetly. I start to move back toward the balcony outside, but she approaches Tessa and me quickly.

For a moment, she watches me, and then she reaches out to touch my bare arm.

I shudder under her cold hand.

"I want you to fit in here. I hope tonight will be a step in the right direction," Ester says.

"Only four more days, Ester," I remind her.

She smiles wider and instantly reminds me of Cassandra. Ester leans in closer, inches away from my ear.

"I hope it all works out for you," she says.

I know there is something completely unreachable in Ester and she is as bad as Cassandra and Alexander. I think she is a true believer. I'd never be able to talk her out of anything. I know I have to stop trying and start fighting.

Right now I feel helpless. Barnabas might have to make it through this situation on his own because I have no idea how I'd get him out of it without all hell breaking loose.

Ester disappears and comes back with a large black bowl full of water. Some of it sloshes up the side, but it doesn't spill on the floor. Her bare feet trudge along the wood toward the center of the room. She bends down gracefully to place the bowl on the floor.

I'll find out what it's for later.

Tessa and I find a private place in the hospital room to relax. I try to clear my mind while we play a game of cards.

We spend over an hour making a new deck of cards from torn pieces of paper, but it wastes enough time to keep me distracted. No one comes to bother us because they're too busy setting everything up.

When we finish, I decide to lay down on one of the cots for a little while. Tessa heads out to see what everyone else is up to, so I find myself alone. Before long, I'm fast asleep.

Tessa comes to wake me right before the ceremony. I sit up, groggy, and look around. I can hear the thunder and rain outside and the compound is dark. Did the power go out? I see that Tessa is holding a lit candle.

She grabs my arm and pulls me close.

"It's starting soon," Tessa whispers. I can feel her trembling. "Everything is dark."

"It'll be okay," I whisper.

I'm not sure if it will be, but I don't know what else to say. I'm scared, too. I'm scared for Tessa and myself. I'm scared for Enzo and I'm scared for Barnabas.

What will happen to him? Will he change? Is this some sort of trick devised by Alexander and Cassandra?

I remain quiet as Tessa leads me down the dark hallway and into the main room. I see now that all the candles are lit and all the girls are sitting on the floor. Ester is not among them. After I take my place next to Tessa, the boys walk in slowly, holding their own candles. Enzo catches my eye as he sits in one of the chairs behind us.

All the boys take their seats on the chairs while all the girls except Ester remain on the floor with our legs underneath us.

Barnabas is still missing.

I watch as Ester walks in next, with her white dress and a halo of flowers on top of her head. I find myself in awe of the whole situation. I want it to stop, especially when I see the large butcher's knife in Ester's hand.

Cassandra and Alexander are behind her with serious expressions on their faces. As they part, Barnabas steps past them.

He is wearing a white long sleeved collared shirt with a black tie that reaches the waist of his black pants. His hair is styled as usual and his cheeks are slightly pink. It looks like he's trembling.

I want to get up and go to him, but I stay where I am. I place my hands on the wooden floor as Barnabas takes a seat in a chair designated for him.

Ester sits next to him, looking pleased. It looks like she might be the happiest person in this whole situation.

Alexander says a few prayers over Barnabas and then places both his hands on the top of Barnabas's head. He closes his eyes

187

for a few moments, mumbling to himself, and I find myself peering out the windows.

I see lightning strike far in the distance. It startles me, but I keep my composure. I'm not sure how well I'm doing because I think I look terrified, just like Barnabas does.

His eyes find me. No one else notices because they're all peering down at the floor like I should be doing. I feel like he's willing me to help, but I know I can't. Something bad will happen to me if I do. I feel my body frozen where it is as he stares at me helplessly.

Alexander opens his eyes and catches our exchange. I know he does because he watches me for a moment before moving onto his next task.

My heart is beating faster. What will happen? Am I in trouble? Will he punish me later?

I'm not sure if I've done anything wrong.

Barnabas looks away when Cassandra grabs his hand. She places it in Ester's and they both gaze at each other. Ester looks happier than ever. Barnabas stares back at her blankly.

He doesn't want this and I think it's clearer than day. He has to play along better than that, but I feel like he's lost all will to do that.

When their hands are joined, Ester stands up and leads Barnabas to the bowl of water in the middle of our circle. Barnabas is inches away as Ester hands him the knife. He presses it against his palm and swipes it across his skin. His blood trickles down as he holds his hand over the water, where it drips in.

Ester takes the knife back, and does the same. Then Cassandra brings them both handkerchiefs that they tie across their bloody palms. Some of Barnabas's blood drips on the floor as he heads back to his seat.

Cassandra instructs us all to hold onto our candles and form a straight line in front of Barnabas. Eden is the first one to approach him and she bends down in front of him. He leans forward and gives her a kiss on the forehead.

After Barnabas kisses her, Eden stands up and moves into the kitchen.

When it is my turn, I kneel down on the hard floor and peer up at him. His soft lips press against my skin and I close my eyes. I feel something warm on my cheek that causes my eyes to snap open. I see that Barnabas has his palms pressed against both sides of my face.

Alexander swoops his arms down and pulls me up harshly. He places a hand on my back ushering me back to where the other girls are waiting.

I'm not sure why Barnabas did that, but I feel uneasy about it. What was he trying to do? Didn't he realize he would get us both in trouble?

I stand in the kitchen with the other girls and slowly the boys trickle in. Since I'm obviously already in trouble, I peer back into the main room and see Barnabas and Ester disappear down the stairs and out of sight.

Without missing a beat, we all start cleaning up the kitchen and place the furniture back where it belongs. Alexander plays a song on the piano while we take our seats on the couch. Eventually, he disappears with Cassandra downstairs too, and we are all left alone.

I finally realize that Titus is sitting next to me. I bite my lip as he takes my hands in his and doesn't say anything for a while.

"We have to wait here," Titus whispers to me.

I know what he means and I turn away from him. I taste blood in my mouth, but I continue to chew on my lip. This shouldn't bother me. I should be able to sit here until it's time to go to bed. I can't wait to go to sleep and forget about all this.

I'm worried because I don't know what Barnabas will do. I hope he won't do anything drastic because I need him to be around for the next few days. I need him to be free so that we can get him away from here. Basically, I need him to play along with Alexander's rules the best he can, without actually following them.

Even if that means being with Ester for the night.

"This is sick. Us…all waiting like this," I mumble.

I lean my head against Titus's shoulder as Tessa plops down next to me. I can see Enzo watching me from across the room, but there's nothing to say to him right now. I know the plans haven't changed. I wouldn't want to talk about them near any of the other people here anyway.

Time goes by slowly and I spend it staring out the window at the passing storm. It's an hour later and I can see the stars twinkling outside. Eventually I stand up and head outside myself.

The sky is too beautiful to miss out on it but no one follows me.

After spending some time watching the chickens in the coup, I ease myself into one of the chairs and throw my legs over its arms. The air is cool and refreshing and I suddenly feel peaceful. I haven't enjoyed a night like this in a long time.

My thoughts wander to Verus. I wonder if it's as nice there as it is here and I think about whether or not my parents are sitting outside. Are they asleep now? Are they thinking about me? I wonder if they're worried or if they think I'm okay.

They haven't heard from me in a while and I'm sure they are starting to have some doubts about my safety. Maybe they'll ignore Alexander's request and come for me earlier than they're supposed to. I'm not sure whether or not that'll help, because we wouldn't be prepared to get Titus, Barnabas and some of the others out.

My eyes spot the wreckage of our plane crash in the distance. It's even more scattered now because of the intensity of other storms that there have been since the crash, but I still feel like the sight of the wreckage is mocking me. I should have listened to my instincts. I should have never decided to go the training camp. I should have never gotten on that plane.

Then I think about Barnabas and how he believes that I can help him. I feel like I've done nothing but mess him up since we've met. Would he have been better off without me or did I make him realize that there's something else out there for him?

I need to keep going and help him. I need to make sure everything turns out okay for him because I know this is all my fault. If I hadn't crash-landed here, he would have never known I exist. Even though I had no control over the plane, somehow I believe that the crash was my fault.

Isn't that right?

I struggle with my guilt until Tessa comes to get me. Apparently, whatever was supposed to happen has happened and now we're allowed to head down into the basement and sleep. Tonight, I dread the darkness, so I talk Tessa into keeping me company and we waste some more time outside. Tessa makes me laugh with a story from home and I feel slightly better.

Finally, Cassandra peeks her head out and frowns at us.

"Let's get going. I don't know what you've done, but I'll figure out what it is. This is all your fault," Cassandra says harshly.

She grabs my arm so I am forced to follow her down the stairs. Tessa follows. Cassandra pauses and holds onto my shoulders, turning me so I have to look at her.

I open my mouth to say something, but I am speechless. I have no idea what Cassandra is talking about when she says that it's all my fault and I don't know where her anger is coming from.

Tessa and I watch as she storms back up to the first floor.

"What was that about?" Tessa asks softly.

I rub at my shoulder and shrug.

"I guess we'll find out tomorrow," I reply nervously.

I hold onto Tessa's hand until I find my room before I let her go. I want to tell Tessa to sleep in my bed tonight, but I feel like it's too risky because Cassandra is already threatening me.

I'm concerned she'll lock me up for the three days that I have left before my parents come for me.

I lie on top of the covers and try to steady my breathing. I want to cry again, but I know I can't. II clench my fists in anger thinking about Alexander.

After a full hour of being awake and formulating a weak plan in my head, I hear a scuffle near my door. Immediately, I know it's Barnabas and I sit up, pressing my back against the wall. I reach my hands out in the darkness until he grabs onto them.

I touch his face to make sure it's him. He inches onto my bed. I run my fingers through his hair. I feel how unruly it is. I'm not sure what he's been doing. I don't ask.

His lips find my cheek and linger near my neck. He pulls me down, keeping his face buried in my hair.

I feel him reach up and unbutton his shirt. After he's finished, I wrap my arms around his bare skin and hold him close. I know right away he's crying.

Barnabas cries silently for a long time.

I let him cry and run my fingers up and down his back without saying anything. I'm not sure what he wants or needs, but this feels right.

Finally, he whispers something in my ear.

"I am in so much trouble," Barnabas says, his voice shaking.

My heart beat speeds up until I am sure that he can hear it.

He reaches up to touch my hair and then rests his hand on my shoulder.

I hear Barnabas's breath become slow and steady. He is asleep. Barnabas is in trouble because Ester told on him. Cassandra's threats begin to make sense because she thinks that Barnabas is in trouble because of me.

I hope she punishes me instead of Barnabas.

Chapter Fourteen

Day Eleven

When I wake, I immediately stretch out my arms for Barnabas, but he's not there. I run my hands along the warm spot that was once occupied by him and realize that he hasn't been gone for long. Instantly I'm filled with worry remembering last night.

Something is terribly wrong! Barnabas has been discovered disobeying their strict rules here at the compound. This is the first time he's done anything like this.

Not staying with Ester is a major transgression. Considering there's only three days before they believe the world is going to end, they're going to want to get Barnabas back on track – and fast. I'll never see him again. I won't be able to take him back to Verus with me.

I force myself out of bed and slip on the white dress from last night. I shove my boots on and stumble upstairs.

Tessa is waiting for me in the hallway. She grabs onto my arm and hurries me upstairs.

"You missed your time to shower! I was about to head down there to get you. We're late for breakfast," Tessa explains quickly.

I shrug. I don't care because I'm sick of playing by their rules. However, I head to breakfast with Tessa without taking the time to change.

If they liked the dress so much last night, they'll like it this morning.

When I enter the dining room, I see a few people are missing. Alexander eyes me as I take a seat next to Enzo, but no one is talking at all. Barnabas, Ester, and Cassandra are all absent. Everyone is tense.

"Slept late today?" Alexander asks, raising an eyebrow.

I don't even bother to reply.

I don't care about being rude to Alexander today because I think Barnabas has already defied him. Whatever punishment waits for him will come no matter what I say.

"Things are going to get serious in a couple of days and I need you to follow simple instructions," Alexander says, glaring at me.

"I won't be here," I reply. "Remember? I'll be gone."

"Sweetheart...your father won't be able to save you. No one will be able to save you," Alexander hisses. He slams his fist on the table, knocking over some of the dishes. "You don't know what you're messing with, but you soon will. You've gone too far."

I swallow hard, but do my best to remain silent. No matter how brave I am, my life is still in danger.

We finish breakfast in a terrible silence. I need to find out where Barnabas is, so we can all get out of here right away and hide out somewhere. I don't have a plan, but I'm desperate.

Demetri smirks at me. I glare back. He leans over to whisper something to Alexander and they both chuckle. My face burns red with anger and I can feel my fists clench.

I want to hurt both of them. I want to see them suffer.

After breakfast, I go into the main room. As soon as Ester sees me, she goes crazy.

She lunges from Cassandra's grasp and grabs at me. Her hands tighten in my hair and she yanks me onto the ground. I control my instinct to fight back. Inching away from her, I lean against the wall.

Eden and Cassandra do their best to restrain her.

"You stupid bitch! It's all your fault! What did you do to him?" Ester screams.

I'm not even sure what "bitch" means. I have only heard it used in biology. "Bitch" is a female dog.

Ester is seething with anger, but I can see tears running down her cheeks.

"What did you do? What did all of you do to him? Where is Barnabas?" I shout back.

I look at Cassandra, but she is silent.

"That's none of your business, you idiot! Leave him alone! You've already done enough damage. You ruined what was supposed to be the best day of my life," Ester screams.

"Tell me where he is," I demand.

When no one answers me, I run past them into the hallway that leads to the infirmary.

I quickly find that Barnabas isn't there, but Alexander is waiting for me. He sits on the edge of the cot and stares at me.

"Where is Barnabas?" I ask desperately.

"He's being punished. Maybe he told you about the silent rooms in the basement. He'll be there until tomorrow so that he can think about how he's failed to perform his duty. He must understand that he cannot stray from the path that has been set for him."

I take a good swing at Alexander, but he catches my wrist easily. My anger weakens me. I want to see Alexander hurt and I'm not thinking straight.

"Let him out!" I scream. "I'll let him out!"

Alexander holds me tightly. I can't get out of his grasp.

"This is all your fault. Things are going to change around here, starting now. You've seen what I can do to Barnabas and you'll soon see what I can do to you. You better start behaving, girl."

"No! You're all crazy! You're all nuts and I need to get out of here. You can't tell me what to do."

It takes all my strength to pull away. I feel tight restricting sobs coming up from my throat, but I try to repress them.

"Says the little girl," Alexander says, laughing.

I can hear his laughter as I run back into the main room and fly out the door to the balcony. I rush down the ladder and run toward Shiloh. I need to be alone and rethink things. I need to figure out a way to protect everyone. I will beg the townspeople to help me if I have to.

My chest begins to burn, but I keep going and I don't look back. I consider that Enzo, Tessa, Barnabas, and Titus are still there, but they might be safer without me anyway.

Dark clouds loom in the sky. I see Edward and Penelope at their fruit stand in the distance. Everyone is staring at me as I run by. I know I am making a scene. When I finally get to the elderly couple, I grab their hands and fall to my knees. My legs feel weak and I can't seem to get a breath. My mind is in such a turmoil that I don't know where to begin.

"What is it? You better go back. There's no use running away," Penelope says, helping me up.

She places a hand on my back.

She's seen this before. The terrifying realization finally hits me.

"Please, I need your help."

"We can't help you. It would be best for everyone if you went back," Edward says nervously.

I grasp their hands tighter and refuse to let go.

"Don't make me go back. I need some time. Please let me stay here for tonight," I cry desperately.

"Alright," Edward sighs. "Only for tonight." Get inside our house and don't come out. If Alexander comes around, we'll say we haven't seen you."

Alexander will know where I am. He owns the town and everything around it. I will have to return. My friends are there. Barnabas is there. But for now, this couple has given me time to think.

"Thank you," I say thankfully.

Penelope escorts me into their house. The buildings are so close together that it would be impossible to walk in between any of them. They are also taller and narrower than any houses in Verus.

The first floor consists of a small living room with two arm chairs, a book shelf, and a wooden bench. Off to the side is a half kitchen with a stove and a refrigerator. Some plants are growing under bright lights against the wall.

Penelope nods to the stairs and says, "Why don't you relax and clean yourself up? You're free to take anything you might need. Keep yourself occupied until tonight but don't come outside."

She leaves and I look around the room. The couple's home is quaint and cozy. I find myself relaxing.

I urge myself up the creaky steps to the second floor. There's a large bed and dresser and a door that leads into a bathroom. I enter the bathroom, close the door behind me and stare longingly at the beautiful porcelain tub. I let the water run while I strip off my clothes and undo my braid.

The water is hot as I ease myself in.

It's hard for me to completely relax knowing that I'll have to leave and go back to the compound. Still, I have to return for my friends. It's cruel enough that I'm leaving them for this long.

I sit in the tub for over an hour. I finally get out and wrap myself in a warm blue towel. I slip on the white dress again because it's not too dirty and it's comfortable. I wipe the fog off the mirrors and run my fingers through my shoulder length hair.

My hair.

For a second it makes me furious. It reminds me of my mother. It reminds me of Barnabas. It reminds me of my own femininity and that seems to be what Alexander uses against me the most. It's a weapon against myself. I dig into one of the drawers until I find a pair of scissors.

Once my hair is combed out, I begin to chop it off. My chin-length hair doesn't make me look like a boy, but at least I can't be made to put it up anymore. I run my fingers through it and clean up the mess I've made. When I'm done, I head back downstairs to find something to eat.

I find an apple and then prepare myself some tea on the stove. While I wait for the water to boil, I search through the bookshelves. There are only about twelve books. Of those, only one piques my interest.

It is a handwritten history of Shiloh. I tuck it under my arm, prepare my tea, and head back to the staircase. I find that the third floor is a guest room and the top floor seems to be an observatory.

The windows completely surround the room and I can see in all directions. On one side, I can see the compound with its cliffs and mountains. On the other side I see something much more interesting.

What is that?

I have to squint to see it, but in the distance is a castle. It might be nearly twenty miles away, but I can see that it's extremely high.

In fact, it's gigantic. There's a brick wall surrounding the entire structure. But why is it so protected and who lives there?

I see a bright yellow light coming from the highest tower. I have only seen castles in old films about knights and princesses. I feel compelled to go there.

Thoughts of the castle swirl through my head but eventually I pull myself away from the windows and sit down against with my back against one of the dusty walls. I look around and see cobwebs.

Edward and Penelope must not use this room much.

The tea that I made earlier has cooled but still tastes good and I close my eyes for a moment. I haven't had tea since I've been home, so of course it reminds me of my family. I brush back hair from my chin before picking up the tattered history of Shiloh.

I pull it open and place it on my knees, making sure to brush off most of the dust. The handwriting is small and neat, but no author is listed. It starts with the year the town was formed, about two hundred years ago. There is a list of Alexander's relatives.

I learn his full name is Alexander Ford and the ownership of Shiloh goes back two centuries to its inception. Alexander's family has owned this place forever.

I also find an updated census of everyone in the town. There's only about fifty, none of them Fords, so I know Alexander is the last of his line.

Beside each name on the list is an identification column labeled "status." Of all the names listed, only one of them is labeled as something else besides "present." The final name, Michael Phillips, is identified as "rogue." I look up toward the castle and wonder if he lives there. Why would Alexander let him get away with that? I don't understand how Michael Phillips could even survive on his own.

The back page of the book frightens me. When I turn to it, I nearly drop the book, but I steady it again on my knees. It is a drawing of one of the creatures I saw in my nightmares; the creatures that Barnabas is convinced exist. It has a hunched back with a visible spine that runs all the way down to its dangerous looking tail. Its eyes are large and beady and it's claws…I remember those claws. They scratched at me and tore away my skin in the closet where Asher locked me.

A shudder runs through my entire body. Why would this be drawn in one of Penelope and Edward's books?

I close the book and think about Barnabas. I wonder if he's suffering in the darkness. Instinctively, I feel it. His visions must be overwhelming him and driving him crazy. I sigh and bump my head against the wall in frustration. I should have gotten him out before I ran away. I should have done a lot of things.

Penelope and Edward return after dark and ask me to join them in the living room. They prepare a small dinner that consists of some meat I don't recognize, but it tastes like chicken.

After we eat, I sit on a bench while they take their seats in the armchairs. Edward looks at me smiles.

"Cut your hair?"

I nod and wrap my arms around my knees.

"A boy came looking for you. Big kid. He went back a few hours ago," Penelope tells me.

I'm not sure if it was Titus or Demetri. I don't know if Alexander would send Titus after me because he might know we get along.

Edward eyes the book lying next to me and nods toward it.

"The History of Shiloh, huh? Did you find it interesting?"

"A lot of stuff about Alexander and his family. Are there really only fifty people living here?" I ask.

"Technically," Penelope says.

"One ran away...to that castle?" I ask. I try my luck because I have nothing left to lose. "What do you know about it?"

Edward looks at Penelope.

They hold hands.

"There used to be a lot more people here, well over a hundred. The man who now lives in that castle, Michael, was best friends with Alexander...before Alexander took an interest in a young boy and started that school," Edward tells me.

"What happened?"

"Michael swore that Alexander was murdering some of the parents in town, but he couldn't prove it. A strange illness spread through the town and many people left. Only a few of us stayed behind along with some of the orphans. They had no place to go and no choice in the matter. Alexander took them all in and used the abandoned compound as the school."

"But how did the other villagers leave?"

"Alexander allowed one plane out with everyone who wanted to leave on it. No planes have been back since to transport people, so we're stuck here. This has always been my home, so I don't mind. Alexander mostly leaves us alone and only cares about those kids," Penelope answers.

"How could Alexander get away with murder? Isn't there any law here?" I ask.

How is this place so completely off the grid, that there's nothing they can do about murder? Then I remember Shiloh is not like other towns. They live differently and they don't have to answer to anyone. They're so far removed from society.

Verus is like that, too, but we still have law enforcement and rules. We still have ways of dealing with our problems.

"Alexander is the only law. There's nothing anyone can do about it and it did seem like a plague ran through here. Alexander tried to get us to capture Michael and bring him in, but Michael ran away. We never went after him at the castle because Alexander called off the search. There was no use to it, anyway. Michael hasn't come back and I don't think he plans to. He wants to be away from Alexander."

Join the club.

Michael sounds like someone I'd get along with.

"Are you sure Michael's still at the castle?" I probe.

"There's always a light on at the top tower, like he's waiting for something. It's a beacon. At first, Michael believed what Alexander and that boy were saying, that the world was going to end, but then Michael started to hate Alexander. He disagreed with how Alexander was handling preparations for what was supposed to be the apocalypse. Alexander started to lose all reason. He became deeply religious and talked about making the world right for God," Penelope says.

"But God does not want cruelty. I'm not sure which religion Alexander believes in now," Edward adds.

I open the book to show them the picture drawn in the back and they stare unfazed at the strange alien creature.

"That was Alexander's book. He left all his things behind. That was the book he used to scribble down that boy's thoughts...the crazy one that started all this nonsense," Penelope says.

I know Barnabas isn't crazy. I know he sees something others don't see, but is he correct in believing that the world ends in three days? I've seen the same visions that Barnabas has seen. I've seen his monsters.

What will happen if he's right?

Penelope and Edward let me take some blankets up to the top floor and sleep there. I peer out toward the castle before lying down on the floor. The light is still on, but I can't see anything else.

It *is* a beacon.

What is Michael doing? Is he waiting for someone?

I think about how lonely he must be, but at least he doesn't have to worry about Alexander. I also wonder if he will be protected if the world does end.

After I get comfortable, I stare up at the ceiling and let my thoughts linger one last time on what Barnabas is doing. I know tonight I will have trouble sleeping. I've gotten used to falling asleep in complete darkness and I'm not sure I can sleep without it. I frown thinking of the ways Alexander has already changed my life. My sleeping patterns being the least of what he has done to me.

Even if I get away from here, Alexander will forever be in my nightmares.

Right now, it doesn't seem possible that I will ever be free of Alexander.

Tomorrow I will find a way to tilt things in my favor. I will think of a way to take down Alexander and free the rest of the people under his control, including my friends. I'll only have two days left to do it.

Chapter Fifteen

Day Twelve

I am startled awake by the sound of footsteps coming up the staircase.

I jump up and press my back against the windows, but the shape of the room and the early morning sunlight makes it impossible to hide. Titus is the first face I see.

Edward and Penelope run up after him and look at me with frightened expressions, but Titus raises a hand, keeping them from moving any closer to me.

"We didn't know," Edward says in a shaky voice.

"It's okay. I won't tell on you," Titus tells them softly.

Titus approaches me slowly and bends down to carry me in his arms. I think this is unnecessary. I'm not going to run from Titus. I will go with him on my own.

As he cradles me and brings me down the long flights of stairs, I watch his stern face.

"I can walk, you know," I say.

When we reach the door, he adjusts me so that I'm slung over his shoulder. This hurts my stomach, but I don't protest.

"It has to look like we're against each other. Alexander will be watching. He can't know we're friends," Titus explains.

"He doesn't know already?"

"I don't think so."

"Has anything changed?" I ask.

"Haven't seen Barnabas, but I got the guns. Hope you know how to use them," Titus whispers to me.

"I do."

We walk for a while before the compound comes into view. The blood is rushing to my head and I feel dizzy, but I pretend to struggle with Titus anyway. He brings me up the stairs to the compound and shoves me inside.

A few people see me but it is Cassandra who grabs my arm roughly. She kneels down close to me so that we're face to face.

Her grip is tight.

"You'll join us for breakfast before you receive your punishment. Change your clothes," Cassandra orders.

She loosens her fingers on my arm so that I am able to pull away.

I head to the bathroom, but not to shower or change. I check to see that my other clothes are still in my locker before I wash my face and hands in the sink.

Tessa finds me, but she is followed close behind by Ariel and Eden. They are either watching Tessa or they're curious, but Ester isn't with them.

"Where were you?" Tessa asks. "I didn't think you'd ever come back."

"Of course I would. I'm fine," I say.

I grab onto Tessa's shoulders tightly and turn her to me. She eyes my shorter hair, but doesn't say anything.

I hope Tessa understands that we still have a plan to leave and that I won't leave them again. I need her to know that we are going to get out of here alive.

"We have to go to breakfast now," Eden says.

I wrap my hand around Tessa's and we follow them out. I'm afraid, but I'll take my punishment. I hope it won't be so bad for me.

Maybe it's bad for Barnabas because his visions are so intense.

Everyone is in the dining room, including Barnabas and Ester. As I take my seat, Alexander doesn't even look me. I don't have an appetite, even though I haven't eaten since yesterday morning.

This place makes me too uneasy and the way Barnabas is acting is worrying me.

He keeps his eyes low and doesn't even notice or care that I'm there. His skin is paler than usual and he is having trouble keeping his eyes open. The expression on his face is bleak.

What did they do to him? What will they do to me?

I see Demetri and Asa watch him with smiles on their faces. For the first time, I realize they might be conspiring against him. If something happens to Barnabas they will become leaders.

I look away when their eyes find me because I don't want to see their evil, grinning faces. I want to them to leave everyone I love alone.

I panic for a moment.

I'm not sure what I will do if Barnabas has completely changed or if he's lost the will to fight back. I think about whether or not I'd leave him here, but I know I can't. I'll have to get Titus to carry him and we'll drag him out of here if we have to.

Barnabas's hands shake when he struggles to lift his fork to his mouth. He manages to swallow a bit of food, but that's it. He stops trying and puts his hands under the table, continuing to look down.

I nearly jump when Enzo's hand rests on my leg in order to get my attention. Everyone seems like they're back to normal and acting like nothing is wrong, so I turn to him keeping my eyes low.

"Should we leave today? We can make it I think. We can get out of here," Enzo whispers.

It is dangerous to talk here, but I know we have to. We won't have another chance.

"Not yet. I can make it through today. I'll be fine," I reply.

Enzo looks like he's about to cry. I can see how worried he is. I understand that he doesn't want me to become like Barnabas. He's afraid I won't be able to handle it.

I can. I will.

We don't say any more because Alexander is watching us. Demetri and Asa help Barnabas from the table and lead him out and soon after Cassandra comes to get me and I follow her to the basement.

Right before we enter, she turns and slaps me hard. I try to hold back the instinctive tears from my eyes. My cheek stings painfully. It doesn't hurt as much as it embarrasses me. I hate having that horrible feeling of shame and I hate Cassandra.

"You're an embarrassment. Girls need to learn how to behave. They need to learn how to obey," Cassandra hisses.

I keep my lips pressed together. I don't want to argue. I have nothing to say to this woman.

Instead, I do something worse than talk. I spit in her face.

Cassandra slowly wipes it from her cheek and looks at me dangerously. She grabs my arm roughly and we head into the darkness. She leads me forward quickly, obviously aware of where she's going.

I struggle to keep up, feeling my elbows scrape against the jagged wall and blood rolls down my arm.

It feels like we've been through a maze before we finally reach our destination, where Cassandra unlocks the door and shoves me inside.

Once the door closes behind me, I can hear nothing. I can't even hear her footsteps as she heads back upstairs.

My hands reach around to find something to sit on, but the room is empty. It's no bigger than a closet and I can reach every inch of it without moving from a single spot, so I sit on the hard, cold floor and wrap my arms around my bare knees.

I don't know how I can stand spending all day here because within the first five minutes, I feel like my head is going to explode. I know why Barnabas thinks it's so terrible. I can't hear anything, not even my own heartbeat.

After spending an hour trying to will myself to sleep, I hear noises. I hear a low growling, like a wolf, and it grows louder and louder until it is echoing throughout the whole room. I cover my ears in order to make it stop. I have no idea where it's coming from. I cry out in frustration.

That's when the hallucinations start.

The growling stops abruptly and I start hallucinating. I'm still not sure if I am dreaming or awake, but everything around me feels so real. I am standing in front of a mirror. I'm wearing the white dress, which is spotted with dirt and I reach up to touch my short hair. I run my fingers over it and feel its softness.

I know this is really how I am right now, but where did the mirror come from? Why can I see in the darkness?

The mirror disappears and the outside world materializes before me.

I see the castle in the distance. I'm not that far away now. Someone is calling my name. I start to run, but the castle doesn't get any closer. No matter how fast I run or how much my legs burn, I can't get there.

Barnabas is next to me now. I smile at him, but he tackles me to the ground. His face is stern as he scratches at my skin. Little streams of blood come out from where he's cut me and he won't stop. I scream and throw punches at him. No matter how hard I hit him, he's still stronger than me. He pins me and holds my arms down as I struggle against him. I can feel his body pressed against mine.

His eyes are distant and cold, like they were during breakfast. He stops and stares at me.

"Barnabas. It's me, Alva. We have to get to the castle," I say breathlessly.

Barnabas watches me curiously and then releases my wrists. He helps me up, but steps back to examine me. As he reaches his hand out for me, he is yanked away abruptly.

He has been sucked into some sort of swirling black hole.

The ground starts to explode underneath me, so I'm forced to run again. The whole area behind me is being destroyed as I finally start moving. This time the castle is getting closer and I can make it there. Right before I reach the gates, I feel something bite my shoulder.

When I peer down, I see that blood is streaming from a deep wound. I wasn't bitten, I was shot. I turn around and see Alexander with a gun pointed at me. He smiles when I collapse to the ground. He looms over me and pressed the metal against my skull.

He pulls the trigger again.

Long after I wake up, I find myself reliving that nightmare over and over and over again until I feel like I'd rather die than go through it again. I never save Barnabas. I never make it to the castle. I never outrun or outsmart Alexander. No matter what I do, I can't make it out alive.

Still, each time I drift off, the visions return. The last time I have the vision, I am able to grab the gun from Alexander and I pull the trigger myself. I'd rather die by my own hand than have Alexander kill me.

Another nightmare takes me somewhere else. By this time, I'm not sure whether these are dreams or reality.

Barnabas is behind some sort of glass being operated on by people wearing with thick suits. I can't see what they look like because their faces are covered by orange plastic. I can only see they have Barnabas strapped down and he is wearing nothing but his underwear. He is struggling but I know he can even see me through the glass. I can tell he is yelling for me, but I can't help him.

I slam against the glass, calling his name, until my fists are bloody and raw. I can't break through it. I can't stop the sick experiment. I'm brought back to the room sobbing and screaming. I am in complete darkness again.

I find the door and try to pry it open, but it's impossible. I have to get out of this room. I can't go through this again. My body is shaking uncontrollably and I'm freezing. If they let me out, I will obey Alexander and Cassandra. I can never be in here again.

No one comes for me and I struggle not to cry for a long time. I don't want Alexander to know that he is stronger than me. I don't want him to defeat me, but it's becoming harder and harder.

The pit in my stomach has become a solid rock.

The image of Barnabas dying stays in my mind. I love him and I'll admit it to anyone. It doesn't make me weaker. It doesn't make me any less myself. I love him so much, I feel braver because of it. I will sacrifice myself to make sure he gets out alive. I will take on Alexander and Cassandra.

I love him so much I'd let Alexander kill me ten times over. When did this happen? How have we become so emotionally connected in such a short amount of time? It doesn't seem to make sense, but I know it's real. I have never felt anything more real in my life.

I curl up on the floor. My hands start to throb, forcing me to sit up. I feel that my palms are wet and I'm not sure what is happening. I begin to yell again. I'm afraid the hallucinations will start again.

The door creaks open and someone gathers me up in their arms—someone unusually strong— and I can smell the familiar laundry scent. I bury my face in Barnabas's shoulder. As I run my hand up to his face, I know it's him. I begin to cry again as he carries me up the stairs.

I don't open my eyes until Barnabas sets me down. When I peer up at him, I see the blood streaked across his face and matted into his hair. It's my blood. I look down at my hands and see the same type of wounds that Barnabas once had.

Holes in my palms.

"What is this?" I ask.

"Visions. I knew you were as powerful as me," Barnabas responds.

Some color has returned to his face and I see we're in the hospital room. He is sitting on the edge of the cot, watching me closely.

The room fades in and out and I don't have a chance to talk to Barnabas again. I can feel him wrapping up my hands and tucking me under a blanket. I feel like I'm in a hazy dream and it's impossible to focus on anything.

A warm hand touches my forehead and then I hear someone shouting. I open my eyes long enough to see Alexander and Barnabas fighting in the hallway.

Alexander shoves Barnabas, but that doesn't stop him. Barnabas is screaming at him. Eventually some of the other boys grab Barnabas and they restrain him, dragging him away.

That's when I realize that Barnabas has lost all control. I don't think anyone will respect him anymore and no one will think he's the right leader for the compound, but I'm not sure if this is a good thing or a bad thing.

He can no longer hide the fact that he's unhappy here. He can no longer pretend that he is on his "path." Barnabas no longer has any power.

I wonder what will happen to him now, but I can't keep my mind clear long enough to think about it for long. I pull the blanket over me and hope that no one will disturb me for at least a little while.

I just want them to let me rest.

I have a few unpleasant dreams, but I can't remember them when I wake. I find Ester looming over me when I open my eyes. She is not smiling. I pull myself up in a sitting position and look down at my hands. The bandages are off and I try to figure out whether or not they were ever on me at all.

"What are you doing here? I have nothing to say to you," I say, rubbing at my hands.

My hands seem fine—there's no blood.

"I have something to say to you. So you should listen," Ester says.

She tries to smile, but it looks more like she's baring her teeth at me.

"What is it?"

"Now that Barnabas has been…compromised…" she pauses for a moment before continuing, "When it's Demetri's birthday, he'll chose me. I'm not sure where you'll fit in here, but if you follow our instructions and stop misbehaving I can stop the others from picking on you."

"Like you'd do that," I say bitterly.

"Some of the students here are bent on teaching you a lesson and personally I think you deserve it," Ester says.

"Why?"

"You ruined Barnabas. I guess they want to ruin you, too," Ester says, shrugging.

I do my best to hold back my anger. I know everyone hates me and I'm stuck here. They're going to make it difficult for us to get away. I don't mind that they hate me because I hate them too. I don't want to see what they have in store for me. I'm afraid they'll make sure I suffer in every way possible.

I know I have to leave while there's still some of me intact.

"You're a terrible person. I hope one day you get what you deserve," I say to Ester.

Ester smiles.

I feel with everything inside me that she is a terrible person. I feel the same about Demetri, Asher, Asa, James, Rufus, and Jethro. I feel it with Alexander and Cassandra. Deep down, I know now they can't be changed.

"I'm not the only one you have to worry about. You should get some rest. We have a big day of preparation tomorrow and you'll have to go out hunting. Jethro and Titus will be keeping an eye on you," Ester says.

She leaves me alone and shuts the door behind her.

I know it's locked, so there's no use trying to sneak out tonight. I'm not sure where I'd find Barnabas and the others anyway. I have no idea where Enzo and Titus sleep and we're not prepared. I'm scared because tomorrow we'll have to get everything done. I know we have to make it to the castle and I'll find some way to contact my parents. It'll be better to hide out there than wait here.

Anything is better than here.

I struggle to the medical cabinets, but I can't find anything of use. It seems like most of the sharp items were removed and I can only find bandages. I'll have to search harder tomorrow, even though I know it'll be difficult because everyone will be keeping an eye on me.

Before getting back to bed, I head to the bathroom. I stare at my reflection to make sure I'm still there. I look a bit different, but it's still me. I'm still Alva.

"I'm still Alva," I repeat to myself.

And I'm going to get everyone out of here.

Chapter Sixteen

Day Thirteen

It's the last day before The Culling.

I wonder if Barnabas still believes it, but I am more concerned with how we will escape tomorrow while everyone is preoccupied.

Instead of changing out of my white dress, Titus brings me an oversized brown jacket to wear while we're hunting outside. He tells me that the weather has gotten colder, which is strange for this time of year. I shove my arms inside the large sleeves and wait for him to return to the main room. I'm the only one sitting in there.

Jethro joins me before Titus returns. He watches me with a cold expression on his face and the shotgun is slung over his shoulder. His lips curl into a creepy smile.

I sit still as he points it right at me.

"You're not much bigger than a mountain lion. Maybe we'll skin you and eat you," Jethro says.

The hood from his jacket is up over his head and it casts mysterious shadows over his face.

"Good joke," I say bitterly.

Titus jogs up to join us and grabs Jethro's gun. He takes it and puts it over his own shoulder instead. In turn, Titus is handed a pistol from Jethro.

"Who says I'm joking?" Jethro says before turning toward the door.

Titus gives me a quizzical look, but we follow him outside.

A bitter wind cuts through the jacket and chills the tip of my nose. It feels like winter.

"We have a lot to do today," Titus says.

As we walk toward the cliffs, I can see that the sky is dark and ominous. It doesn't make me feel better about the approaching apocalypse because at this rate it looks like it might happen. I wonder if everyone else is thinking the same thing.

"Is that why we're up before everyone else?" I ask.

"We won't have meat for a while unless we get some today. Alexander thinks everything will die," Jethro replies.

Every time he talks, it sounds like he's irritated with me. There's a chance he's still angry he couldn't kill me a few days ago.

We get to a fork in the road, one leads higher up on the mountain and the other stays level.

Titus grabs onto my arm, halting me in place.

"We should split up," Titus suggests. He turns to Jethro before saying, "We don't have much time."

Jethro eyes Titus and then eventually shrugs.

"I guess that makes sense."

"I'll keep an eye on her, don't worry," Titus says in an annoyed tone.

He's good at pretending I'm a burden. I gasp as he lifts me up by the back of my coat and starts walking toward the level path.

When Jethro is out of earshot, Titus finally puts me down.

"Maybe he thinks I'm going to kill you myself. I thought we needed some time alone." Titus says.

"How is Barnabas?" I ask right away.

I have been waiting to find out after he was dragged away last night. I wonder if he's back in that terrible silent room. I tremble thinking about it. I still don't feel right.

"He threw a fit last night. It got worse. He was screaming about something and he wouldn't stop. I think they've sedated him. He'll be awake when we get back.

Titus shrugs and adjusts his gun. After another moment, he smiles slightly and nudges me with his shoulder.

"He shouldn't have come to get me," I say, but I know he saved me.

I'm not sure I would have made it much longer.

"I think they were trying to drive you crazy. It was good he did what he did. It's important that we get him out."

"I need you to pack up my bag in the bathroom. Fill it with whatever we need. Tessa's bag is also in her locker. You're the only one Alexander still trusts, so it's up to you."

He pauses and places a soft hand on my cheek. He is massive as he looms over me, but there is undeniable kindness in his eyes. He is a good person and he doesn't deserve to be here.

"Everything will be okay, Alva. I know you're what we needed. I will help you in any way I can," Titus says.

"But why?"

"I've never had a friend before," Titus responds.

We walk in silence for a little while until Titus spots some sort of big bird and I cover my ears as he readies his shotgun and shoots.

I watch as the bird flutters to the ground and flaps its wings a couple of times before it dies. I can't help staring at it as life leaves its eyes.

It looks like it's watching me as Titus lifts it up. It's about the size of a turkey.

Titus is able to get a few more before we start to head back. We walk slowly because both of us are dreading going back to the compound.

"Can Junia come with us? I don't think she wants to be there," I ask softly as I kick a stone with my boot.

Titus looks are me curiously. "

"I guess so," Titus replies. "We sometimes played when we were little. That was before she wasn't allowed to talk."

"Why can't she talk?"

"Alexander doesn't allow it. He says she's a servant, not worthy of saying anything important."

"That's horrible. I guess that's what would happen to me if I stayed here, if my father never came," I reply.

"You're too loud for that. You never shut up when you're supposed to," Titus says with a smile.

I laugh. It's nice to find something funny even if it's only for a moment. The hard truth is that I know I can be controlled if Alexander threatened me in the right way. If he was going to my friends' lives in danger, I'd do whatever he wanted. I'd have to.

He places a hand on the back of my neck.

"We don't have to worry about that though. We'll be long gone."

"I hope."

We meet back up with Jethro on the walk back.

I see he has been dragging a few birds, but no mountain lions.

"Everything go okay?" Jethro asks Titus.

Titus nods.

"Glad to be back with someone who isn't brain dead," he replies.

Jethro laughs at my expense and I glare at Titus—he's a little bit too good at playing along.

For the rest of the morning, we work on preparing the birds and putting the meat in containers to be frozen.

I see there is a big freezer in a small room off the kitchen where everything else is contained. I wonder what Alexander plans on doing with it all, considering I don't think it'll stay fresh for long.

"There's a big feast. To celebrate the restart of humanity. It'll be tomorrow night," Titus says, answering my question.

I cringe. I hope we aren't around for that.

Jethro watches us carefully for most of our time outside.

I know that Alexander told him to keep an eye on me. I see some of the others filtering back in from the village and realize that not many people were in the compound, but Tessa finds me when the rest of them head inside.

They seem busy and nervous.

Some of the boys are carrying several wooden boards, but I'm not sure what they're for. I'm sure I'll find out later, but I'm worried because I don't see Barnabas.

Titus and Jethro head inside to help them while Tessa aids me in finishing up. We carry the containers inside and bring them to the kitchen where Ester, Eden, and Ariel are all working on something in there.

They watch us put the meat into the freezer and Ester puts a hand on her hip.

She points to the pile of food stuff on the kitchen table.

"You're going to help us organize. Alexander wants everything perfect before tomorrow. Maybe this is one thing you'll be good at," Ester says.

I have a feeling it was Alexander's idea to keep us occupied, but the task doesn't look too daunting. I think it'll be relaxing to be working with Tessa for the afternoon and we might even get a chance to talk about things if the other girls leave.

"So when does the world end tomorrow?" Tessa asks, somewhat sarcastically. She continues to mock them, "Is there a time or…"

Ester doesn't look at us as she clears out some of the cabinets. She pulls out a lot of canned and dried food, including tons of gallons of water.

"I'm sure you'll be laughing tomorrow when you find out we were right. Maybe you two will be saved, but I doubt it. I don't think any of you are pure enough," Ester says.

"What happens if we're not? Do we get sucked out of here? Does someone come and find us?" I ask.

"Stop making jokes," Ester says, glaring at me. "You've got a lot of bad things coming to you, Alva."

"I'm not too worried about it."

She shoves a few cans at me and points to the highest shelf, so I climb up on the counter and place them neatly inside. Ester and the other girls hand me up some stuff.

The bottom of my dress keeps getting caught on the edge of the shelves, so I bend down to rip some of it off.

Ester pauses before handing me the next few cans.

"Do you ever act like a girl?" she asks me.

"I am a girl...therefore, I always act like one. Don't you ever realize how stupid you sound?" I ask.

Ester glares at me and we continue working without any other delays.

It takes about two hours to finish everything and I realize how much food Alexander has stored. The cabinets are filled and there's still another closet to be organized. Ester, Eden, and Ariel take over that when Tessa and I head into the main room to see what everyone else is doing.

Demetri is boarding up all the windows. The others, Asher, Asa, and Rufus are holding the planks in place for him.

Demetri smiles at me and pauses for a moment.

"My two favorite girls," Demetri calls enthusiastically. He pauses before asking, "Alva, will you marry me?"

The other boys laugh and whistle. It makes me uncomfortable.

"Thought you picked Ester?" I ask, with an eyebrow raised.

"You're the only one for me, Alva. We'll have a good life together. Maybe we wouldn't have to kill you, then," Demetri says, with a wink.

Demetri's words linger in my mind while I watch him and the other boys. I wonder where Enzo and Barnabas are. I hear sounds of hammering coming from the hallway, so Tessa and I go to investigate.

Barnabas grabs me almost immediately, but I stop myself before yelling out. He ushers Tessa toward the hospital room and holds onto my hand.

He has a bruise underneath his right eye and a few scratches along his cheek, which is most likely Alexander's doing.

"Go help Enzo and Titus in there," Barnabas says to Tessa. He turns to me and adds, "We don't have much time."

"Where are we going?" I ask as Barnabas pulls me farther down the hallway.

"There's something I need to get before I leave," Barnabas tells me.

We head all the way to the entrance of the basement, walking as quietly as we possibly can.

I'm afraid to breathe. If Alexander catches us together, we're toast.

"Where is Alexander?" I ask.

Barnabas presses a finger against his lips and points down into the darkness.

"He's outside for now. No talking," Barnabas replies.

He holds my hand tighter and leads me into the basement. I'm immediately engulfed in darkness, but Barnabas is too close for me to be afraid. I bump up against him a few times before I find my bearings. He is leading me somewhere I've never been.

It feels like we walk forever before Barnabas places a gentle hand on my back. After a few moments, I feel a step with my foot. In a couple more steps, I know we're in an entirely new area.

Barnabas stops me and I hear him opening a door. He gently pushes me inside and I hear the door click shut behind us. He lets go of my hand and a light turns on, taking me by surprise.

I blink a couple of times to adjust my eyes.

We're in a bedroom with a queen sized bed and a couple of dressers with personal items strewn on top.

I see the gun right away, along with discarded clothes and some jewelry.

"What is this?" I ask, moving around.

The room is spacious and comfortable looking. I am both emotionally and physically spent, but I resist the urge to sprawl onto the bed.

"What do you think?" Barnabas asks, with a slight smile. He leans against the dresser, watching me before saying, "Take one guess."

"Alexander and Cassandra's room? Why do they have lights?"

"They live a bit better than us," Barnabas replies.

"How do you know about this?"

Barnabas shrugs and runs a hand through his hair. He's obviously lost the need to even look like he cares about having a clean cut appearance. His sleeves are rolled up. More rules broken!

The color of his shirt is also a lighter blue than his other, the one that set him apart from the others.

"I was close with Alexander once. I saw this whole place while we were still allowed to have lights down here. Alexander and I were friends. He was like a father to me once."

"You trusted him," I say.

I understand Barnabas's initial reluctance to disobey Alexander. He was never a strong believer in Alexander's cause. I think he loved being around Alexander. He had feared that he was losing family, even though he was learning that they were sick and twisted.

Barnabas turns away and digs through some of the drawers. He pulls out a silver pocket watch and pulls it open.

There's a picture of a woman on the right side, a woman who looks like him.

"I need to bring this. It's my mother," Barnabas says, slipping it into his pocket. "It just doesn't seem right to leave it with Alexander."

"I understand." I pause and he stares back at me. "Does it feel weird…being treated differently?"

"A little. I like being myself though. I'm still trying to figure out who that is," Barnabas says.

"Don't worry. You'll have a lot of time to figure it out."

I watch as Barnabas smiles a genuine smile. I can finally see some happiness in his eyes.

We hear a sound that makes the happiness we were feeling only seconds before disappear.

"Let's go!" I say.

I grab his hand and shut off the lights. I ease open the door as quietly as possible and shut it the same way.

We hear footsteps on the stairs.

With nowhere to go, I move toward the wall and pull Barnabas closer to me. As I crouch down to the floor, I can feel how rigid his body is. I am afraid that the sound of his breathing will give us away, so I reach up and cover his mouth. I pull him even closer.

I can feel Barnabas's heart beating against my own chest. The footsteps get closer. Despite our precarious situation I have my body under control.

The air cools when someone breezes by us and enters the room we just left.

I can see light under the door. Some light lets me see the fear on Barnabas's face. I put my finger to my lips when I remove my hand from his mouth. We hurry back up to the second floor.

Barnabas is breathing heavily by the time we get to one of the classrooms. He leans against a while he catches his breath.

"Should have grabbed that gun," Barnabas pants.

"Whoever that was would have noticed it missing," I say.

It takes a few moments for Barnabas to calm down and we head back to the main room to help them board up the rest of the windows, as if nothing happened.

I move back to the kitchen to avoid suspicion. When I spot Cassandra in the kitchen, I realize that it's important that she doesn't know that Barnabas and I were. I wipe my hands on my dress and turn to her when she calls me.

"And, where were you, Alva?" she asks, raising an eyebrow.

"Helping with the windows," I answer innocently. "Can I do anything else?"

She believes me so I think she hasn't had time to check up on me. I wonder why she's not keeping a closer watch on me and my friends.

It takes another hour to help them finish organizing the stores and by that time my stomach is screaming for food. Ignoring my hunger, I glance around the compound. Now that all the windows are boarded, I feel more trapped than ever.

I sit with Tessa in the main room while dinner is being prepared. I don't feel like helping them so we both listen to Enzo play the piano.

He's not allowed to talk to us, so we don't say anything to him, but the music calms me.

Junia and the other two mute girls sit on the couch across from us. She smiles at me just as Cassandra enters the room to fetch us for dinner. That convinces me Titus has talked to her about leaving and I think she'll come with us.

228

Dinner is silent and tense, except for a long prayer that Alexander recites before we eat. Barnabas doesn't sit next to him anymore, Asa has moved up to Barnabas's old spot. Barnabas has been relegated a seat that is all the way down the table, next to Rufus and James.

About halfway through dinner, Alexander looks at me condescendingly.

"Are you ever going to change your clothes?" he asks.

Some of the girls giggle and the boys smirk.

I wait, seeing that Barnabas's expression remains bleak. He doesn't even pause. In a way, this makes me happy because I haven't seen him eat anything substantial in a long time.

"Later," I say, forcing a smile. I remind myself that I only have to be here for a little while longer. "Maybe I'll even wash myself."

"It's about time," Demetri jokes.

I ignore them.

Ester looks satisfied that I have been chastised in front of the entire group.

After dinner, I take my time in the shower. I let the warm water run over my body for a long time before getting dressed into the few clothes I have left. I find a pair of shorts, a sweatshirt, and my boots. I wrap the large jacket around me, so I'll have it with me tomorrow. I check my locker before I leave and find that my backpack is gone.

I panic. I hope Alexander didn't take it, but then I remember I told Titus to take it. I check Tessa's locker and see that hers is gone, too. I pray that we're all ready to go tomorrow morning because preparation is no longer in my hands.

We all are forced to go to sleep early.

I'm exhausted anyway and we have a long journey ahead of us. I'm worried, but happy because we will finally be getting out of here. I can't stand another day.

I toss and turn for a few moments before I get out of bed. I find Barnabas in his room and slip under the blanket with him. His arms wrap around me, covering me in wonderful warmth that I only feel when I'm with him.

"Titus has our things hidden in the classrooms. We're all ready to go," Barnabas whispers.

"This is your last night here, then? How do you feel?" I ask.

"Terrified," Barnabas replies.

"That's okay. I'm scared, too," I say.

He turns closer to me. I lift my chin and he kisses me for the first time.

He presses his hand against the small of my back and kisses me again, more intensely this time.

I know I will have terrible dreams tonight, so I don't want to fall asleep right away. I'm also afraid of what tomorrow will bring.

Alexander must know that I'll run if my father doesn't isn't allowed to pick us up. He knows that I will never follow his rules.

Before I finally sleep, I run my fingers along Barnabas's face, trying to remember everything about him. I don't want this it be the last time I get to touch him. I don't want there to only be a couple of kisses between us. I want us to have all the time we want together.

I'm not entirely sure if that will be the case, and that's what scares me the most. I'm not sure I'll be able to protect everyone. I'm not sure how tomorrow will end or if we'll even live to see a day after that.

Chapter Seventeen

C-Day

This morning, I learn who Michael Phillips is. I see his young face, much more youthful looking then Alexander's, but I know they have to be the same age since they were once friends. Michael's dark, short hair and the set determined look on his face stick in my mind. I don't see him smile, but I know he is kind. I know he will accept us.

I wake up early with my arms still clutching Barnabas. I can feel his chest rise and fall evenly and I know he's still asleep. I gently shake him awake and feel his breath on my neck.

We have to get ready to leave. We have to get everything ready to go before breakfast.

"Good morning. It's C-Day, he says.

"Do you still believe that?" I ask.

"I don't know. It doesn't matter," Barnabas replies. He keeps his face close to mine so we can keep talking. "I had a dream about Michael Phillips."

My heart beats faster. Barnabas has had the same dream that I had.

This is a sign we're onto something important. This is a sign we're connected in more ways than I thought. Barnabas was right about me. I was sent here to help them.

Despite the dream, I still have doubts. It's probable that not all of us will make it out of here. My horrible thoughts float away when Barnabas kisses me again.

"That's where we're supposed to go, to the castle," I say.

"Yes. That's the plan."

"Michael's important."

"He is," Barnabas says.

I smile even though Barnabas can't see it. Today is the day my father is supposed to arrive, but I'm not even sure that'll happen. I'm not even convinced he knows where to find us.

I miss my father. I miss my whole family and everything back home.

Barnabas sits up, shifting the mattress toward the edge of the bed. He gets up first and I wrap the brown jacket around me, leaving on the same outfit from yesterday. It's the only thing I have left to wear and I want to get out of here in my own clothes.

After I ascend the stairs, Titus finds me right away. He brings me into one of the classrooms where the others are waiting— Tessa, Enzo, Barnabas and Junia.

Barnabas has his arms folded across his chest and looks worried, but he still smiles when he sees me. He nods his head toward all of our backpacks that are shoved under the desks.

No one ever uses these rooms, so I know it'll be fine. Plus, Alexander and Cassandra will be worried about the "Culling" that is supposed to happen today.

Barnabas unfolds his arms and stands in front of us. He seems younger today, like he's a teenager again.

I wonder if he'll ever be able to recover from what Alexander has done to him.

We watch as he checks over his shoulder before saying anything.

"We'll leave after breakfast during the free time schedule. I'm not sure what Alexander is planning for today, but we have to leave right after breakfast. I want to make sure we're safely at the castle before anything happens…if anything happens," Barnabas says, in a low voice.

He goes over the plan again, even though we know it anyway, but I think it puts everyone at ease.

Enzo is smiling again and Tessa is holding onto his arm, trying to hold back tears. Everyone is happy we are leaving and it's a great feeling.

"Thank you for including me," Junia says before she leaves.

I head out right before Barnabas and make my way into the bathroom. I shower quickly and dress. I spend some time drying my hair and watching myself in the mirror.

I understand that I'm putting everyone's life in danger, but I know I have to. I have to appear as if I believe that everything is normal. I will go to breakfast. I will begin our escape.

I run my fingers through my dry hair and take a deep breath. When I step into the main room, I see everyone heading to the dining room.

Barnabas, Enzo, and Titus keep their heads low and Alexander is right behind them.

On the way through the door, Asher and Demetri both bump into Barnabas, slamming him into the wall.

I watch as he rubs at his shoulder and the other boys laugh. I see Alexander does nothing to stop it, so I know that Alexander is behind Barnabas being punished. Even though Alexander has caused him nothing but grief and pain, I know this still hurts

Barnabas. I know Barnabas feels like he's being rejected by a family member.

I'm thankful Barnabas does nothing to retaliate because it's imperative that we all lay low this morning and avoid getting into trouble.

I try to eat, but everyone seems on edge.

Finally, Alexander looks at me with a forced smile.

"Ready to go home today? I know that's what you think is going to happen," he says.

I try to steady my breathing because I think he's onto us. I think he knows what we're doing. Then I realize he's still pretending that my father is really coming today. I know in my heart that Alexander is still playing his own game.

"Have you spoken to my father?" I ask.

Alexander shrugs, still gazing at me.

"I haven't been able to get in touch. Communications are off today. If he shows up, he shows up," Alexander says.

"He'll come," I say confidently.

"And if not?"

I pause and everyone stares at me. Barnabas continues to look down.

"What are my choices?"

Alexander folds his hands in front of him like this is the question he's been waiting for. He doesn't seem to notice or care I want to punch the sly smile off his face.

"You're welcome here, but you'll have to follow our rules...completely," Alexander explains. He looks at me before saying, "All of you."

I exchange glances with Enzo and Tessa. I can't find anything to say. I feel like this is a trick somehow.

"If the world ends today, we'll follow your rules. But Alva's dad is coming, so we won't have to worry about that," Tessa answers for me.

The tone in her voice tells me she is trying to stop this conversation. She sounds nervous.

"Okay," Alexander says with a nod. He somehow got the answer he wanted. "That's settled."

He takes his attention away from us and watches Barnabas for a few moments.

Barnabas peers up at him and then back down at his food, which he isn't eating. He bites his lip.

"Don't bother packing. You're going to be here for a while," Demetri hisses.

The others laugh.

He grins cruelly before taking a massive forkful of his food. Some of it sticks to his chin and I find myself completely disgusted by him.

When breakfast finally comes to an end, I try to stop myself from shaking. I feel nauseous and I want to scream. This is it. I know we have to leave right after breakfast if we want to get to the castle before dark, but we have to wait a little while longer.

Junia walks past me helping the two other girls clear off the table.

Cassandra announces that there will be a meeting downstairs in ten minutes. She disappears with Alexander down to the second floor.

We don't have much time.

Once Junia reenters the main room, Titus and I hurry into the hallway and down the stairs toward the classrooms. We each heave a pack onto our backs and Titus holds onto the third one.

He digs into one of the old lockers and pulls out a couple pistols. I'm surprised by this, but he hands me one and I tuck one into the back of my pants. I can feel the weight of it as we hurry back upstairs.

Tessa and Enzo are already waiting outside when we get back into the main room. No one seems to notice us. Barnabas grabs my hand and pulls me onto the balcony. Titus and Junia are right behind us.

The darkness of the sky immediately alarms me. I've never seen weather like this. It could start pouring at any moment. I see faint outlines of lightning in the distance. I see the others are already at the cobblestone paths leading up to the village when they look back, but Barnabas is going slowly and he looks sick. I know there isn't time to deal with his uncertainty.

I'm a few steps ahead of him when Barnabas turns back. I try to grab for his arm, but he's running back toward the compound. I feel strange as I see his hands grasp onto the metal fence as he peers into the distance.

"Barnabas! We have to hurry!" I call, as I jog back.

I try to pull him back toward everyone who is waiting, but he yanks himself away.

This isn't going well at all and my adrenaline is starting to turn into panic. I try to support him under his shoulders and pull him back up.

He looks at me, his eyes full of fear. He places his hands on my cheeks.

A storm is starting behind us and the lightning is brighter now.

"Alva, I saw all of it. It all flashed before my eyes in an instant. I was the first one they were able to communicate with. The others. We're a part of them. We're an experiment," Barnabas says.

His nose is bleeding, but what he's saying is too important. I don't say anything about it.

"What are you talking about? Who are we a part of?" I shout over the roar of the wind.

The weather has turned even worse than when we started out and I know we are out of time.

"They want to destroy us because we mean nothing to them. Earth is an alien experiment and it's over today, but we can fix it.

There are three of us who are destined to rebuild...the ones they see goodness in. You, me, and Michael. The triumvirate."

I can feel tears forming in my eyes because I want him to stop talking. I want him to come with us and I can't make sense of anything.

"Barnabas ..."

He cuts me off again and his hands go down to my shoulders.

"They speak to me telepathically. I was the first one to let them know we were capable of intelligent thought. The three of us are the only ones who can understand them and figure out what they want. Our whole species was created by them, don't you get it?" Barnabas is shouting now. "It's happening."

Barnabas holds me around my waist as we turn back toward the cliff.

The lightning is blinding as I stare back at it. I can hear Titus yelling something at us, but the thunder is too loud to hear what he's saying. The weather has become extreme.

I watch as lightning strikes the canyon and although it's terrifying, it's also beautiful. I see greens and blues and reds as it crashes to the ground near the wreckage. Streams of lights are everywhere and rain has started. I can't look away.

The scene turns horrifying as the ground begins to rip apart where the lightning strikes.

I see that the flashes of light are getting closer and closer. The destruction around us is incredible yet it's hard to look away, but we have to get somewhere safe. I swing around and see our friends running back to us. I am too overwhelmed by what's going on to move and I can barely make out what the others are doing.

Barnabas picks me up. I am surprised by his strength, but he lifts me with ease and we all rush back to the compound.

"No! We can't go back there. We have to keep going," I shout.

Barnabas can't hear me. I can't hear anyone.

Barnabas is shouting something back to me, but the rain is too heavy for me to understand what he's saying. I am soaked by the time we make it inside. I crane my body in time to see the grassy area we were just standing being torn apart by the lightning. I can feel the heat from it.

The door shuts behind us, but it is nearly pitch black inside the compound. Someone struggles to board up the door.

A hand digs into the back of my pants and pulls out the gun. I reach for it, but someone grabs onto my wrist.

"It's okay. We have to hide them for now," Titus's voice whispers to me.

I see his silhouette, along with Enzo's, disappear down the hallway with the backpacks. They are heading toward the hospital room. I steady myself against the door and see Barnabas sitting on one of the couches wiping the blood from his nose. I focus on him for a while, trying to ignore the chaos around me

I feel someone bump into me. A pain pulsates through my shoulder as I'm slammed against the wall. My head jerks back and bangs against something hard. I reach up to grab onto something, but my body hits the ground.

All my senses fade out completely. The last thing I remember is Tessa's voice calling out for me.

Chapter Eighteen

Aftermath

When I open my eyes, I realize right away that I'm in the hospital room. I'm shivering. I can't see outside because of all the boarded up windows.

Lit candles line the dark room.

Barnabas is sitting on a chair. He has his head in his hands and there are a blood stains on his shirt. When I sit up, he looks at me. He is tapping his right foot on the floor demonstrating just how anxious.

I ease myself up over the side of the cot and press my palm against a bump on the back of my head. I feel dizzy.

"What happened?" I ask.

He gives me a sympathetic look, and then he hurries out into the hallway.

I know right away he's up to something, but I'm not sure what. I jump off my cot and run after him.

"Barnabas. Talk to me. What happened? Why are we back here?" I call.

No one else is in the main room.

Barnabas doesn't turn back but continues into the dining room, so I continue to follow him.

Barnabas stops abruptly in the doorway and I stand behind him. Everyone is sitting down, dressed in their best clothing. A massive celebratory dinner is sitting in china plates in front of everyone as they wait to eat, but the mood is ominous. Candles cast eerie shadows over everyone's faces.

Tessa and Enzo watch me nervously. I watch Barnabas's fists bawl together as he gains confidence. I watch as he inches closer to Alexander and he addresses everyone in the room.

"I'm sorry. I was wrong. I shouldn't have doubted you, Alexander. I shouldn't have let everyone down," Barnabas says.

"No! What are you doing?" I ask desperately.

I try to pull Barnabas back out into the main room, but he shoves me away. I stand rigid against the wall as Alexander and the other boys stare at him.

Titus looks angry and Junia is peering down at her empty plate.

"I would like to still be considered as your leader. I should have never strayed," Barnabas adds.

"Barnabas!" I shout.

I see Alexander watching us with a look of amusement on his face. I move closer to Barnabas and he turns to me, almost annoyed.

"I have to do this," he hisses.

I don't remember thinking about striking Barnabas, but I do. I hit him hard, but I stand there with my hand raised after it's over. I thought he was going to retaliate and hurt me too. I'm more afraid of him hurting me than anyone else because I know I wouldn't defend myself from Barnabas.

A strange look comes over his face as he holds onto his reddening cheek. He looks confused and scandalized. He opens his mouth to say something to me, but no words come out.

I won't apologize.

"Please be seated," Alexander finally says.

Barnabas sits down next to Demetri, but I stay pressed against the wall. I can't sit with them. I can't pretend anymore.

Alexander eyes me.

"There's a lot we have to do. It all begins today. This vision originally came from our brother Barnabas, but he has left the path and I'm afraid there's no way he can get back on it.

It's now convenient for you to join us, but this life has never been about convenience. There will be punishment for your actions and you can never be leader," Alexander says, directly to Barnabas. He pauses. "Unless one of your brothers thinks otherwise."

I watch while Barnabas looks up at his old friends, the children he grew up with. Demetri and Asa are smiling at him, but they don't say anything. Their smiles are cruel and conniving. They like seeing Barnabas this way.

"I don't trust him. He wanted to abandon us for one of them," Demetri says, finally.

Demetri points at me and I glare back at him.

"We'll deal with them later. I think with some time, they'll be useful to us. It's not like they have a choice…they promised me they'd behave if "The Culling" did happen."

"He was a nonbeliever," Asa adds, looking at Barnabas.

I see Barnabas looking down at the table in shame. I'm not sure what he's thinking because I don't know him anymore. My heart is broken. Everything is over for me and the rest of my friends. I want to scream and punch him again, but I know it won't do any good.

Alexander starts to go on about the rebuilding process, so I turn and find some privacy in the hallway in front of the hospital room. I sit down on the floor and run my fingers over the cool wood. It's dark and chilling and I don't want to see what it's like outside. I don't want to think about whether or not my family is dead or alive.

If Barnabas is right about everything, they are dead. They can't be gone.

My home can't be gone.

There's no way that these maniacs are right, but I saw it with my own eyes. I saw the ground being torn up and I felt the heat from the lightning. I know deep down that was the destruction everyone has been predicting. I know the outside world isn't pretty. I'm not sure how this changes how I feel about everyone in the compound. They're still cruel and evil and I hate them all. I'm even staring to hate Barnabas, which I never thought possible.

Enzo and Tessa come find me and we all sit together in silence.

I know that they're thinking about home, because I am too. I also know that they are hurting. I'm not sure what to do besides run. I feel more trapped than ever.

We have to get to the castle with or without Barnabas. We have to go through with the plan or die trying.

"You're still in, right?" I ask.

"We don't know what it's like outside. Everything could be destroyed. This could be the only place left on Earth," Enzo responds.

I see that he's back to wearing his tank tops and his tattoos are now clearly visible. I know he wants to get away, like I do.

"It isn't," I say confidently. "I'd rather take my chances out there, no matter what."

"They're going to be reassigning new jobs," Tessa tells me. "I'm sure it'll be nothing we want to do."

"Definitely not," I reply.

Enzo and Tessa head back into the main room to check out what everyone's doing, while I go back into the hospital room to collect the brown jacket that I left behind. I need a way to stay warm. After I pull the jacket on over my shoulders, I lean against

242

the wall and shut my eyes. I want to make sure this isn't one long extended nightmare.

When I open my eyes, I see Barnabas standing in the doorway. He walks past me and sits on one of the metal tables. He runs his hands through his hair. I don't want to look back at him, but of course I do. I want to know why he's here.

The small red spot is still on his cheek where I struck him.

"Thanks for hitting me. I think I needed to be brought back to my senses," he says.

"Can anyone trust you?" I shoot back. "Are you lying to me, too?"

"No...no, it's hard to explain. I thought it would help us in the end. I thought I could gain Alexander's trust again." Barnabas pauses. "Alva, please. I'm sorry."

"You can't do that to me. I trusted you," I say, through gritted teeth.

"It wasn't about you. I would never let them hurt you. I thought it would be safer this way, if we started to fit in again. I could protect you that way. If I was leader again....I could save you."

"I don't need to be protected. You scared me."

I stand in front of him. I lean my hands on his thighs to steady myself. I feel dizzy and nauseous again.

"I'm sorry. We still have to rebuild. We still have to go. You're right. Alexander is still the enemy," he replies, softly.

This fills me with relief. I know I have to forgive him. I know my temporary anger and mistrust is less important than our need to work together and get us all out of here.

"I know."

"Let's see what's going on, then," Barnabas says, hopping off the table. He starts toward the door, more determined than ever. He turns back to say, "I'll see if I can check outside."

I wait a long time before wandering back into the main room. Everyone is busy doing something, but I have no idea what they're planning. I see Alexander has them rearranging furniture and some of the boys are working on some of the generators. I'm sure he has big plans for this place and I don't want to be involved.

Enzo and Barnabas eventually return and sit with Tessa and me on one of the couches. Everyone is too absorbed and robotic to notice us, so we still do our best to talk in hushed voices and quiet down if anyone is close to us. The way everyone is acting is creeping me out.

"The whole area is flooded out, but the village was high enough to be spared. We can go there and see about the castle. We'll have to take our chances."

"I know a house we can see it from. Do you think any of them are alive?" I ask.

"I'm not sure. I doubt it. We should head out as soon as we can," Barnabas says.

He would know more than me about what's going on outside and why it happened. He told me right before all the destruction started. *We're a science experiment.*

Asher calls Barnabas and Enzo over to help them, so it's up to Tessa and me to gather up the stuff before we leave.

No one wants to wait any longer. No one can spend another night here.

I watch for a while as they start to rip off the boards from the windows and light begins to pour in. It's still cloudy out, but it's much better than the candles. I don't know how long I've been asleep for because it's already getting dark out. It'll be about a half hour before night hits.

They take about twenty minutes to remove all of them and the full world outside is revealed to me. It's all incredible and I find myself in shock. The pit where our plane wreckage was is completely filled in by water with lapping waves. There is an ocean where the desert was, but the cobblestone path I took up to the village is still intact. I think there might be a lot of damage done to the houses, but it's all we have.

That's where we'll head.

Hopefully, Alexander won't follow us. He doesn't need Barnabas any more.

I press my hands against the glass and stare out at the destruction until it gets dark. Finally, Titus taps my shoulder and I am brought back to life.

"I'll get everyone together. Grab one of the packs in the locker and two of the guns. That'll be enough to get away," Titus whispers to me.

Ester is staring at us, but I don't think she could hear.

I wait until she turns away before heading down the stairs. The hallway is desolate and dark as I make my way down.

This is it. Our second attempt. If we don't make it this time, we're stuck here and Alexander will make sure we'll never be able to leave.

I sneak into the classroom and pull out my pack, slinging it over my shoulder. I stick one gun inside it and tuck the other one back into my pants.

Unfortunately, someone is waiting for me when I reemerge into the hallway.

I immediately know it's Alexander's outline and I step further to see his full figure. I'm alone with him. There's nowhere I can go unless I shoot him.

"I know a few things about you, Alva, which I didn't realize before," Alexander starts in a cool voice. "I was right about you being a menace, but now I know why. Now I know you've been sent here to destroy us."

"Why do you think that?" I say, stopping where I am.

Alexander looks more dangerous than ever and I see something in his hand. It could be a weapon.

"You're the girl Barnabas had dreams about all those years ago. You're the one who started his immature behavior. I should have seen it earlier. I should have noticed his infatuation for you."

"What are you going to do about it?" I ask.

"Since I know you're the evil that wants to tear apart what we have left, I'll have to destroy you. I was told by Barnabas years ago you could destroy me. Those were his visions, Alva. I take them seriously."

"You're going to kill a teenager? You're going to murder me because you think I'm a threat to you?"

"You're saying you're not?" Alexander says.

I don't say anything and Alexander takes a step forward. He is an arm's length away and I see he is only carrying a book with him. I see he has no weapon. I do wish to kill Alexander but only because of everything he's done, but it's not because I'm evil.

He's got it all wrong.

"Let us go," I reply.

I raise my hands up to show I'm weaponless. I think he'll understand and he'll want to get rid of us as soon as possible.

"I need Barnabas here. I'll send you off to die, but not him. He tells me what I need to know and I can get him back on my side. He'll be punished first, but he knows he deserves it. You're a bad seed we can get rid of. You can go only if you promise never to come back."

I know I can't leave without Barnabas, but Alexander is assuming I would. He thought I'd take him up on his offer.

"I can't promise that. I won't leave him here."

"That's not your choice to make," Alexander says, anger rising up in his voice. "You're still a guest. You have no right to meddle in this. I'm giving you the opportunity to get out and never look back."

"I'm offering you the same thing. Let us go and I won't kill you. I'll spare your life," I say.

246

Alexander smiles at me.

"You're a bold little girl. I can crush you. I can turn Barnabas against you again. You're nothing."

"No, you're nothing. You know you're nothing without Barnabas so that's why you want to keep him close. You want to humiliate him and crush him to the point that he can't live without you, but I know he can. You don't have the same hold over him that you used to."

He blinks a couple of time, looking surprised. I know I'm reading him correctly. I know there's a reason he hasn't completely forsaken Barnabas yet. I know there's a reason he still wants to keep him here. I think he knows he's still not safe from the destruction. It's not over yet.

"You have no chance out there," Alexander says, his eyes burning with anger. "Where do you think you'll go?"

"We have somewhere to go. I'm sure you have an old friend who lives close by here."

Alexander stares at me with the most shocked look I've seen yet. He has to know who I'm talking about, but he doesn't understand how I know.

"Michael?" He forces an incredulous laugh, but I know he's worried. "He was a nonbeliever and you think he was spared? You think he's safe?"

"He believed. He just didn't believe in you. He knew you weren't right. He knew you were messed up in what you were doing to these kids. I'm sure he knows all about your dark little secrets."

"Oh, Alva," Alexander says gently. He reaches out to grasp onto my shoulder before I'm able to pull away. I know I have to reach my gun, but his grip is too tight. I stand rigidly where I am. "You don't know what's right from what's wrong, but I will teach you. I will teach you how to be pure and respectful. I will do whatever is necessary to teach you all those things. You will understand that I've been nothing but good to these children. You'll know I saved their lives and made them good in turn."

"What did you do to them? How did you convince them to follow you?" I ask, through gritted teeth.

Alexander's fingers dig painfully into my shoulder.

I want to cry out, but I don't.

"I'm a psychologist, Alva. I'm good at what I do. When we have some time alone, I'm sure I'll be able to convince you as well."

As I reach out my free hand toward the back of my shorts, Alexander grabs onto my wrist.

"Stop it!" I shout. My voice echoes through the hallway, but Alexander shoves me onto the ground. I force out, "Let me go!"

When he drops me, my head strikes the hard tile again. Pain radiates through my skull, but I force myself up in sitting position. I know how to fight and this is the perfect opportunity to do it. I've never fought anyone as big as Alexander before, but I will try. I will try to take him down.

Alexander kicks me his hard before I'm able to readjust myself. He connects with my jaw and makes the room spin.

I can taste blood in my mouth as I steady myself on the floor. I hear Alexander's cruel voice. I blink a few times.

"I think Barnabas loves you," Alexander teases. "He has since he was a little boy. I think that's sweet. I'll even let you two see each other every once in a while. I'll let him hold your hand while I kill you. It would be nice to convince him to be the one to do it."

"He won't," I shout out in a strained voice.

Blood is in my throat and I'm choking on it. I force myself back up and face Alexander again with my fists clenched. My vision becomes clear once more.

"He can be rehabilitated. He can be fixed. You, however, haven't had the right upbringing," Alexander continues to talk. "Asher was up for the task. Maybe he can try."

I swing my fists and get Alexander right in the nose. I watch as he stumbles back and grabs onto it. Blood begins to pour. I steady myself when he pulls his hand away and smiles again. Blood streams down onto his shirt. The sight of him makes me nauseous.

"I can hurt you," I remind him. "I won't stand here and take it."

"Impressive, Alva," Alexander says, with a laugh. "But I never expected you to give up so quickly."

He grabs my shirt at lightning fast speed and slams me against the wall. He lifts me up against it so that my feet no longer touch the floor.

I try to kick out him, but I can't reach. I know he is much too strong. My only hope is getting to my gun, which is now pinned between the wall and my body.

I scratch at his face, but then he presses himself against me. The weight of his body causes me to gasp for breath. I spit out a wad of blood.

"One day you'll get what you deserve," I groan.

I feel like a rib is broken. I feel like I'm falling apart, but I know I will continue to fight. I inch my right hand behind my back and try to dig into the back of my shorts. Alexander might be able to grab it from me anyway before I can fire a shot.

"Today's not that day, Alva. It's your day. I'm going to fix all the mistakes you've made," Alexander says.

Anger takes over and I scream out loudly before I bring my boot up to his groin. I am able to get out one swift kick, causing him to drop me. I know someone has heard my scream by now. I'm able to pull out my gun and point it at Alexander. For once, something is going my way.

Alexander raises his hands defensively and backs away. He's still smiling.

I wipe the blood from my face and reach down to ease on my backpack. I feel much more powerful now even though the gun is shaking in my hands.

"If you move from this spot and come after me, I will kill you. I promise you," I growl. My voice sounds foreign, like it's not coming from me. "Don't move from here. I don't ever want to see your face again."

I turn away from him and start to run up the stairs. As I clatter along the metal, I can hear Alexander's laughter echoing from the hallway.

Chapter Nineteen

Escape

I know right away that Alexander will not follow my instructions.

Titus is waiting for me at the top of the stairs, like he was about the descend them to find me. He runs with me all the way to the main room and stops when he gets to Barnabas.

I grasp the heavy metal gun in my hand. I see Barnabas eyeing it, but I keep myself in front of him.

Enzo, Tessa and Junia hurry up to join us. They all look worried.

"We have to go now," I say, turning toward Barnabas.

Barnabas's hand pushes the door open, but his eyes grow wide as he peers over my shoulder.

I swing around to see Alexander at the hallway entrance, pointing a pistol at me. I get nervous when I notice the rest of the kids from the compound have gathered around him. I point my own gun back at Alexander and Titus stands at my shoulder. I'm breathing heavily and I can barely hold it straight.

"You said you would kill me. I think you're a liar," Alexander says.

"Believe me," I reply. "I have no problem killing you. Lower your gun and I won't kill anyone. We're getting out of here."

"I don't think so. Come here, Barnabas. You're staying here with us," Alexander orders.

He cocks the gun and takes a step forward with the others remaining behind him.

I know they've never seen anything like this. I feel Barnabas's hand on my shoulder.

"No, I'm not," I hear Barnabas's voice behind my head.

"Listen to me, Barnabas," Alexander growls. "You come join us and you'll be their leader again. This is a way for you to prove yourself."

I don't look behind me because I need to keep my eyes on Alexander. I'm ready to fire at any moment.

His eyes are focused on me even though he is talking to Barnabas.

"I'm fine with them," Barnabas replies calmly. He removes his hand from my shoulder. "You need to let me go."

"That's not your choice," Alexander shouts, making me jump a bit.

"It is my choice!" Barnabas shouts back.

"I'll kill her and it'll be your fault."

"You won't shoot," Barnabas tests him. "You'll kill me, too."

For a moment, I feel like Barnabas is crazy, but then I realize what's going on. It's too late when I try to stop it.

Alexander's gun goes off right after Barnabas steps in front of me.

I watch as the bullet rips through Barnabas's upper body. Titus has already shoved me back and grabbed the gun. I hear him fire a shot at Alexander and watch as Alexander topples to the ground.

He is not dead. He sits up as a pool of blood flows around him. His eyes go to Barnabas with his back pressed against the wall near the door.

Barnabas stares back at Alexander with wide eyes.

I figure it's not only physical pain he's feeling, but something deeply emotional I won't understand.

Tessa and Enzo drag me outside before I can get a good look at where Barnabas has been shot. I watch helplessly as Titus heaves him over his shoulder and I run blindly ahead. I know they'll come after us especially now that we've harmed Alexander.

We don't have much time.

The whole run up to the village is a blur. I'm too worried about Barnabas and who is chasing us to concentrate. Tessa has to grab me and shake me before I am able to tell them where to go.

We slip into Edward and Penelope's house right as the others head out from the compound. Some of the boys have torches, which I can clearly see in the darkness.

Enzo locks the door and keeps watch as Titus eases Barnabas into his arms. I throw everything from the kitchen table and then we are able to get him on top of it. His body is sprawled out and he is having trouble keeping his eyes open. I place a hand on his cheek as Titus and Junia look over him.

"Stay awake," I say, gently. "Why did you do that? You didn't have to..."

He isn't looking at me, however. His head is leaned toward Titus and the spot where he was struck with a bullet. His right shoulder is bleeding and raw.

Barnabas turns back to me and holds onto my hands as Titus looks for something in the kitchen to work with.

"I didn't think he would do it," he says weakly. "I didn't think he would shoot me. I was wrong about him..."

Now I understand where Barnabas's hurt is coming from.

I get that he never thought Alexander would harm him and he thought he'd be able to protect us both. It is clear that Barnabas is realizing that Alexander never loved him or cared about him in any way.

I have to look away from the wound when Junia and Titus work on getting the bullet out. I can see how hard it is for Barnabas not to scream in pain, but he remains as calm as he can.

Tessa is able to find something to clean out the wound and they wrap it up with some of the medical tape we packed.

Titus orders Barnabas to lie down and he heads upstairs with me to check out the situation outside. He also tells Enzo to remain by the door with one of our guns.

I bring him to the top floor so we can peer out the windows. The air is chilly because some of them have been busted by the storm, but I can see clearly into the distance. I breathe a sigh of relief when we see the castle is still there, which seems relatively unaffected by the storm and a light is still glowing in the top window. I smile and Titus wraps an arm around my shoulder.

"That's where we'll go. We'll finally be free there. I know it," Titus says.

"We have to head out tonight, we can't wait. Do you think Barnabas will be okay to travel?"

"He'll have to be."

We head back all the way downstairs as quickly as possible and see Enzo and Tessa are both peering out the windows into the darkness. They turn to us when we reenter the room.

"They're starting to burn down the town, starting with the house closest to the compound," Enzo explains, exasperated.

I push him aside and peer out myself. I see the torches moving swiftly away from the first house and it's quickly going up in flames. I know it'll spread fast because the houses are so close together. I swing back around to see Barnabas is sitting up on the edge of the table.

"Everyone take ten minutes and we'll get out of here. Try to find anything that'll help us," Titus orders.

Barnabas motions for me and I help him back onto the ground. He wraps an arm around my shoulder and I support him around the waist. He needs to make it as far as we have to walk.

"I'll be okay," Barnabas says. "Take me upstairs? I want to get changed before we leave."

"Sure," I reply.

I'm so happy that he's alive, I'd literally do anything for him. The warmth of his body against mine calms me.

I walk with him as quickly as he can to the second floor, which was Penelope and Edward's bedroom. I search through the dresser drawers while Barnabas waits by the bed and find a long sleeved flannel shirt and a pair of tan pants, similar to what he is wearing. I leave them on the bed and back up toward the door.

"Close it," he says. He stops me when I start to walk out. "Stay here with me…please."

I nod and shut the door behind us, leaning against it.

He unbuttons and pulls of his bloody shirt and then steps out of his pants, so that he's only in his underwear. It feels strange to see him so bare, considering he's spent most of his time around me completely covered up.

I am able to see a few scars and bruises along his pale skin, along with the thick bandage that is starting to soak with blood.

"How are you feeling?" I ask.

Barnabas shrugs and then winces.

"Fine," he says. "I was just thinking about something. Remember during prayers around the time you first arrived when we talked about the one who could destroy everything and everyone thought it was you?"

"Yes," I reply, with an eyebrow raised.

"The visions were talking about Alexander, not you. I've known this for a long time, but I never believed it. I never knew how he would handle it or if he would punish me. He was too powerful to confront him about it."

"Alexander was the one they were telling you to get away from. They knew all along."

"Whoever they are," Barnabas replies, bitterly. "We are at their mercy."

I laugh for a moment, thinking how true that statement has always been. At least I won't have to worry about being at the mercy of Alexander and Cassandra, but will someone step in and take their place?

Are those horrible creatures just as bad? What if Michael is?

Before he dresses, he motions me over. I can see his muscles tense up as I approach him.

"Do you feel weird like this?" I ask.

"Not really," he says, with a curious smile. "Not with you, at least."

He pulls me closer and I begin to kiss him, the feeling of his warm lips against my own revitalizes me. I'm so happy I get to experience it again and we're both alive. It's not over yet, but I won't let him die. He obviously won't let me die either.

Barnabas backs up onto the bed, easing me carefully over him. We continue to kiss with my body pressed against his. I run my fingers along his soft skin and stop at his waist. He groans and I rest into the nook of his right shoulder, facing him.

"Sorry, that hurt," he says, patting his recently acquired wound. He gazes at me curiously. "But we can do this again soon, right?"

I know he's joking, but I can't do it. I know we aren't even close to being safe yet.

"If we don't die," I remind him. "If Michael isn't a psychopath like Alexander is."

"He's not," Barnabas says, squeezing my shoulder tighter. "We have to get there. We aren't going to die."

He forces himself up and pulls on the flannel I got out for him. His fingers fumble with the buttons as he looks back up at me. He shoves on the pants and his own boots as I look around the room.

There's nothing useful except clothing, but I'm not worried about that. As I open the door to leave the room, he reaches down to wipe off some blood from my hairline.

The way he's staring at me is different than he's ever looked at me before.

"What is it?" I ask.

"You're the strongest and bravest person I've ever known," Barnabas says fondly.

"There are people a lot braver than me. I wish you could have met them all," I reply.

Barnabas nods sadly and digs into his pocket. He pulls out the stop watch that belonged to his parents and pops it open.

"It's just us now. Time has stopped."

I look and see that he's right. I slip it into my own pocket when he hands it to me and follow him back downstairs.

"You sure took your time," Titus says as everyone looks over at us.

Junia, Enzo, and Tessa are all sitting at the kitchen table, looking distressed. They start to gather everything up and get moving when they notice us.

"They'll be here soon," Junia reminds us. "Maybe we should leave three at time."

This is the first time I've ever heard Junia say a full sentence and she makes a lot of sense. I know we shouldn't all leave together.

Titus grabs onto the pack and takes out one of the guns for himself. He hands another one to Tessa, who stares back at him.

"Enzo, Tessa, and Junia can head out first. Head straight toward the castle and don't worry about keeping pace with us. It'll take a while to get there," Titus says.

Tessa nods and looks at me. She wraps me in a hug and kisses my cheek. She has wet tears on the side of her face.

"You'll be fine. We'll be right behind you," I tell her.

Enzo leans in and kisses my cheek as well.

I hold onto his arms tightly before letting go. I don't want to see anything bad happen to them, but they'll be safer getting a head start.

Titus hands over the pack to Enzo and he slips it over his shoulder. He makes sure the coast is clear and they hurry out into the night.

"I don't see them anymore. Maybe they returned to the compound," Titus says. "Let's go."

I can see the yellow and orange flames from where I stand. The fire must be close and reflecting off the water. The smoke is filling the air outside.

Titus leads us outside and I immediately feel disoriented, but Barnabas keeps a firm hand on my arm and leads me down the path. We trail a bit behind Titus, but I can still see him in front of us. The smoke is almost unbearable and I can feel the heat from the fire approaching.

Barnabas lets go of me. We run and I can barely hear him as calls something to me.

"I'm going to get the gun from Titus," I think he says.

I am amazed by how much the smoke is accumulating around us, but we are almost past all the houses. I pause for a moment trying to stop coughing and end up puking on the path. I'm down on my knees. I realize that I can no longer see Barnabas and Titus. I can barely see anything.

After peering back, I lift myself up. I see something strange coming toward me…a bright glowing red light. I realize too late that I won't have time to run away.

Asher and Demetri grab me and start laughing. Their faces are a blur, like something out of a nightmare.

I hear Barnabas calling for me somewhere up ahead and I scream out for him. I don't think I can take on these two boys, the two people who ended up hating me the most. Now they have me right where they want me.

I struggle as Demetri lifts me up despite my thrashing and kicks open one of the doors to the houses. I see we're in a small kitchen and he slams me onto the wooden floor. I groan and roll onto my back to see them looming over me.

Asher kicks my side to drive the point home.

"Well, well, well," Asher says, smiling at Demetri. "I wanted to catch someone, but I never dreamt it would be you. This is a quite a surprise."

I watch helplessly as Demetri kneels down next to me, but I'm too exhausted to move. His face is close to mine.

"Alexander won't be angry if we killed her, would he? Could we just bash her up a bit?" Demetri asks jokingly to Asher. "I'm sure Barnabas won't mind either. What happened to him anyway? Did he abandon you to save himself?"

"Get away from me," I hiss.

Before I'm able to get up, Demetri is straddling me, pinning my body to the ground. He pulls out a knife from his belt loop and runs it along my cheek. Something tells me he is trying to enjoy this. He is trying to make it as unpleasant as possible.

I will die.

I try to yank myself free, but he's much too heavy. Besides, Asher has his own gun. Why did Alexander keep so many weapons at the compound and why are they all so ready to use them? Had he been planning on war?

I continue to struggle against him as runs the knife along my side and he pushes the knife tip in far enough to puncture the sensitive skin over my ribs. I want to scream out, but I don't. He wants to terrify me, but I am stronger than his intentions.

After a few moments, he pulls the knife back out and holds it up in front of me. It's covered in my dark red blood.

Without hesitation, I take the only action I have and I bash my forehead into his nose. He cries out and I free myself from him. Asher still has his gun pointed at me, however, as Demetri writhes around on the floor.

Asher turns away from me when someone steps in the room with us and I see Titus and Barnabas are in the doorway. I smash Asher with my elbow and he drops the gun, causing a round to go off. Luckily, the bullet rams into the ceiling far away from me or anyone else.

Demetri reaches out and grabs the fallen gun before I can. He points it at Barnabas and Titus, who also has a gun pointed at him. He forces himself up and motions for me to stand to the side.

I'm afraid how this will end. I'm afraid his bullet will find one of them. I obey.

His eyes dart around the room because we outnumber him. I wouldn't dare charge at him when he has a gun on my friends, however, and Demetri knows that.

"Good to see you all again," Demetri sneers. "Someone isn't making it out of here."

Asher gets up and stands beside Demetri. He eyes me, blood streaming down his face, but he doesn't try to grab me. We are both equally useless at this point.

"It doesn't have to be like this," Barnabas argues. "Come with us. You don't have to stay with Alexander anymore."

"Shut up, Barnabas. I never liked you anyway," Demetri shouts.

Barnabas looks me up and down to make sure I'm okay. When he sees the blood stain forming on my jacket, his demeanor changes.

I don't want this to make him angry. I don't want him to feel like he needs to take on Demetri because of it. I shake my head and Barnabas's jaw clenches with determination.

Titus's hands are steady as he continues to point the gun at Demetri.

"You all deserve to die like animals. Then I'll go back to killing her slowly," Demetri says, his eyes boring into Barnabas's.

Both guns go off at the same time and I nearly jump a foot in the air. I watch as Demetri collapses first and then Titus. I know Demetri is dead instantly.

Asher goes to grab the gun, but I wrestle him to the ground. He is not as strong as Demetri, so it's much easier. He tries to leap over me to get the gun first, kicking it farther away.

"Go! Get out of here. Go, now!" Titus shouts at me.

Barnabas motions for me to come to him and I forget about the gun. He tries to help Titus up, but he pushes us away.

I hesitate and struggle against Barnabas's grip. He has to lift me up off the floor and drag me out.

"He won't make it anyway. He's trying to give us a head start!" Barnabas shouts, as he continues to pull me down the cobblestone path.

The smoke has gotten much worse.

"No!" I call, struggling against him again. "He can make it. He wasn't shot too badly."

"Yes, he was," Barnabas argues, holding on my wrist. "He is going to die."

I'm torn about what to do until I hear another gunshot go off. I can hear Asher's voice, so I know he is still alive. I grab Barnabas's hand and we take off as fast as we can.

We are completely defenseless now.

A few yards after the path runs out, the smoke begins to clear and I can see. I turn back for a moment to see Shiloh burning to the ground. The blaze is so intense I can feel it from where we stand. I wipe some ash from my face and we continue on.

The path ahead of us slopes back down again for about a mile and then it's desert for another few miles before the castle.

I have no idea how it hasn't flooded out like everything else. I conclude the cliffs have been able to block the water from gushing into this specific canyon and they are contained to the one side of the compound. I hope that doesn't change any time soon.

It's dark and only the light shining in the distance from the castle is giving us any direction. It'll be a long walk before we get there and hopefully we can catch up to Tessa, Enzo, and Junia.

After about a half hour of walking down the path, I have to pause and lean against the jagged cliff wall. Barnabas waits next to me, also breathing heavily. I feel wet tears on my cheeks when I think about Titus, but I don't make any noise.

I am sad that we lost him. I'm sad that'll he'll never know life without Alexander. I hope that in the time we spent together he was happy and I'm forever grateful for all of his help. I can never, ever repay him for it.

Barnabas places his hand back in mine and we continue to jog along once again.

I peer up to see that the clouds seem to be clearing and the moon is doing its best to peek out. That is starting to give us some light and I think I see a few figures far ahead of us. I figure our friends might be okay after all.

I know we're not safe yet.

Chapter Twenty

Contact

The sun is starting to come up.

I haven't seen it like this for weeks. I can already tell it's going to be a beautiful day because the clouds are completely gone and there's a warm breeze coming across the massive canyon we're trudging through. I look back briefly to see that the town of Shiloh is completely burnt down and smoldering, except for the compound.

Up ahead, Enzo, Tessa, and Junia have stopped to let us catch up. We're about to reach them and then we'll have to explain about Titus.

I don't want to talk about him. I want to get to the castle and then cry my eyes out. That sounds like a weird plan, but it works for me. I can't break down yet.

When we reach our friends, Barnabas and I collapse on the ground. They sit down around us and no one asks about Titus, but I think they've figured it out by now. They've been waiting for us for about a half hour.

"No one's coming, so why don't you rest?" Enzo says.

They move a few yards away and keep watch.

I can tell they're exhausted, too. I move in closer to Barnabas and snuggle up against him. It doesn't take me long to fall asleep.

When I wake something strange happens. I run my fingers over long green grass and to the left of us is a massive dense forest. I shake Barnabas awake as the others also begin to rouse.

We're in a gigantic green field full of yellow flowers that leads to the castle in the distance, all the dirt and dust is gone. The warm sun is refreshing on my skin as I peel off my jacket.

Barnabas is in awe as he stands up quickly and peers around. He walks a bit toward the forest and undoes a few buttons on his shirt. His collar bones are clearly visible and the bandage on his shoulder sticks out. He closes his eyes and smiles widely up toward the sun.

I recognize this scene, but I can't remember from what.

This is my dream. This is when I saw that Barnabas could be happy and right now I know he is. He turns to me still grinning and I smile back at him. He runs back to me and holds onto my arms as he laughs. I am happy, too.

Barnabas kisses me before he drags me back down into the grass. I stare up at the sky and listen to Enzo, Tessa, and Junia's laughter. I like the way it sounds.

Suddenly, a grim expression comes across Barnabas's face and he shoots up.

The moment is over and I expect the worst. I know deep down it couldn't have lasted for long. He gets up without saying anything and starts toward the forest. Considering his quick pace, I know he's not going to slow down or turn back. I look at my friends for help, but they're too busy talking and enjoying themselves to notice us. I don't catch up to Barnabas until he's a few feet under the tree line.

"Barnabas, stop!" I call. "Where are you going?"

He doesn't listen, so I know there's something wrong. He pushes aside low tree branches, so I have to duck under them to catch up. Whatever he's doing is important and I follow silently.

When we come to a clearing, I start to see what he sees. There's some sort of metal craft halfway into the ground, like its crashed there, and a blue light is radiating from the center. My mind immediately becomes fuzzy, so I stay back as Barnabas approaches it cautiously.

There is something wrong with him. He doesn't seem to care about the danger he might be putting himself in.

I take a few steps closer as Barnabas extends the palms of his hands toward the glowing metal. I want to tell him to stop, but I'm too curious. I find myself wanting to do the same thing.

Right before Barnabas can touch it, the scene from my nightmare begins.

Long scaly arms with extended claws at the end reach out of the ground and grab onto Barnabas's legs. The ground rips up and sucks him down into the grass.

I cover a hand over my mouth and rush forward to help him, but it's too late. I stare down into the blackness below.

After attempting to build up my courage for a while, I ease myself down into the hole until I can reach the bottom with my outstretched feet. I let myself drop the rest of the way down and walk toward the blue light at the end of the tunnel.

Barnabas is standing alone in a large room that looks like it's been carved out of the middle of a cave. He doesn't stop looking ahead, so I follow his gaze. One of the terrible creatures is staring back at him with its terrifying lifeless black eyes.

Its slimy skin clings to long, bony limbs and I find myself involuntarily gasping.

It moves a lot more smoothly than I expect and stops itself right in front of Barnabas. He can't seem to look away, so I stay back against one of the cave walls. These are the creatures that decided to destroy us. These are the creatures that are a hundred times smarter than us and can wipe us out in a matter of moments.

I hate them, but I'm fascinated by them.

It lifts up its clawed hands and places them on top of Barnabas's head. I suddenly feel everything he's feeling. I suddenly know everything that's going on, not only now, but for the past thousands of years. In seconds, I know the history of everything. It's impossible to explain to anyone and I'm not sure I ever can. It's the most beautiful thing in the world.

As the information rushes in my head, I collapse to my knees on the ground. I know all about what those creatures have been planning, how they've suffered for so long, and how they didn't know we were capable of understanding them. My life, Michael's life, and Barnabas's life flashes before my eyes and I know what we're supposed to do. Nothing has ever been clearer to me.

What's more important is suddenly I know how to fix everything that we've done wrong for so long. I know why the creatures want us to restart and why they chose us. Barnabas, Michael, and I are the perfect blend of what we'll need to rebuild. There's a small group that Michael has gathered back at the castle. We won't be disturbed by the creatures. They will leave us alone from now on.

When the creature lets go of Barnabas I feel their grasp over me is gone too. It backs up into one of the many tunnels and leaves us alone. Barnabas finally brings his attention back to me. There's a look of understanding on his face that I feel myself. I feel different somehow. I feel like I've changed and I'm more powerful than ever.

We climb out of the hole and walk back out of the forest in silence. The others are looking around for us and are relieved when they find us.

"Where were you?" Tessa asks, sounding a bit annoyed. "We were looking all over."

Barnabas doesn't say anything. He peers back up at the sky and then back toward the compound. He senses something and I feel it too.

"Let's get going," Barnabas says, placing a hand on my back.

Enzo collects up his backpack and we start back on our way.

I feel numb as we trudge through the ankle high grass. I'm not sure what to think about what happened, even though I feel stronger.

Barnabas keeps his hand on my back keeping me steady. He seems to understand it more than I do. He seems much more confident than he's ever been. He looks ahead at the castle with hope and acceptance.

"Everything is going to be okay," Barnabas whispers in my ear.

I believe him. He removes his hand from my back and I can now go forward on my own. I know everything is going to be okay.

Barnabas walks ahead as I trail behind everyone else. The more I watch him, the more in love with him I feel. For a moment, I think I can hear his thoughts, but they're muffled and far away.

How would that be possible anyway? How come I hear his voice in my head?

The triumvirate, comes his voice. *Alva, Michael, and I.*

Why am I so strongly pulled toward someone I've only known for two weeks and someone I haven't met? I know we all belong together. I know we're supposed to meet. The creatures made that clear and they filled my heart with the acceptance of their plan.

We were always meant to work together.

I start to wonder why I was chosen to help Barnabas and Michael. What makes me more capable than anyone else? I am a citizen of Verus, nothing more, nothing less. But obviously those creatures thought I was worth more. Obviously there is a reason Barnabas dreamt about me. I wonder if I'll ever find out the reasons, but there doesn't seem to be any. It all seems random.

"Hurry up, Alva," Tessa calls to me, lagging behind. "Everything okay?"

Everyone stops and waits for me to catch up. Barnabas watches me curiously, but doesn't say anything. His eyes search the field behind us before he turns back around.

"Yes," I reply. "As okay as it can be."

Tessa wraps an arm around my shoulder, but pulls away suddenly when her hand touches the bare skin on my arm. She looks at me accusingly.

"You're freezing! It's so warm out. Are you sure you're okay?" Tessa asks,

I rub at my arms, but there's no way to feel what she felt. What happened to me when I was with those creatures? Did the same thing happen to Barnabas? Why do I feel so strange? I shake away my thoughts and try to focus on the immediate problem. Hopefully, we'll have time to think about it all later.

"I'm fine," I say, firmly.

We walk for about another hour until the full magnitude of the castle becomes apparent to me. It's gigantic and I love the feel of it as we get closer. It feels more like home than the compound. It feels more like home than Verus even. That immediately makes me feel guilty.

I know we still have about a half hour to walk until we reach it, however. We're exhausted. At this moment, I'm not ever sure I can make it much farther without a rest.

The only one who doesn't seem to have lost his stamina is Barnabas.

"Enzo," Barnabas calls, catching up to him.

I can't hear what they're saying, but Enzo hands him over a small knife, which Barnabas shoves into his belt loop. I'm not sure why he needs it, but I know something is up. I know he is preparing for something that's coming.

Something soon.

As a bad thought passes through my mind, Barnabas suddenly swings around and sees Asher facing us a few yards away. He has a gun pointed right at us, but mostly at Barnabas. He looks so confident that I know he won't hesitate to fire it. He will kill us if he has to.

"Go!" Barnabas shouts at us. "Get to the castle! Do it!"

The tone of Barnabas's voice gets everyone moving, including me. It takes me a moment to realize what I'm doing and I turn back. I can't leave Barnabas.

Tessa locks eyes with me, but she gives me a knowing glance. She runs off with Enzo and Junia as fast as they can. Someone needs to get to safety if it can't be us.

I'm a few feet behind Barnabas and I stay there. Coming up next to him will only distract him. He needs to stay focused. He needs to figure out how to take down Asher and then we're home free. Then we can finally find home. His new found confidence tells me that he's ready for this.

"You're unarmed, aren't you?" Asher says, with a satisfied grin. "You should get going, Alva. You've got a lot coming to you and Barnabas won't be able to protect you soon. You're both either pretty brave or dumb as rocks."

"Yes," Barnabas says, without looking back. He's frozen in place and his fists are clenched at his sides. "You should follow them, Alva. Don't worry about me."

"Don't tell me what to do," I say.

Somehow, I know that Barnabas is smiling. I take a few steps closer to him and try to look around for anything that can help us. It's only us and Asher. I turn back briefly to see that our friends are far ahead of us.

"Why are you doing this, Asher?" Barnabas asks, his voice steady. He has a plan. I don't know what it is, but I know I should trust him. "Go back to the compound or join us. You don't have to kill."

"I want to kill you," Asher says. He tightens his hand around the gun to steady his arms. "I really do, Barnabas."

"You'd kill for Alexander? Would someone who has your best interests in mind want you to take someone else's life?"

"Yes," Asher replies. "If I don't do this, I can't go back. This is my job now to keep us safe. I never liked you Barnabas. I never liked how everyone idolized you."

I feel like he could fire at Barnabas at any moment and that terrifies me. I take another step forward to stand next to Barnabas. I resist my urge to charge at Asher when Barnabas looks at me briefly.

He seems to know what I'm thinking now.

"I didn't like it either," Barnabas says.

"It was your choice to leave. It was your choice to abandon us."

"That's the only choice I've ever made on my own. Don't you understand that? I never had a choice in anything. I never wanted to be in the compound. I wanted a family."

"So, she's your family now?" Asher asks, glaring at me. He points the gun at me for a moment, but Barnabas shifts his body in front of me. "You trust her over us?"

"She's the only one who ever let me know I could make my own decisions, Asher. You admitted you never wanted the best for me. What kind of family is that?"

"A normal one. A structured one. One that makes sense," Asher shoots back. "Now you have to die. You can't be in charge of rebuilding this world."

"Go home. Let us be," I urge.

Barnabas puts a hand on my shoulder while he continues to look at Asher.

"Shut up!" Asher shouts at me.

He looks confused and on edge. He's about to lose it. I think about what he's done to me and anger surges through me. I think about how he treated me in the compound and during Demetri's attack. He didn't do anything to stop it.

"Put down the gun and I won't kill you. I don't want to do it."

I wonder where Barnabas's threats are coming from because he's unarmed besides the knife in the belt loop.

There's no way he can use it at this distance anyway. There's no way it matches up to Asher's gun.

"You couldn't do it!" Asher screams. He points the gun more at me and motions to his left. "Move away from him or I'll shoot him right now. Do it!"

I raise up my hands and move a few feet away from Barnabas. I don't know why I'm following his orders, but something is telling me I need to listen. I hear Barnabas's voice inside my head somehow.

He tells me not to fight.

Am I going crazy?

I notice that Asher still has the gun pointed at me and my heart starts to race faster. Was this a trick to kill me right now?

"She's away," Barnabas says. "She's not going to help me or do anything rash."

Asher nods and points the gun back at Barnabas.

This doesn't make me any less nervous. I don't want him to be threatening Barnabas either.

"Good. Now get down on your knees and put your hands on the back of your head," Asher insists. Barnabas stares back at him for a moment, testing him. He doesn't move. "Do it or I'll shoot her!"

This time, Barnabas doesn't hesitate. He follows Asher's instructions, but keeps his head held high. He stares back at Asher with a slight smirk on his face.

Asher begins to approach him slowly and I feel my body tense up.

271

"Don't kill him," I plead. I'm unsure of what to do, so I stay where I am. I can't do anything stupid. "Asher, you can walk away right now."

He ignores me and stops right in front of Barnabas. He extends the gun and presses it against Barnabas's forehead. Barnabas is surprisingly calm with the metal weapon threatening his life.

The smirk never leaves his face.

"Do it," Barnabas urges.

"No, stop it!" I shout.

I take a step forward, but Asher gives me a dangerous look. I know there's nothing I can do.

"Say goodbye, Barnabas," Asher says.

I know he's going to do it. I watch as his finger squeezes the trigger. I want to look away, but I can't.

Barnabas should be dead, but he isn't. I stare in disbelief after the gun jams. Asher pulls the trigger a couple more times, but still nothing happens. Barnabas reaches up and holds onto the barrel of the gun. I watch as it somehow melts and becomes uselessly distorted. Asher drops the defective gun to the ground with his eyes wide.

"Get out of here," Barnabas says, standing up.

I see his hand on the knife.

I want Asher to finally leave us alone, but I can see he's too angry for that. He grabs Barnabas around the stomach and pushes him down onto the ground. His fist connects with Barnabas's jaw, stunning him for a moment.

I try to pull Asher away, but he elbows me hard in the face. I see stars and fall back onto the ground. It takes me a few moments to push myself up. When my eyes finally clear, I see Barnabas and Asher are still fighting.

Barnabas punches Asher hard in the stomach. He is somehow much stronger than he was and he doesn't need my help.

In one swift motion, he pins Asher to the ground and buries the knife into his leg. Asher screams out in pain when Barnabas backs away.

"If you follow us, we'll kill you. I promise," Barnabas threatens. "Get going."

Asher hobbles up and watches Barnabas with curiosity and fear. He turns and starts to walk away slowly. He pulls the knife from his leg and drops it on the ground.

Barnabas chest rises and falls rapidly, but he seems satisfied with Asher's response to the situation.

"You think he'll be back? Any of them?" I ask.

"No," Barnabas responds confidently. "Can't you feel it? Can't you feel everything?"

Somehow I do know that none of them will be back, but I assumed it was a hunch. I can feel it. I understand what he's saying.

"We're safe now," I say.

Barnabas smiles and he pulls his eyes away from Asher. He picks up the melted gun and drops it back down on the ground, laughing.

"I bet you could do something like that," he says, grabbing my hand.

"I'm not sure, Barnabas."

He laughs again and we start back toward the castle.

We don't have too much farther to go.

Chapter Twenty-One

Home

I'm sweating by the time we get to the gates, where Enzo, Tessa, and Junia are waiting for us.

Enzo hugs me right when we get to them and grasps onto the firm iron gate that is blocking us from the long path inside. I think we can climb it, but it's pointy on top and it'll take a while to maneuver around it.

An interesting thing happens when Barnabas grabs onto the gate next to us. A motorized noise is heard and it starts to open by itself. We gather up our remaining things and walk slowly inside it. We watch as it shuts behind us with a loud clang.

"That was easy," Enzo says, furrowing his brow.

We stare up toward the entrance of the castle and marvel at how high it extends above us. I know we are supposed to be here.

I know this is our only option, but also the right one. I also know Michael will be waiting for us inside.

When we reach the massive wooden doors, I pull at it and swing it open. It's a lot lighter than I first thought it would be, so I stumble back into Barnabas. With his hand on my waist, he urges me forward.

It's much cooler and darker in the castle. The large entranceway leads up to a stone staircase and at least four different confusing hallways. The passageways are lined with lit torches. It feels old, but it's inviting and I'm comfortable.

"Alva?" I hear a familiar voice.

I look up and see Penelope looking down at us from the staircase. I smile as she starts to run down and presses her hands against my cheeks once she reaches me.

"You're alive? But how?" I ask, in awe.

I didn't think anyone from the village would be alive because they didn't believe in any of this. I know they never thought the world would end, so why would they prepare for it?

"Michael gathered us up and offered the castle to us. Only about fifteen of us came. I'm pretty sure everyone else is dead," Penelope says sadly. "Edward has been resting. He was injured on the way here."

"What convinced you?" I ask.

"He described you in detail and I'm certain he's never met you. I started to believe all of it. I knew we had to get away from Alexander," Penelope explains.

I nod and introduce her to my friends. She smiles at me and then her eyes linger on Barnabas. She must remember him from something. He's the boy she never understood until now.

A few more people wander down from the staircase, watching us curiously. Some of them are young like us, but there's a few older people scattered in the mix. Everyone seems tired, yet happy. They seem relieved.

Penelope leaves to fetch Michael, but comes back without him. She motions for us to follow her up the staircase which reveals another maze of hallways.

I feel like I could easily get lost inside this place.

"This is beautiful," I say, staring out some of the old paintings illuminated by the torches.

"There's more light in the rooms with the windows," Penelope explains. She gestures down another long hallway. "Take whatever ones you want. There are hundreds. We're in the hallway to the left. Come down whenever you wish."

Penelope somehow knows that we need some alone time. She smiles at us before turning back to the others.

The five of us stand by ourselves, unsure of what to do.

"I guess we can have our own rooms for a while," Enzo suggests.

None of us have had any privacy in a while, but we are scared about breaking up...even if it's only for some rest. I've become so attached to all of them through the compound that I'm still afraid of losing them.

I nod, taking a deep breath.

Enzo and Tessa take a couple of rooms next to each other, while Junia takes the one across the hall. I guess we have a long time to figure it all out. I'm pretty sure I could sleep in a different room every night of the week if I wanted to.

Barnabas turns to me before heading into one of the rooms farther down the hall.

"You're going to be okay?" he asks.

"Yes," I reply. "I think I need some time alone."

He smiles at me curiously before slipping into the room. He disappears behind the door and it closes loudly behind him.

I find a room across the hallway from him and peer inside curiously. There's a big bed with a warm red blanket folded up neatly across it. I see a bench near an open window, where a beautiful stream of light is floating in. It looks out into a courtyard in the middle of the castle. I love this room almost immediately.

Once I tuck myself into bed, I spend the next couple hours crying my eyes out. After letting everything build up for so long, I finally feel comfortable enough to let it all out. I think about my family, my old home, Titus, all the kids from the compound, the people who died in the village, Asher and the other horrible ones that tormented me, along with anything else I can think of. I want to cry as much as possible now because I don't think I'll have much to cry about later on. I think I can be happy here, even if it isn't Verus.

I'm trying to get rid of as much horrible feelings as I can because soon I will find out how I'll spend the rest of my life.

I fall asleep for a long time. I remember waking up in the middle of the night and seeing the darkness outside, but I'm so exhausted I can't stay awake for long. When I finally wake up again, it's day time. I think I've been asleep for almost a day.

No one comes for me, so I search through some of the drawers. I find a boy's long sleeved shirt, which doesn't make a difference to me, and I slip it on. I run my fingers through my hair a few times until all the loose strands are back in place. I make my way slowly back into the hallway.

Some noise is coming from downstairs, so I head into the main entrance and keep going to the right.

There's a large open room where everyone is eating. The wooden dining table is massive and I can smell heaps of wonderful food surrounding me. A large, lit chandelier is overhead, casting lovely shadows around the room.

Tessa and Enzo wave at me. Junia smiles. The rest watch me curiously, but there is admiration behind their eyes. I'm not sure why. I don't see Barnabas, but Penelope points toward a room off to the side. I can see the book shelves right away.

I'm amazed by how happy everyone looks and how quickly my friends seem to fit in. Junia is already talking to a few other kids, laughing and smiling about something they've said. I never saw her like that once in the compound.

I am more concerned about finding Barnabas. As I step into the library, I see them standing near a large open window. I shut the door behind them and they turn to me immediately. When they're watching me, I feel different. I feel like something has changed.

"You're awake," Barnabas says, with a smile.

I step closer to them and look mostly at Michael.

He is exactly how I saw him in my dreams. His kind face shows some age, but he is still young. He looks hopeful, a strange contrast from Alexander's constantly stern and malicious expression.

"I'm Alva," I say.

He grins wider and accepts my handshake.

"I know. I'm Michael."

"I know."

The three of us share a strange unexplained connection and I feel stronger being around them. I somehow feel complete. For the first time, I have hope for something better.

We talk for a long time about everything. About Alexander. About the compound. About the creatures. We laugh and sometimes cry about some of it, but Michael mostly always has a smile on his face. Barnabas grabs my hand and seems to be filled with much less pain. He's finally able to live his own life.

Michael puts a hand on each of our shoulders and starts to walk toward the door. I feel power pulse through me like I've never felt before.

"Come on. I have something to show you," Michael says. "Something that will help us change the world together."

The End

ABOUT THE AUTHOR

Kris Noel was born and raised in central New Jersey. She is a graduate of Montclair State University where she earned a degree in Anthropology while minoring in Film. Kris began writing at a young age and has always aspired to be a novelist. Her favorite authors include Alex Garland, C.S. Lewis, J.M. Barrie, and Chuck Palahniuk. Along with her love of writing, Kris is a film enthusiast and an avid reader.

The Serenity Compound is her second novel.

www.ingramcontent.com/pod-product-compliance
Lightning Source LLC
Chambersburg PA
CBHW051249260626
47162CB00002B/681